Randa Abdel-Fattah is a twenty-six-year-old lawyer. *Does My Head Look Big In This?* is her first novel, and, like its fictional heroine, she has her own identity hyphens to contend with as an Australian-born-Muslim-Palestinian-Egyptian-chocaholic.

Randa grew up in Melbourne, but now lives in Sydney where she is active in the inter-faith community. She is also a member of Palestinian human rights campaigns and the Australian Arabic Council. She loves travelling to Egypt and Palestine and being spoilt by relatives. She also loves reading, watching romantic comedies, her husband's sense of humour, getting a seat on the train, and any movie starring Colin Firth. Randa has a baby daughter and is working on her second novel.

She says: "I wanted to write a book which allowed readers to enter the world of the average Muslim teenage girl and see past the headlines and stereotypes; to realize that she was experiencing the same dramas and challenges of adolescence as her non-Muslim peers and to have a giggle in the process."

Does My Head Look Big In This?

Randa Abdel-Fattah

mlb

MARION LLOYD BOOKS

First published in the UK in 2006 by
Marion Lloyd Books
An imprint of Scholastic
Euston House, 24 Eversholt Street
London NW1 1DB, UK
A division of Scholastic Ltd
London ~ New York ~ Toronto ~ Sydney ~ Auckland
Mexico City ~ New Delhi ~ Hong Kong

10 digit ISBN: 0 439 95058 9
13 digit ISBN: 978 0439 95058 9

Copyright © Randa Abdel-Fattah, 2005
First published in Australia by Pan Macmillan Australia Pty Ltd, 2005

Typeset by M Rules
Printed and bound in Great Britain by Bookmarque Ltd, Croydon

10 9 8 7 6 5

The right of Randa Abdel-Fattah to be identified as the author of
this work has been asserted by her in accordance with the
Copyright, Designs and Patents Act, 1988.

Papers used by Scholastic Children's Books are
made from wood grown in sustainable forests.

www.scholastic.co.uk/zone

To Mum and Dad for your faith in me.
To Nada, my sister, for encouraging me.
To Ibrahim, my husband, for supporting me.

ACKNOWLEDGEMENTS

Many thanks to Sheila Drummond for all her effort, enthusiasm and smiles! And I am grateful to Marion Lloyd for all her support, and for so faithfully understanding why I wrote this book.

1

It hit me when I was power-walking on the treadmill at home, watching a *Friends* rerun for about the ninetieth time.

It's that scene when Jennifer Aniston is dressed in a hideous bridesmaid's outfit at her ex's wedding. Everyone's making fun of her and she wants to run away and hide. Then she suddenly gets the guts to jump onstage and sing some song called "Copacabana", whatever that means. I'm telling you, this rush of absolute power and conviction surged through me. I pressed the emergency stop button and stood in my Adidas shorts and Winnie-the-Pooh T-shirt, utterly captivated by that scene. It was like stepping out of one room, closing the door behind me, and stepping into another. One minute it was the last thing on my mind. The next minute this courage flowed through me and it just felt unbelievably right.

I was ready to wear the hijab.

That's right. Rachel from *Friends* inspired me. The sheikhs will be holding emergency conferences.

That was at four thirty yesterday afternoon. It's now three twenty in the morning and I'm lying in bed trying to figure out if I'm really ready to go ahead with my decision as I watch a guy on television try to persuade me that for forty-nine dollars and ninety-nine cents I can buy a can opener that will also slice a watermelon and probably pluck my eyebrows.

I can't sleep from stressing about whether I've got the guts to do it. To wear the hijab, the head scarf, full-time. "Full-timers" are what my Muslim friends and I call girls who wear the hijab all the time, which basically means wearing it whenever you're in the presence of males who aren't immediate family. "Part-timers" like me wear the hijab as part of our uniform at an Islamic school or when we go to the mosque or maybe even when we're having a bad hair day.

I've got four days left of my school holidays. Four days to decide whether I'm going to actually start only my third term at McCleans Grammar School as a full-timer. You should know that right now the thought of stepping into my home room with the hijab on is making my nostril hair stand on end.

At this stage you should probably also know that my

name is Amal Mohamed Nasrullah Abdel-Hakim. You can thank my father, paternal grandfather, and paternal great-grandfather for that one. The teachers labelled me slow in preschool because I was the last child to learn how to spell her name.

My dad's a doctor and my mum's a dentist. Two major nerds who fell in love during their hibernations in Monash University medical library. They were both born in Bethlehem, but there are fifty-two years of Australian citizenship between them.

My dad's name is Mohamed. He drives a metallic-red convertible because he's under the misguided delusion that he's still young and cool. He fails to remember that he has a receding hairline and Italian opera or Palestinian folk songs blasting from his car stereo system. My mum's name is Jamila, which means beautiful in Arabic. She's loud and energetic, loves to laugh, and is neurotically clean. The type who Sprays and Wipes doorknobs and dusts extension cords. Who actually has a spotless laundry (even the cupboard under the sink) and folds back toilet-paper rolls into a pretty triangle even when we don't have guests. What did I tell you? Neurotic.

Apart from our daily clashes over the state of my bedroom and the million and one insane chores she puts my dad and me up to (he has to get up the ladder and wipe non-existent dust off the light bulbs every month), I'm afraid I can't say (and I really am quite embarrassed about this) that we have the typical mother–teenage daughter hate–hate relationship. We actually do the whole bonding-at-the-shops-together thing and I can talk to her about personal stuff and gang up on my dad with her. I suppose our relationship detracts from the whole point of my being a teenager but at least I can say there are always ways to provoke her into an argument (leave microscopic crumbs on the kitchen bench, a towel on the bathroom floor, a fly screen open). This allows me to let off some steam and have a go at blaming my mum for every problem confronting me in my life. After all, it's a rule: every teenager should have the chance to say "you're ruining my life" to their mother at least four times a week.

As for my dad, I just need to hint that I'm experiencing "cramps" or a "girl problem" and I can get my way. Dad says I shouldn't watch *Sex and the City* because it corrupts my mind. I respond, in a weary I-need-sympathy tone of voice, that I have bad cramps and would he mind getting me a Panadol as I am incapable of moving from the couch. He forgets about the programme and goes to talk to my mother. This buys me some time to see whether Samantha picks up the mailman. See, you just need to develop a system to manage parents.

Did I mention my mum's obsessed with diets? (Or, as she calls it, "achieving the healthy lifestyle".) My lunch box in primary school was filled with 97% fat-free yoghurt bars and containers of oil-free tabouleh. Oil-free tabouleh is basically wheat with parsley. Gross. I suspect she had me intravenously drinking wheatgrass juice when I was a foetus.

4

My mum's been trying to lose ten kilos for the past ten years. My dad gets dragged through every phase: the Eight-Day Banana Diet, the Soup Diet, the Low-Carb Diet, the High-Carb Diet; she even made him go to her Weight Watchers meeting. After one attendance my dad swore he would never return. Apparently the discussion topic was "How to cope with partners who jeopardize your weight loss efforts".

At the moment she's walking around the block after dinner with my dad. She's been trying to get me to join them but there's fat chance I'm going to be seen with two middle-aged power-walkers in matching fluorescent parachute tracksuits puffing along Riversdale Road.

We live in Camberwell, one of Melbourne's trendy suburbs. Beautiful tree-lined streets, Federation homes, manicured front lawns and winding driveways. We moved here last year because my dad started working at a clinic in a nearby suburb, and my mum wanted to live a little closer to the city. Before that we lived in Donvale, a very leafy, hilly suburb with lots of acreages and owls hooting at night. There were a lot more Aussies with ethnic backgrounds there, so being a Muslim family wasn't such a big deal. In Donvale our street was a cocktail. There were the Chongs, the Papadopoulouses, the Wilsons, the Slaviks, the Xiangs and us, the Abdel-Hakims.

Our street in Camberwell is different. We've got the Taylors, the Johns and Mrs Vaselli. Wouldn't have a clue who the rest are. Everybody pretty much keeps to themself.

I'm an Australian-Muslim-Palestinian. That means I was born an Aussie and whacked with some seriously confusing identity hyphens. I'm in Year Eleven and in four days' time I'll be entering my first day of term three at McCleans. My Jennifer Aniston experience couldn't have come at a worse time. I mean, it's hard enough being an Arab Muslim at a new school with your hair tumbling down your shoulders. Shawling up is just plain psychotic.

2

I'm terrified. But at the same time I feel like my passion and conviction in Islam are bursting inside me and I want to prove to myself that I'm strong enough to wear a badge of my faith. I believe it will make me feel so close to God. Because it's damn hard to walk around with people staring at your "nappy head" and not feel kind of pleased with yourself – if you manage to get through the stares and comments with your head held high. That's when this warm feeling buzzes through you and you smile to yourself, knowing God's watching you, knowing that He knows you're trying to be strong to please Him. Like you're both in on a private joke and something special and warm and extraordinary is happening and nobody in the world knows about it because it's your own experience, your own personal friendship with your Creator. I guess when I'm not wearing the hijab I feel like I'm missing out. I feel cheated out of that special bond.

I'm ready for the next step, I'm sure of that. But I'm still nervous. Agh! There are a million different voices in my head scaring me off.

But why should I be scared? As I do my all-time best thinking through making lists, I think I should set this one out as follows:

1. The Religious/Scriptures/Sacred stuff: I believe in Allah/God's commandments contained in the Koran. God says men and women should act and dress modestly. The way I see it, I'd rather follow God's fashion dictates than some ugly solarium-tanned old fart in Milan who's getting by on a pretty self-serving theory of less is more when it comes to female dress.

2. OK, cool, I've got modesty covered.

3. Now the next thing, and it's really very simple, is that while I'm not going to abandon my fashion sense – you'd better believe I'd never give up my Portmans and Sportsgirl shopping sprees – I'm sick of obsessing about my body, what guys are going to think about my cleavage and calves and shoulder to hip ratio. And for the love of everything that is good and holy I am really sick of worrying what

people are going to think if I put on a kilo or have a pimple. I mean, home room on Monday morning can be such a stress attack. There's one girl, Tia Tamos, the resident Year Eleven bitch, who has a field day if you have a pimple. You might as well call a funeral parlour because she makes it seem like you'd be better off dead than walk around with a zit. And some of the guys have this disgusting Monday morning habit of talking about the pornos they watched on the weekend loud enough so us girls can hear. They're the biggest bloody stirrers. According to them, fat chicks should be deported, girls should starve and implants should be a civic duty. Then we all get into this massive fight about respecting girls for their minds not their bra sizes. Well that basically has them sharing around an asthma pump because they lose their breath laughing.

4. At this point, I should say that this is no longer a list, and that I am well and truly writing an essay.

I can't imagine what my class will say if I walk in with the hijab on. Oh boy, does this give the walking-into-class-naked dream another dimension. Except in my case, I'm not walking in naked. I'm walking in fully covered and yet I'm still breaking out into a sweat.

Come to think of it, though, it's not like I'm not used to being the odd one out. I attended a Catholic primary school because we lived too far away from an Islamic school and my parents didn't have the time to travel the distance twice a day. Plus, all that "love thy neighbour", "respect your parents" and "cleanliness is next to godliness" stuff was basically what I would have been taught in RE in an Islamic school anyway. So I went from Prep to Grade Six as the only Muslim kid at St Mary Immaculate, where we had to sing the Lord's Prayer and declare salvation through Jesus every morning at assembly. Not that there's anything wrong with that. If you're Catholic, by all means sing as loudly as you want. When I was in primary school, different coloured socks were enough to get you teased. So when you're a non-pork eating, *Eid*-celebrating Mossie (as in taunting nickname for Muslim, not mosquito) with an unpronounceable surname and a mum who picks you up from school wearing a hijab and Gucci sunnies, and drives a car with an "Islam means peace" bumper sticker, a quiet existence is impossible.

Hey Amal, why does a sneeze sound like a letter in the Arabic language?

Hey Amal, want a cheese and bacon chip?

Hey Amal, do you have a camel as a pet?

Hey Amal, did you notice the sub teacher called you "Anal" at rollcall this morning?

Forget sanity if you're the only one with a pass to sit in the back of church during service. Well, not every time. I remember the time I attended confession. I was in Grade Four. I was standing with my class in a queue to take the

Eucharist. I wasn't supposed to be in line but I didn't feel like sitting like a loner in a back pew till the end of the service. We took turns as Brother Andrew offered us the Eucharist. I wanted to try the holy bread. I took a taste and spat the rest into my hands. I don't know what I was expecting. Tip Top slice? I slipped the chewed-up remains in my jacket pocket and made my way to the line outside the confession box.

Mrs Piogarni was too busy telling Chris Barkley off for asking Brother Andrew if the bread was low GI to notice a Muslim kid standing in line for confession. When it was my turn I walked into the confessional and sat down on the bench.

The slide opened and I heard a gentle, kind voice. "What is your confession, my child?"

I was stuffed. The priest would declare me a heretic, my parents would call me a traitor and Mrs Piogarni would give me detention. I had no idea what to say. I mean, what does a Muslim confess to a priest? I could only think of one thing. That every time Chris Barkley called me a wog, or teased me about my mum's nappy head, I made a silent prayer asking God to drop a tree on his stupid head.

The priest asked me again: "What is your confession, my child?"

"I'm Muslim," I whispered.

"Five Hail Marys and five of the Lord's Prayer."

That was my first and last participation in a church service.

Don't get me wrong. I wasn't one of those children who

had a mixed-up, "syndrome" childhood. Yeah, sure, it didn't matter how much my parents told me to feel proud of my identity, there was always somebody in the playground to tell the wogs to go home. But as it turns out, I was pathetic at sport and obsessed with boy bands featured in *Dolly* magazine, so there were plenty of other ways to make me feel like an idiot. I learnt how to suppress my Muslimness, and I pretty much got on with having a fun and religiously anonymous primary school life.

School from Year Seven to Year Ten was Hidaya – The Guidance – Islamic College. Where they indoctrinate students and teach them how to form Muslim ghettos, where they train with Al-Qaeda for school camp and sing national anthems from the Middle East. Not.

I can't stop thinking about Hidaya and I feel sick with longing for my friends and teachers. Sick with longing for a school where you learnt what every other student in any other Melbourne school learnt but you could also pray and fast and wear a hijab and get on with being a teenager without having to answer questions or defend yourself against news headlines. Where you sang "Advance Australia Fair" every morning at assembly and got detention if you didn't take it seriously. Where you could deal with puberty and the teenage angst thing and have your crushes and go through your diets without being a prefix to terrorism, extremism, radicalism, any ism.

At Hidaya the hijab was part of the uniform. But I used to take it off as soon as I stepped outside the school gates because man oh man do you need guts to get on public transport with it on. At the end of the school day the trains would be absolutely choc-a-bloc with schoolkids. I could stay wearing it if I hopped on with a group of Hidaya students because I wouldn't feel so exposed. But the problem was that I had to change trains to get home and there was no way I had the courage to go the distance *alone* with it on.

When I first started at Hidaya I hated wearing the hijab. I found it itchy and I absolutely despised wearing it during sport. I also thought it looked daggy on me and in the first two weeks I was always styling my fringe and letting it out at the front so that everybody knew I had nice hair. Talk about being a love-me-do. But then I got to know the other kids and it no longer felt awkward. I got used to it and I met girls who were wearing it full-time outside of school, like, *voluntarily*, and I started to really respect their courage. I was even a bit jealous because there I would be ripping it off as soon as I was off school property and there they would be, calmly and proudly stepping on to a train filled with students from schools all over without so much as a hint of fear or doubt. They looked so at peace with their identity and everybody got to know and respect them on their own terms.

I hate the fact that I had to leave Hidaya. But it only goes up to Year Ten because it doesn't have enough funding to offer Year Eleven and Year Twelve. My best friends, Leila Okulgen and Yasmeen Khan, moved on to a public high school close to Coburg, where they lived. I begged my parents to let me go with them but Mum and Dad insisted that I go to a private school. I tried everything. At first I sucked up to them big time, making them coffee after dinner, offering to set the table before Mum had a chance to ask me, letting them watch SBS documentaries when I wanted to watch *Big Brother*. That didn't work. So I turned political, ranting about them *perpetuating the snobby bourgeoisie power trip of our educational system which forges aristocratic divisions between social classes* (I got that from an SBS documentary). Talk about having no compassion or social conscience. They just laughed at me and gave me a pile of literature about the school. What a puke job that was. I mean how excited would you feel reading a school mission statement which had "moulding students in the image of the school's traditions and values" as their top priority?

The more I think about my parents' sadistic decision to send me to McCleans, the more I wonder whether I harbour severe masochistic tendencies. I can't believe I'm actually contemplating wearing the hijab to a snotty grammar school where you're seriously doomed to the non-cool list if you're one issue behind on the latest *Cleo* fashion. I mean, *hello*, wake up and smell the frappaccino, what am I doing being all holy and stuff when I know I've got more chance of getting away with a Kelly Osbourne look than I do covering my hair?

I can't sleep. What will Adam say?

Adam? Who gives a crap about Adam?

Not me. Uh-uh. Nope.

He'll probably laugh.

Hey, that's not fair. He's not like that.

I should have auditioned for *Lord of the Rings*. I'm really making heads turn as a Gollum tonight.

Allah, please let me fall asleep now. Otherwise I'll wake up with a Qantas baggage belt under my eyes, and seeing as I left my concealer at Yasmeen's last week there's no way foundation is going to fix this one.

3

The next day I resolve to write an official To Wear or Not To Wear List. In the left-hand column I'm going to write a list of all the people I know who won't hassle me for wearing the hijab. On the right-hand side I'm going to list all the people I suspect might give me attitude, stare ozone holes into me or tut-tut behind my back.

Here is what I come up with:

To Wear or Not To Wear List

☺OK People☺   ☹Not So OK People☹

1. Mum and Dad

2. Leila and her family (excluding her brother as I don't give a crap what he thinks anyway)

3. Yasmeen and her family

4. Simone and Eileen

5. Samantha my cousin

6. Mr Pearse???

7. Nuns

8. Orthodox Jewish women who wear the wig

9. Monks and other religious people

1. Everybody at McCleans (especially Tia Tamos, Claire Foster and Rita Mason)

2. Milk bar owner down the road from our house

3. Check-out girls and guys at local Safeway/ Coles/all fresh food establishments

4. Uncle Joe and Aunt Mandy

5. Spunky sales rep working at Sanity

6. All spunky sales reps

7. Future university students & staff

8. Hard-core feminists who don't get that this is me exercising my right to choose

9. Ms Walsh, principal

10. Bald women

11. Hippies who don't care what you wear so long as there is peace and goodwill and pot

12. People who appreciate good fabric

13. Nudists (if they believe in the right to take it all off, surely they believe in the right to keep it all on?)

10. Nudists who are offended by people who keep it all on

11. Our neighbours, *especially* Mrs Vaselli

12. People who will interview me if and when I apply for a job one day

13. Adam (please not ADAM!)

OK, done.

Now, as it's a weekday I have the whole house to myself because my parents are at work. So I turn the stereo up loud and throw my entire wardrobe on to the family room couch. I pull my floor-length mirror off my bedroom wall and put it up against an armchair. I then try on every single outfit I have and mix and match all my clothes with assorted coloured scarves as I dance to a J.Lo track. I try different styles with the scarves and attempt to figure out which shape makes my face look slimmest. After three hours I'm exhausted, so I collapse on top of a pile of clothes and telephone Leila.

I've known Leila since Year Seven. Leila's like a child prodigy. She's never got anything below an A+ and if she did she'd probably be hospitalized for post-traumatic stress disorder. She's fanatically determined to become a lawyer. The only problem is that her parents are more interested in her getting a marriage certificate than a high school certificate.

Leila already wears the hijab full-time. She was in Year Seven when she came to school one day, sat down next to Yasmeen and me in class and told us she'd decided to wear it. We weren't even surprised because she's always been more religious than us. She has more guts than anybody I know. If we're out and somebody throws a comment at her, her tongue whips out a comeback before they've had a chance to finish their sentence. So she's naturally the first person I call for a pep talk.

"I'm bored," she tells me as soon as we've said hello. "There's nothing on TV. Either I'm stuck watching Oprah give away holidays and cry about her book club or I've got to watch Dr Phil tell me why carrots provide self-esteem."

"Guess what?"

"What?"

"I'm thinking of going full-time."

"You got a job?"

"Not that full-time! The *other* full-time."

"Get out!"

"Yeah. I mean, I haven't decided completely yet, but I'm seriously thinking about it. I'm going to get Mum to take me to Chadstone tonight. See how I go with it."

"I can't believe it! We'll both be wearing it now! How cool is that?"

We talk through *The Price is Right* and then I hang up and call Yasmeen. Yasmeen is the Arabic word for Jasmine. When we go out, Yasmeen likes to call herself Jasmine because she thinks it sounds more exotic. When I point out that it's usually non-English words which are considered exotic, she tells me to shut up.

Yasmeen's dad is Pakistani and her mum is British. Her mum converted to Islam when she was a History and Sociology student at university in London. That's where she met Yasmeen's dad who, spending most of his free time at the pub, wasn't exactly Islam's champion ambassador. Cassandra was in the middle of her thesis on British Muslims. At an on-campus bar one night, she overheard an "Abdel-Tariq" raising a beer to loudly toast "Cat Stevens, the Queen Mum and the glorious mini". She had found chapter one of her thesis, and her future husband.

Yasmeen has long curly hair down to her waist. At Hidaya she was always getting into trouble for letting it hang out from the bottom of her hijab. The thing is, she's obsessed with straightening it. Sometimes when I sat next to her I'd detect the distinct scent of ironing aid and Pantene.

Yasmeen's first response is to tell me I've lost the plot. "How can you even think about wearing it at *McCleans Grammar*?"

"Yeah, well, that's what's holding up the decision."

"Well duh! What are you trying to do to yourself? Isn't it hard enough with a surname the length of the alphabet? Now you want people to wonder if you're batting for Osama's team? Stick with anonymity, girl!"

I know Yasmeen is just mucking around and I snort with laughter. "What can I say? No pain no gain."

"Are you sure though?"

"Nope."

"How will you know when you're sure?"

"Don't know . . . I've got until Monday to decide."

"Why? There's no time line, you know."

"Yeah, well, I just reckon it's better if I do it from the start of semester. Less complicated that way."

"Well, you know I'll support you no matter what. I know you've got guts. If anybody at school says anything tell them to piss off.

"Anyway, this means we have to go shopping soon and get you a whole new wardrobe. Mix and match spree. What do you think?"

Hmm. Sounds like a plan. My afternoon home fashion parade gave me about ten outfits at the most. If I decide to wear the hijab I'll be wearing clothes which cover my entire body except for my face and hands. So that means long skirts or pants. I've got a zillion singlets and short-sleeved tops but I'll need more denim and linen jackets to wear when I go out. Something tells me my pocket money isn't going to be going towards my DVD collection any more.

Later that evening, after my parents have come home, I'm in my bedroom pretending to be absorbed in my chemistry holiday homework in order to avoid setting the dinner table. I take out my To Wear or Not To Wear List and review my candidates. I add a couple of people to my right-hand column. Upon further consideration I've decided that our local bus driver's consistently bad mood on school mornings (he once kicked a kid off because the kid had let out an enormous pizza-breath burp as he bought his ticket) doesn't give me much comfort that he'll flash a winning smile at my new fashion sense. But, admittedly, there are those I suspect I've underestimated and so I negotiate some people out of one column and into the other. I'm just not convinced Lee Ng down at the milk bar warrants a right-hand column place given he's half blind and wouldn't notice if I walked in dressed as a Teletubby.

As I'm amending my list my mum's voice yells out: "Ya Amal! Dinner! Come and set the table!"

I knew it wouldn't last.

"*Yallah!* You had all day to study and you wait until we come home? Do you think I'm silly? *Yallah!*"

Even though my parents speak to me predominantly in English there are some Arabic words which are instinctively part of their everyday vocabulary. *Yallah* means "come on" or "hurry up". When my parents are in a particularly

22

affectionate mood they sometimes prefix my name with *ya* so I'm "ya Amal", which means "oh Amal". When I was little, I actually thought my name was Yaamal.

If I'm in trouble the *ya* is dropped and I'm addressed as a mere "Amal". It's not good news.

At dinner I tell my parents that I'm thinking about wearing the hijab and to my disbelief they look at each other nervously. I was expecting a cheerleader routine around the family room. Not two faces staring anxiously at me.

"Hmm, would you prefer I get a tongue ring?"

My dad rolls his eyes at me and my mum sips on her soda water, her eyes fixed intently on my face, as though trying to work out if I'm joking.

"Wow, bring the enthusiasm on." I slam some mashed potato on my plate and proceed to make a potato castle, scraping the fork against the plate until my mum raises her eyebrows at me, daring me to ruin her dinner set. I proceed to throw a tantrum instead.

"I can't believe you guys aren't even happy for me! I thought you'd be ecstatic! Sheez! A little support would be nice! You're always encouraging me to pray more and talking to me about *finding spirituality* and all that, so why aren't you happy that I'm taking the extra step? Like you did, Mum? Huh?"

My dad looks away awkwardly, scratching his head. My mum sighs and then leans over and takes my hand in hers.

"We're proud of you. But it's a big decision, honey, and you're not at Hidaya any more. It's a different environment at McCleans. It might not even be allowed."

"Yeah right! How can they stop me? It's up to me whether I want to or not!" I'm acting like I've already made the decision. I haven't, but the thought that somebody else might take that choice away from me is energizing something inside me. Call it what you want. Defiance. Pig-headedness. It's burning me to think that I might not have the right to choose.

"Ya Amal, don't be so unreasonable," my dad says. "Of course it's your right to wear it. But don't be under any delusions as to the power of school rules and tradition. Especially at a school like McCleans. It's not a public school. The system is entirely different."

"They don't scare me!"

"Ya Amal, calm down," my dad says, smiling at me. "We'll support you but you have to think this through. Are you sure you are ready to cope with such a huge change in your life?"

"What's the big deal? It's a piece of material."

My mother snorts. "Since when do people see it as a mere piece of material? You and I both know that's being a tad optimistic, ya Amal."

"So what? I can deal with all the crap . . . I want to try . . . and I want that identity. You know, that symbol of my faith. I want to know what it means to be strong enough to walk around with it on and stick up for my right to wear it."

My parents don't say anything for a couple of seconds and then my mum pulls me into a hug.

"How about you give it a go until Monday?"

"You both treat me like I'm some kid," I say indignantly.

"I'm an adult. I can think like an adult too. That's *exactly* what I planned on doing."

My parents gaze at me affectionately. "Don't try to grow up so quickly, ya Amal," my dad says. "You'll remember your teenage years when you're old and wise and treasure the memories of your school days. When I was a kid—"

"Dad!" I moan. "That wasn't an invitation to tell me about your life!"

"Don't be so rude, ya Amal," he says, sitting upright and rolling his sleeves up as though he's preparing himself for a three-hour lecture.

"I'm not being rude. It's self-preservation. You're going to tell me for the zillionth time about how you used to walk through the bitter cold between Bethlehem and your village just to get to school."

"That's right!" He's beaming at me proudly because I've managed to remember a story I hear, on average, about twice a week. "We were living under Israeli occupation. The occupiers were making our lives as oppressive as possible to try to force us to leave. My parents insisted I go to school and I valued that privilege!"

"Maa!" I groan. "Tell Dad to give me a break."

She gives me a disapproving look and then glances away, her shoulders starting to shake. My dad catches her and she bursts out laughing. "Ya Mohamed, maybe tonight you could spare us?"

He pretends to look wounded and she flashes him a disturbingly flirtatious smile. He winks at her and they laugh

25

away like they're on a first date or something. Watching my parents act all lovey-dovey is barf-worthy.

"So how about we go for a test run tonight?" Mum asks me. "Let's go to Chadstone."

My dad snorts. "How did I know you'd suggest that? It's your second home. Jamila, Amal normally takes an hour to get ready when she goes to Chadstone. If she can cope with Chadstone, she can cope with anything."

If you're my age and you're at Chadstone shopping centre on a Thursday night with your friends, you're not there for the sock sales. You're there to make an impression, muck about at Timezone, hang around the entrances for a smoke and a perve, and to piss off the security guards who see a midriff top or goatee and think "troublemaker". I wouldn't ever make an appearance in the tracksuit pants and daggy pullover tops I wear to the local supermarket. Chadstone means make-up, designer clothes, great hair. So basically I've got to replace great hair with great hijab in the equation and I'm all set.

At the moment, wearing a tarantula as a brooch sounds less intimidating.

I've decided on a navy blue veil and baby blue cotton headband to match my jeans and blue cardigan. I pull my hair back into a low bun and put the headband on. I need the headband as the veil is a silk fabric and will slip off without the headband to grip it underneath. The contrasting shades of blue also spice the look up a little. I fold the veil in half, into a triangular shape, and even it out over the headband. I wrap it around my head and face, taking care that there are no creases and that the front part of my headband is showing. When I've perfected the shape I fasten the veil with a small safety pin at my neck. I fling the tail ends across my shoulders and join them together with a brooch.

My top three greatest fears, of which (1) makes me slightly incontinent just thinking about it and (3) gives me a twitchy eye, are these:

1. smart-arse comments (*e.g. I'm standing on the escalator and a group of guys yell out "nappy head" or some equally original comment*);
2. humiliation (*e.g. toilet paper on my shoes, tripping on my heels, the painful public moments made even more excruciating when you already stand out like a Big Mac in a health food store*);
3. fixated staring (*e.g. I'm trying to order chips at the food court and the girl at the counter can't register that I don't want sauce because she's too preoccupied burning her retina*).

So you can understand why I'm walking around the shops as if I'm in combat mode, avoiding eye contact with other people and waiting for something to happen. But as I browse through the shops I realize how uncomfortable and irrational I'm acting because it feels like most people really couldn't care less. I mean, sure there's staring, but it's not

27

enough to rate in my fears list. There are the occasional goggle-eyes but most people give me the once-over top to bottom, which I can deal with. I'm just one more late-night shopper, one more person to bump shoulders with, negotiate a crowded queue with. My mum gets this. She walks and talks as though she doesn't even realize she's wearing the hijab. It makes me feel kind of protected because she's so confident and dignified. I wonder how long it will take me to feel and act that way.

While I'm walking through the food court I pass three women who are all wearing the hijab. They're huddled around a table, talking and eating ice cream. One of them catches my eye and smiles.

"*Assalamu Alaykom*," she says, greeting me with the universal Islamic greeting, *Peace be upon you.*

"*Walaykom Wassalam*," I reply, smiling back at her. The other two girls also greet me and I reply and they all smile warmly at me. They go back to their conversation and I walk off with a big grin because it is now that I think I begin to understand that there's more to this hijab than the whole modesty thing. These girls are strangers to me but I know that we all felt an amazing connection, a sense that this cloth binds us in some kind of universal sisterhood.

I lie in bed that night and replay the scene over and over in my head. I'm experiencing a new identity, a new expression of who I am on the inside, but I know that I'm not alone. I'm not breaking new ground. I'm sharing something with millions of other women around the world and it feels so exciting. I know some people might find it hard to believe but walking around Chadstone tonight I'd never felt so free and sure of who I am. I felt safe that people weren't judging me and making assumptions about my character from the length of my skirt or the size of my bra. I felt protected from all the crap about beauty and image. As scared as I was walking around the shops in the hijab, I was also experiencing a feeling of empowerment and freedom. I know I have a long way to go. I still dressed to impress and I took ages to get my make-up, clothes and hijab just right. But I didn't feel I was compromising myself by wanting to make an impression. I was looking and feeling good on my own terms, and boy did that feel awesome.

My dad wakes me up for the morning *fajr*, prayer. I'm not my best at dawn and sometimes I throw the pillow and tell him to go away. But most mornings I get up with them to pray. The walk to the bathroom is always a zombie-steps experience. Some mornings I manage to knock into a wall, but that's actually quite useful for waking me up. Then I perform the *wuduh*, the ablution, wetting my hands, face, arms, feet and crown of my head. And then we pray. My dad leads the prayer and his voice as he reads the Koran is soft and melodious. And it's when I'm standing there this morning, in my PJs and a hijab, next to my mum and my dad, kneeling before God, that I feel a strange sense of calm. I feel like nothing can hurt me, and nothing else matters. And that's when I know I'm ready.

4

I'm fast asleep, dreaming of my first day at school, when my alarm goes berserk. I hit the snooze button and slip into that deepest of sleeps, where you know that nothing in the entire universe could offer the slightest temptation for you to get out of bed. Then four minutes pass and that sadistic shrilling device sounds off again. If that's not bad enough, my mum walks into my room and jumps on me, kissing my face and head.

"Come on, ya Amal! First day at school!"

"Five more minutes," I groan.

"Ya Amal! Come on! *Yallah!*" In an act of severe child abuse my bed quilt is mercilessly pulled off my body.

"Maa! Leave me alone!"

"I'm making you a nice breakfast. A good start for your first day! *Yallah!*"

I eventually manage to fall out of bed and into the shower, where I have a panic attack about my decision. Then the shampoo gets in my eyes. So my panic attack goes from "What will they say about my hijab?" to "Is this soap going to blind me?" I eventually salvage my eyeballs, towel off, put on my uniform and plait my hair. Then I sit on the edge of my bed and study my list. Yep, no doubt about it, the majority of people at school are right-hand columners.

I've just got to take the plunge; that's the only way to do it. Wear it and then deal with the consequences as they come along. It's a new term. It'll be like a fresh start for me. I feel like I'm ready but that my fears have ganged up on my confidence and grabbed it in a headlock. Every minute or so it manages to escape their clutches and come up for fresh air, but then my fears attack again and I'm stuck struggling to feel one emotion, have one stable thought, take one solid stance as the gang warfare goes on.

It's like somebody taking weeks to decide to go skydiving. They finally psych themselves up to do it but then they end up standing in the plane ten thousand feet in the air stressing about whether they want to go ahead with it. It's one jump and the decision is made. No turning back. That's how I see it. I don't want to wear it today and then chicken out and rock up to school tomorrow without it. It's not a game or a fashion statement or a new fad. It's more serious than that.

So I take my veil out of the cupboard and stand in front of

the mirror, staring at myself. It's just hair. Follicles attached to my head, which occasionally frizz out anyway. Hair. A piece of material. Hair covered *by* a piece of material. Nothing to it. Sweet.

I've chosen a plain white scarf, made of a soft chiffon. I think white will be the most appropriate match to my school uniform colours of maroon and yellow. The uniform consists of a maroon shirt with yellow stitching and collar. We have the choice of a pleated maroon skirt or tailored pants. As the skirt is knee-length I wear pants.

It's going to be one of those mornings because now my hijab won't work. I want a perfect shape, a symmetrical arch to frame my face. That means no creases, no flops, no thread pulls. As I'm struggling in front of the mirror Mum comes in and offers to help, but whether it's about how to wear a shirt, a pair of jeans or a hijab, my dress sense is out of bounds to motherly advice. After pulling and coaxing the material around my face, I finally have the shape I want, and fasten it with a safety pin at my neck. It's taken me forty-five minutes. Not even moussing my hair takes this long.

At breakfast, in between force-feeding me scrambled eggs and giving me pep talks on studying hard and staying away from drugs, my mum and dad stare proudly at me in my uniform and hijab. I smile at them but as I turn away I catch them darting anxious looks at each other.

"What? What's wrong?" I ask.

"One last time, ya Amal," my dad says. "Are you sure about this?"

"One hundred per cent." OK, a white lie but I don't want anybody to know about the butterfly cheering squad in my stomach. Not even my parents.

"You'll have to see the principal immediately. You know that, don't you?" my mum asks. "If only you could have made an appointment."

"Yeah, but how could I? School's been closed."

"Ms Walsh would have been in her office during the holidays, Amal, and you know it."

"Yeah, well . . . it's better this way."

"What about you talk to her today and start wearing it tomorrow?" my dad suggests.

I lose my temper. "First of all, that makes it open to negotiation – and it's not! Second of all, I want to start school upfront about it from the moment I walk through those gates! And third of all—"

"– you will lower your voice and speak to us with respect."

Parents. Honestly. Sometimes they really do think the world revolves around them.

McCleans is a massive expanse of ovals and courtyards, basketball courts and swimming pools, tree-lined lunch areas, with park benches, shapely hedges, rosebushes and perfectly symmetrical paved tiles. The front gate is lined with mums and dads dropping their kids off in four-wheel drives and BMWs.

I can't help missing my old school. Sure, there was

nothing fancy about Hidaya, but strangely enough I miss going to a school where you sat in class and smelt the pollution of the nearby factories penetrating the recesses of every window. Where lunch times were spent fighting over a space in the tiny playground. There was one asphalt court and it was versatile enough to accommodate a cricket match, basketball game and kick of the footy. You spent half your lunch time dodging balls as you ducked your way from one side of the school to the other. I loved it. I loved the intimacy of it, that you knew everybody's name and history. That you knew the teachers felt it was more than a job. That you could feel they lived and breathed the idea of making the school as big as their dreams. That it didn't matter that you didn't have gyms and courtyards and pools and horse-riding and tennis courts. All that mattered was how hard you studied or bludged and your friendships. And it was no big deal if you didn't have a clue who you were because nobody was asking for an explanation anyway.

There's something about McCleans. I just don't feel at home. How much your dad earns, how many cars you have, whether your money's "old", all that sort of crap counts as your initiation ceremony. But even if you do fit the "financial" résumé, some people still don't make it. Tia Tamos, with her entourage of Mini-Mes, Claire Foster and Rita Mason, made that very clear to me on my first day of school. I was talking to another girl and she asked me where I lived. I overheard Tia snickering with the Mini-Mes about us probably living off the dole. I wanted to smash her porcelain face. That's how I met Eileen Tanaka. She told me I got it mild. Her father, an optometrist, and mum, a biochemist, were apparently sweatshop factory hands.

Whenever I walk through the massive gates I feel like Alice in Wonderland, with one too many forks in the road and no Cheshire cat to direct me around.

This morning, I walk along a fence of perfectly trimmed hedges on my way to the main office to see the headmistress and talk to her about my decision. As I'm walking I notice a group of boys, probably in junior school, standing together laughing. I pass them and I swear to God I have butterflies. Butterflies. Over a group of kids the size of lemmings. I am so idiotic I want to kick myself in the head. They look at me like I'm a biology specimen, but one of them has a Nintendo Game Boy so I'm not worth staring at for long.

When I eventually arrive at the office the secretary, Mrs Duckely, just about chokes on her coffee. She recovers long enough to ask me why I'm not in home room.

"I need to see Ms Walsh."

"Can't it wait until recess? Ms Walsh might not be too happy about you skipping home room."

I grin at her and whisper conspiratorially: "She doesn't know I'm wearing the veil."

She looks at me with wide eyes and tells me to take a seat.

I'm buzzed in soon afterwards and enter a large room

filled with beautiful mahogany furnishings and plush armchairs. The burgundy walls are decorated with massive portraits of earlier principals and framed photographs of past Year Twelve classes. Trophies and plaques line the floor-to-ceiling shelves.

Ms Walsh is seated at her desk, her head down as she continues writing. She motions at me to take a seat on the plain pine chair beside her desk. She does this without looking up. I tiptoe across to the chair, then sit down on the edge.

Please God. Please God. Please God. Don't let her schiz it on me.

After half a minute she stops writing. The countdown in my head begins.

Three.

"So, Amal, what is so important that –"

Two.

". . .you had to see me first thing –"

One.

She looks at me.

". . .today. . ."

I think songs. I think "Take my breath away" and "It's in your eyes".

And then she coughs. Ahh, the comforting sound of an awkward *ahem*. When in doubt as to how to react, buy some time and roll that phlegm.

Twice if you must.

"Ahem . . . er. . ."

"Hi, Ms Walsh. Sorry to barge in on you without an appointment but because it was school holidays I couldn't make one and I thought I should see you first thing this morning, before I go to school, you know what I'm saying? I . . . I've . . . I've decided to wear the hijab. You know how I'm Muslim and all? Well, it's part of my religion to wear the hijab and I'm sorry if I've kind of shocked you like this but it was almost like an overnight decision . . . kind of thing. . ." I stop rambling and look down at my hands nervously, saying a silent prayer that she won't have a fit.

She sounds like she needs a ventilator. She draws in a huge breath of air, leans back in her chair and gazes intently at me: "Well now, Amal Mohamed Nas – Nas – Nasru—" I cut her off. It's too painful to watch. She never fails to stutter like the Rainman when she takes a shot at my surname.

"Mohamed Nasrullah Abdel-Hakim," I complete for her. I smile, trying to send off a million happy vibes with every spasmodic twitch of my facial muscles. I'm under no delusions that she's going to take this easily. After all, she has a reputation for popping a painkiller from the trauma of seeing a student wearing the wrong socks. No chemist will have sufficient supplies for her now.

Instead, she half smiles, half winces and runs her fingers through her hair. I momentarily feel sorry for her because I'm not about to pretend that this is the equivalent of mismatched socks or the wrong coloured hairclip. There seems to be something almost X-Men-like about this piece of material on my head. Too many people look at it as

37

though it has bizarre powers sewn into its micro-fibres. Powers which transform Muslim girls into UCOs (Unidentified Covered Objects), which turn Muslim girls from an "us" into a "them". Ms Walsh probably wants to deal with detentions, board meetings, curriculum changes, teachers' pay rises. Figuring out how to deal with a Muslim kid wearing the veil at her stuffy old grammar school is probably the last thing she expected to pop up in her job description. But although I understand her viewpoint, I've got to stand up for myself. As much as I would like to live a comic-book character's life, I really would rather not be treated like an UCO.

"Amal . . . hmm. . . I don't want to – I mean, I want to tread delicately on this . . . sensitive issue . . . hmm. . . Did you speak to anybody about wearing . . . about abandoning our school uniform?"

"I wouldn't exactly call it abandoning."

Her eyes narrow. One thing about teachers and principals. They hate to be contradicted.

I bite my lip, worried she'll erupt, and then quickly say something before she has a chance to. "I would have spoken to you earlier except today is my first school day wearing it. I made the decision during the holidays."

"Hmm . . . now let me see." She presses her fingers down on her temples. "So your parents have made you wear the veil permanently now? Starting from today? Your *first* day of term three. Couldn't it wait until tomorrow? After they'd spoken to me?"

38

I stare at her in shock. "My parents? Who mentioned my parents?"

"The veil, dear." Her voice is annoyingly phony. "So you've been made to wear it from today?"

"Nobody has *made* me wear it, Ms Walsh. It's my decision." I shift in the chair, my bum numb from the hard wood.

"*Your* decision to cover yourself up?" she asks with the faintest hint of scepticism.

I look at her with a bewildered expression. "Yes, it was my decision."

She gives me another *ahem*. "Well, Amal. I'm not sure what to do here. I hope you appreciate that this isn't Hid—Hida – your old *Coburg* school. This is a reputable educational establishment. We have more than one hundred years of proud history. A history of tradition, Amal. Of conformity with the rules and policies of this institution. We have a strict uniform policy. And you have walked in, on your first day back from holidays, and been so presumptuous as to alter it without authorization."

"But Ms Walsh, it's not like I've put in an eyebrow ring or grown a mohawk or dyed my uniform pink. I'm still in school uniform. I know it's the first time a student has worn it but couldn't you make an exception? I'm not doing this because I'm trying to rebel against the rules."

She looks uncomfortable and leans back in her leather chair. "But you've made no effort to seek the school's permission. This certainly wasn't raised at your enrolment interview. I recall your parents. They seemed like very decent, straightforward people. I'm rather disappointed they never mentioned this. I saw your mum wearing the veil but I never suspected you would be wearing it too."

"But my enrolment interview was more than six months ago! I didn't *seriously* start to contemplate going ahead with this until last week. And even *then* I was still unsure. I only made my final decision four days ago!"

"Why didn't you at least approach me when you were thinking about it? You should have consulted me first."

It takes me a solid minute to realize my jaw is hanging down.

"Er . . . it was personal. . ."

"Well, obviously not. It's rather public, don't you think? Personal is something tucked under your shirt. Personal is rosary beads in your pocket. I would submit, Amal, that your veil is not, of all things, personal. Now don't get me wrong; I respect your religion. We live in a multicultural society and we should accept and tolerate people no matter what their creed, race or colour. But you must understand that I have an educational institution to run and there are certain guidelines. I'm sure your parents will appreciate that."

"I'm not going around preaching or anything. It's something . . . for myself."

She looks at me incredulously.

"My parents had nothing to do with it. They found out last week. They were even concerned for me—"

40

"Concerned?"

"Yes, they were worried I wasn't ready. Actually, they were freaking out more about how I'd be able to cope. Being the only one in the school with it on."

"Let me get this right." She sits up straight in her chair. "They were actually opposed to this decision to cover up?"

"Well, not *opposed*. Just, I don't know, cautious. Worried for me. Because of the reaction I might get." I look at her, but she ignores my tone and is suddenly shuffling papers on her desk and flashing me a large, friendly smile.

"Well, Amal. Let's discuss this later, shall we? You've got class to attend."

She scribbles out a late note and hands it to me.

"Here you go. Now have a wonderful first day and I will speak to you soon."

She gives me a fake smile and resumes writing, an invitation for me to leave pronto. I nod back, careful not to slam the door behind me as I leave.

I end up entering English with everybody already comfortably seated. I close the door behind me and am confronted by an instantly silent classroom, lines of faces staring up at me from their desks.

Mr Pearse is standing at the front of the class. I can tell my hijab has taken him by surprise. I wait, holding my breath, for his response.

Tell me off for being late. Give me detention. Scream, yell, be normal.

41

"*Ahem!* First day of school, Amal. I hope you have a note."
His eyebrows are raised and his hands folded across his
chest; he taps his fingers against his arms impatiently.

He is inaugurated into my hall of fame of all-time
favourite teachers.

"Here you go, Mr Pearse."

He scans it and then smiles at me, nodding at me to take
a seat. My friends, Simone and Eileen, are grinning proudly at
me. Everybody else is staring like I've dyed my hair green or
showed up to school wrapped in toilet paper. Tia Tamos,
Claire Foster and Rita Mason look at me and then snigger
amongst themselves. Predictable. After all, they were top of
the right-hand columners in my To Wear or Not To Wear List.
As I walk past the desks my eyes meet Adam's and he looks
taken aback. He wriggles in his seat and is suddenly
fascinated by the corner of his desk. I feel like somebody has
got a stapler and started punching holes all over my guts.

I met Adam Keane in Chemistry a couple of weeks into my
first semester. We were paired up as lab partners, and we
were assigned together many more times throughout the
term. As this is high school, it's important to understand what
type he is. He's not the loner type. Not the ostracized-nerd
type or stuck-up brainiac type. He's not the pot-head type,
just-wants-to-bonk-girls type, teacher's-pet type, personally-
unhygienic type. He's pretty popular, as any guy who's good
at sport usually is. In that sense, he's a sporty type. Plus,
everybody knows he wants to be a doctor and needs to
pretty much ace every subject to become one. So he's also an

ambitious-but-retains-coolness type. He's just one of those guys who seems to have it all. Back then I wasn't really that impressed with him. We hung out in Chem, did the hi/bye thing in the hall, and that was pretty much it. We had the "classroom relationship". The kind that ends when the bell rings. There's no recess or lunch time thing happening.

Then at approximately 11.45 a.m. on Friday, 24 May, we're in Chemistry and Adam's passing me a gauze mat and bunsen burner when I suddenly notice his sleeves are pulled up and I get a glimpse of his forearms.

I'm telling you, I'm usually a 1) smile, 2) eyes, 3) skin, and 4) six-pack kind of girl. But the sight of Adam's forearms, with his veins bulging against his muscles and his shirt sleeves begging for oxygen just about made me dizzy. I started to notice his eyes — a deep navy-blue. His hair — a dishevelled mess of brown and sandy blond. OK there's a bit of dot-to-dot acne and he almost has a monobrow dilemma, but his imperfections are what kept me up all that Friday and Saturday night as I fantasized about cuddling up to his forearms, stroking his hair and listening to him tell me I'm the most beautiful girl in the world.

So I've been in official crush mode since May 24.

Hence the absolute gastro-inducing experience of being snubbed by him.

I take a seat next to Simone and Eileen and wait for a comment during class. But nobody approaches me and nobody says anything. So I wait for people to say something in-between classes. But nobody does.

In English, Simone and Eileen furiously write notes to me.
You look great!
Boy have you got guts!
Fill us in at recess.

At recess I sit with Simone and Eileen in the northern courtyard overlooking one of the ovals. Simone and I hit it off from my first day at school. I'd walked into home room and approached the closest free seat, next to a gorgeous girl with jet-black hair and cat-green eyes. She was all haughtiness and glamour and took one look at me and told me she was saving the seat for a friend. She's a scanner. You know the type, the kind who looks you up and down, head to toe, and makes it so obvious. Never mind the fact that you're wearing the same uniform every day, she'll still do her scan, as though she's trying to detect if you've put on a gram of fat or something. She's also into the sexy hair tossing thing. Every time she speaks her hair gets tossed from one side to the other. It's a wonder her neck doesn't crack. Anyway, Simone was sitting in the back and waved me over. I sat next to her and she told me I'd had my first encounter with Tia Tamos, aka hair-spinning bitch, and asked me if I watched *Friends*. We've hung out ever since.

I met Eileen Tanaka after the "living off the dole" incident with Tia. Eileen's parents are Japanese. Not Chinese. Or Asian. Japanese. She doesn't have much patience for people who are too lazy to make the distinction.

"So let me get this right," Eileen says. "You don't have to wear it in front of family, kids and females?"

"Basically that's it."

"So it's not like you wear it all the time," Simone says.

"That's right. Of course . . . I wear it in the shower."

Eileen and Simone roll their eyes at me. "Like we're *that* naïve, Amal."

"Seriously, I do. Helps with the conditioning treatment."

"*Please* do us a favour and audition for the Melbourne Comedy Festival."

"Anyway, what did Ms Walsh say about it?" Simone asks, offering me a celery stick.

"What's with the celery?" I ask her.

"New diet," she groans. Simone's incredibly self-conscious about her body. She doesn't understand that it's all in her mind. OK, so she's not a size eight, can't feel her ribcage and doesn't have toothpicks for legs. She's about a size fourteen and really voluptuous and curvy and gorgeous with big blue eyes, creamy, radiant skin and lips that look like she has permanent red lipstick on. When she smiles, her cheeks squash up and her eyes twinkle. But tell that to her and you're up for a fight given that when she looks in the mirror she's seeing one big lipid molecule. She's on a new diet almost every week, but they never last, and then she goes through a binge/purge cycle and comes back on Monday morning with a new celebrity diet that she got from *Women's Weekly*.

"No-carb?" Eileen asks.

"Who knows." She takes another reluctant bite of her celery stick. "So tell us, Amal. Did she crack it?"

"She nearly had an aneurism. She was raving on about breaking tradition and this *institution's* proud history. Why do all principals do that? Make you feel like you're in a mental asylum?"

"Did Adam say anything?"

". . .No. . ."

"Just forget about it. He'll come round."

"Yeah . . . I guess. . ."

I need a place to pray, so at lunch time I go to see Mr Pearse. All through the year I've been carrying out my two afternoon prayers at home after school but I'd go through them at supersonic speed so that I could make it in time to watch *Home and Away*. It never felt right and now I really want to try to pray at the set times, the way it's supposed to be.

"Now let's see." Mr Pearse leans back in his chair and stares at his desk, deep in thought. "Will an empty classroom do? I can arrange one for you if that's suitable."

"Well, have you ever seen news reports where the camera zooms in on a group of Muslims praying? The 'bums up' shot? Forget every other move in the prayers, it's the bums up that really sets the cameras off. So I'd hate to be in a classroom with my rear end in the air and people walk past and start thinking I'm into solo yoga."

He chuckles. "I see what you mean. You can use the

46

storage room adjoining my office. You'll have your privacy as it's nicely tucked away, and it can be accessed through my office so just walk right in when you need to. How long will the prayer take?"

"About ten minutes."

"Oh, is *that* all? It's nice and simple then."

Yep, he's my favourite, favourite, favourite.

5

The first thing I do when I get home from school is jump on my bed and call Leila.

"Oh my God! I wore it! To school! To *McCleans*! And everybody was staring and kind of freaked out and avoiding me and Mr Pearse was so cool and Ms Walsh, well, yeah, she spun out but that was to be expected, and Simone and Eileen were *so* supportive and Tia obviously scrunched up her face at me like I'd walked in covered in cow dung but, hey, I'd be insulted if she ignored me, and Leila, it felt so amazing and scary and—"

"Amal! Chill pill please!"

"OK, OK," I say breathlessly. "Adam ignored me, Leila!"

"He did not!"

"It was brutal."

"So confront him. You're not the type to sit and cry in a corner."

"How long did it take you to feel, you know, *confident*?"

"Sometimes I still get nervous; depends where I am. But I'm used to it now. The hijab's part of me. Hey, got to go! Mum's calling me. She's having a tantrum because I can't be stuffed watching her cook tonight. See ya!"

I hang up the phone and call Yasmeen. Her reaction is to give me a long lecture about the urgency of me applying make-up.

"Tell me you had eyeliner on today."

"Are you scrunching your face up in tension waiting for my answer?"

"Yes."

"I'm happy to disappoint. It's a big fat NOPE."

"You are beyond *pathetic*, Amal. Do you not understand that if you wear eyeliner and eyeshadow your eyes will be devastating with the scarf? Trust me. You've seen my mum. Her eyes are similar to yours, although yours are probably a little more greeny-blue, and only God knows why you got the coloured eyes when I'm the one who knows how to apply cosmetics. When Mum does her eyes up under her hijab she looks hot."

"Yasmeen, my principal would probably put me in front of a school assembly and wash my make-up off with steel wool if I went to school all dolled up."

"Go figure. You're at nerdville. Anyway, back to your

attempt to wear the hijab without the assistance of Revlon. I hate to disappoint you, but there are only a few women in this world who can get away with the natural look. Don't you read *New Weekly*? "Stars without their make-up", etc.? *Hello?* Do you have a big modelling contract you haven't told me about? Are you co-starring in Brad Pitt's next movie? If your answer to either of these questions is no, then go out and buy some cosmetic products this instant."

We talk for ages. I tell Yasmeen about Adam and Ms Walsh and Simone and Eileen and Tia Tamos and Mr Pearse and Adam, Adam, Adam. She fills me in on the goss from her school and all the people from Hidaya who moved on there who say hi to me. We talk and talk and I miss her and Leila so much it aches.

At dinner my parents tell me Ms Walsh called them and wants to see them tomorrow. They've arranged to meet at five. I'm livid. My mum wants me to calm down and my dad wants me to stop with the conspiracy theories.

"I don't want to take it off," I plead. "If she thinks she's going to make me take it off I'll take her to court!"

My dad snorts. "Stop being so dramatic."

"Well, I will!"

"No one's taking anybody to court," my mum scoffs, giving me an amused look. "*Or* making any such threats either."

"OK, fine. I'll ring the tabloids. I'm sure *they'll* be interested. I can just see the cover story now: 'Innocent

Muslim girl – victim of snobby grammar school prejudice'."

My parents laugh. I don't see anything funny.

"Look," my dad says, calmly placing his fork and knife down at a proper angle to his plate and adjusting the napkin on his lap in his usual I-am-such-a-nerd-and-eat-as-though-I'm-at-a-five-star-restaurant fashion. "It's really very simple, Amal. All your mum and I need to know is one thing. Are you convinced?"

"I think I am . . . I mean, yeah sure, it was really hard at school and everybody was staring at me and I just know they're all wondering if I've flipped. I know it kind of looks like I'm asking for it. Do you know what I'm saying? You don't put the hijab on and walk into McCleans expecting people not to wonder what the hell is going on."

"Exactly our point," my dad says. "Why are you doing it if you know what you're up for? Are you mentally prepared for the staring and small-minded stereotyping and mis-conceptions?"

Before I answer, my mum interrupts: "You see how people react and look at *me*, at my age! You're still young and starting out. You've got university and then looking for a job. Have you thought all of it through?"

"Maa! I'm not a kid! I've spent every last minute in these past four days thinking through every single potential obstacle. I've predicted all the smart-arse comments people can throw at me. Nappy-head, tea-towel head, camel jockey, and all the rest. Yeah, I'm scared. OK, there, happy? I'm petrified. I walked into my classroom and I wanted to throw

51

up from how nervous I was. But this decision, it's coming from my heart. I can't explain or rationalize it. OK, I'm doing it because I believe it's my duty and defines me as a Muslim female but it's not as ... I don't know how to put it ... it's more than just that."

I take a big sip of water because there's a lump starting a roadblock in my throat and the last thing I want is for my parents to see me cry. So I swallow my glass of water in seconds and manage to extend the corners of my mouth enough to flash a tiny smile at them. After all, everybody knows that when you're sixteen you don't cry in front of your parents. Not if you're ever planning on bringing up the whole "stop treating me like a kid" argument again.

My parents glance at each other and then smile warmly at me. My mum reaches over and squeezes my hand tightly. "We're proud of you, darling."

My dad says: "OK, ya Amal, we understand. That's all we needed to know, *habibti*. Leave the rest to your mum and me."

"Now pass me the salad," my mum says, "and tell us everything we need to know about this Ms Walsh."

My dad and I toss between taking the garbage out after dinner or wiping the table. I go garbage.

As I walk up to the side of the house and put the rubbish in the bin, I almost don't notice Mrs Vaselli, our next-door neighbour. She's sitting out on her front porch and I suddenly hear a harsh cough and an "In ze name of ze Father, ze Son and ze Holy Ghost".

She's a grump. If you smile at her she scowls. If you nod at her she curses you. If you attempt conversation she pretends that she can't hear you. If you ignore her she yells out Greek swear words. I dread being outside at the same time she is.

I don't know what her constitution is like, but I'm struggling to get the lid off the bin with my fingers all numb from the cold. It's a typical winter evening in Melbourne where you take in a breath of the air and your body goes into a spasm, like when you take a quick sip from a 7-Eleven Slurpie and your head is frozen into agony.

I look over her way and wave a reluctant hello because if I don't she'll probably tell my parents and then I'll get the "she's an old lady, show some manners" lecture.

"Hi, Mrs Vaselli," I call out.

"Why you keeping leave za cigarette pack on my grass?" She has a thick accent and a voice that seems like it's bottling up years of anger.

"I don't smoke, Mrs Vaselli." The cold has obviously reached her head.

"Huh! You *sure*? Maybe you acting innocent to your parent. But you no tricking me!"

"I said I don't smoke," I say firmly. "Maybe somebody was walking down the street and threw it. Maybe it got blown here by the wind. There's a million ways it could have ended up on your grass but me smoking isn't one of them!"

"Huh!" She turns her face away abruptly, indicating to me that the conversation has ended.

*

53

The next morning at *fajr* I pray that Ms Walsh lets me wear the hijab and that Leila's parents grow some brain cells and quit pressuring Leila about marriage. That Simone's next diet works, Adam and I become the best of friends, and Ms Walsh lets me wear my hijab. I pray that Palestinians are granted the same rights and freedom and dignity that the Israelis enjoy and that the streets fill with Israelis and Palestinians walking side by side in peace. And that Ms Walsh lets me wear my hijab. That Tia loses her hair – I mean gets over her power trip – and that my class stops their silent treatment.

And that Ms Walsh lets me wear my hijab.

I'm on edge in home room. Then English, then Maths, then recess. By three o'clock Simone and Eileen are as nervous as I am and we've managed to get through a whole packet of doughnuts in between the last two periods, waiting for five o'clock to come.

They wish me luck as they get on the bus. I've told my parents I'm staying after school to go home with them. There's no way I'm waiting at home while they're in there with Ms Walsh discussing the most important thing I've done in my life. I wait out the rest of the afternoon in the library. I try to do some homework but I see Ms Walsh's name in every line I read. So I go into the music section, put on a set of headphones and listen to an album. But her name is popping up in all the lyrics too. So I just sit and stare at a huge oak tree outside the window.

I fall into a daydream, imagining the whole school ignoring me for weeks and months. And I imagine that one morning at school assembly, while Ms Walsh attacks the microphone with a lecture on the evils of chewing gum, she gets a message that I've been hit by a bus, no make it a tram, and I'm in intensive care. Ms Walsh starts sobbing and drops the microphone in a dramatic crash, then storms to the hospital with a troop of my class, showering me with flowers and apologies. Adam approaches the bed and takes my hand, whispering that he wants me to wake up from my coma because he loves me and thinks I look beautiful in hijab because it accentuates my eyes. I get so caught up in my daydream that pretty soon my eyes start to go fuzzy and my skin all prickly. It's only when I feel my throat choking up that I snap back to reality.

Soon it's five thirty. And then it's five forty-five. Then I start to panic. The librarian, Mr Thompson, approaches me and tells me they're closing at six. So I pack up my things and wait outside on a bench in the quadrangle, wondering, as my teeth are chattering and my nose is turning into a Rudolph, if it would have been the same if I'd waited for them at home.

And then my mobile rings and my mum tells me to meet them at the car park. And I run, which is hard with a backpack filled with textbooks and folders, but I don't care and just run, my scarf lifting up in the wind.

At the car, my parents are looking out for me. I bolt up to

them and my mum tells me off for running with a heavy backpack and asks if I want to be a hunchback when I'm older. My dad gives me a hug and then I stand in front of them, panting and sticky, the cold wind rushing against me.

"Well? What did she say? Can I wear it?" And I don't know why but I burst into tears and then my mum is hugging me and telling me it will be OK and my dad is having his Mr Brady moment and telling me it's been sorted out. And I cry and I cry because until this moment I've never felt so sure about what I wanted.

We go out to a Japanese restaurant on Brunswick Road. We have to take our shoes off and my dad's embarrassed because he's got a massive hole in his right sock and his big toe is sticking out. He dashes past our waitress and plonks himself down on the cushion in case anybody notices.

"So what happened?" I ask after the waitress has taken our order. We didn't speak about it on our way here. All they told me was that I am allowed. And that was enough to send me into a happy trance all the way, my window rolled down, my face being cut by the icy breeze, my scarf blowing in the wind. It felt beautiful.

"Well, it was strange," my dad says, "but she seemed to be under the impression that we disapproved of your decision. Any idea where that came from?"

"She kept insinuating you guys had held a gun to my head and I explained to her that you were actually concerned for me, if anything."

"When we walked in she wanted to talk about how the three of us could talk you out of it."

I look at my mum in shock.

"She didn't?"

"Yes," my mum continues. "She said she understood our concerns completely and had called us to a meeting to discuss a way to convince you not to go ahead. Your mouth is still hanging down, Amal. Close it."

"So what did you tell her?"

My parents look at each other and grin.

"Well," my dad takes a sip of his Coke, "let's just say we cleared that up."

"And?"

"None of your business, Amal," my mum says.

"*What?* We don't have the Fifth Amendment here. You *can* tell me." I start pleading but they refuse to give me the details because they think it "might affect my relationship with Ms Walsh". Affect my relationship? What do they think? That we even had one to begin with?

"She's your principal and you must be on good terms with her," my dad says.

"And don't worry," my mum says, "she was only trying to make sense of your decision, Amal. It's OK, now, we explained *everything* to her."

"That it was entirely your decision and a part of your religious identity," my dad adds.

"That you would wear whatever colour they thought most suitably matched the uniform—"

"What colour did she agree to?" I ask, hoping it isn't the awful maroon or yellow of our official colours.

"Maroon," my mum answers. "And don't scrunch your face like that. You should be—"

"– grateful, yes I know," I groan.

The food arrives and we dig in to our prawn tempura and steamed rice.

"You've got until next Monday to get hijab in that colour," my mum says. "We'll go shopping for material on Saturday."

"OK . . . so what did you think of her?"

But they don't answer. Instead they look at each other and then give me an *ahem*.

I'm called to the office over the loudspeaker during Maths the next day. Everybody always gets the "are you in trouble?" look when that happens. Mr Loafer excuses me and five minutes later I'm sitting on the hard pine chair in Ms Walsh's office, watching her squeeze her temples again.

"I assume your parents have spoken to you?" she begins.

"Yeah. Last night."

"I've decided to allow you to wear your veil."

"Yes, I know! Thanks, Ms Walsh."

"Now, I've decided on maroon. That will at least blend in with the rest of your uniform. Amal, I need to ask you, so that there are no further unexpected announcements, to please advise me whether this is the only religious symbol you intend to display."

For a moment I feel like I'm in a witness box and start to

get a little annoyed by her cross-examination. But then I try to put myself in her high heels and think of it from her perspective.

"Um, yes it is, Ms Walsh."

"*Ahem* ... right. I'm glad that's sorted out. I've put you down as an agenda item in tonight's staff meeting so that your situation can be explained to the teachers. You have nothing to worry about. It will simply serve to allay their curiosity and also give them an opportunity to discuss how to deal with it."

"Deal with what?"

"Amal, I hope you appreciate that this is something ... rather novel. I respect your decision and your right to practise your faith, but you do look different now, dear. I don't want you to interpret this incorrectly but I hope you realize that I am going out of my way to accommodate you. I'm sure that there are grammar schools in Australia which would forbid you from wearing the hijab because of strict uniform codes."

"Oh. I didn't realize ... I ... um ... appreciate your support, Ms Walsh."

"I know you do, Amal. I hope you also appreciate that I have to think of the broader scheme of things. Anything can happen in today's climate. If the media get word of it, I'm sure they'll be interested. McCleans Grammar School is one of Melbourne's most prestigious institutions and it is renowned for its very strict discipline."

"Yeah, I know. .."

"Anyway, I'm sure there will be no problems. But I do need to advise you, Amal, that you are now under an even greater responsibility to represent this institution faithfully. With your veil, all eyes will be on you outside of school, so I trust you will not do our reputation any disservice. Understood, Amal?"

"Yes."

"Very well. You may return to your class now. Have a good day."

"Thanks."

I don't go back to my class straightaway. I go to the toilets and sit on a toilet seat, taking deep breaths.

Breathe.

I'm an agenda item? The media? What have I got myself into?

Breathe.

It's OK. She seems to be on my side. She's not as bad as I thought.

Breathe.

Except, seriously, what's the deal with her and the word institution?

It's Wednesday. The only people who haven't freaked out about my hijab have been Simone and Eileen. Oh, and Josh Goldberg. Josh's Jewish. He's got orthodox Jewish cousins but, from what I can tell, he's a secular Jew. I don't think my hijab's really strange to him, though. Orthodox Jewish women also cover their hair and there are tons more things that are similar with our faiths. We kind of hit it off from my first week at McCleans.

As for the rest of my class, it's been two whole days since the start of term and there's still an uncomfortable *politeness* between me and everybody else. Well, I wouldn't call it politeness with Tia, Claire and Rita, who are still into their sniggering routine, which is fine. That I can handle. At least they're acknowledging I exist. But everyone else is acting way too civil with me.

When it comes to the guys, well, some of them are kind of acting almost scared of me. As though they're not allowed to talk to me, or I'll bark at them if they say something. One of the guys, Tim Manne, accidentally bumped into me while we were walking out of class and then fumbled and *apologized* and moved on quickly, like he didn't want me to think he'd given me an invitation to talk. Since my first day here, I've *never* heard a guy apologize to a girl for bumping into her. I was about to make a joke about it, to ease the tension, but he was already halfway down the hallway.

And then there's Adam. He hasn't spoken a word to me since the start of term. He just smiles awkwardly if our eyes meet and quickly turns his head away. It's gruesome. When he ignores me like this it feels as though somebody has a potato peeler and is torturously peeling away the layers of my skin. This morning I'm in the hallway when I overhear some girls talking about me next to the lockers. One of them says the word "oppressed" and the other one is saying something about me looking like a dag. I can't go up to them, because then they'll know I've been eavesdropping. So I walk slowly away, feeling like a boiling kettle of water about to whistle and screech.

I'd like to say that I walked back to the lockers and planted myself in front of those girls. I'd like to say that I looked them in the eye and gave them a pulverizing comeback line that left them shocked and speechless. But don't you just hate yourself when you always think of the killer line when it's too late? Anyway, by the time I've got the guts to even think about turning back, the bell has rung and the moment has gone.

So I just keep walking.

At lunch time Simone, Eileen and I hang around in the Year Eleven common room. We've got the place to ourselves because it's a gorgeous sunny day and everybody's outside. But Eileen's got stomach cramps and is refusing to move from the wall heater. Simone and I are in a severe mucking-around mood and are taking turns imitating teachers we love to hate. I absolutely suck at mimicking voices but Simone's a pro. She gets the tone and accent to perfection. She can jump from impersonating Ms Walsh to Michael Jackson to Austin Powers. She can do any accent or facial expression. Simone's usually reserved and quiet. You get the feeling that she wishes she had a curtain to hide herself behind. But whenever she gets in this mood, this amazingly confident side flows out of her, blowing Eileen and me away.

Today we're in hysterics as Simone does an absolutely

brilliant impersonation of Mr Taylor, our Legal Studies teacher, talking to us about how the entire course of our lives depends upon us appreciating the Australian Constitution. Mr Taylor has this habit of emphasizing his point by using three adjectives or verbs in a row.

"Class, you must know," Simone begins in a droning voice, flinging her arms around at every syllable, "that should you fail to understand, to comprehend, to *feel* the power of the Constitution's words you will lose, forfeit, *surrender* your ability to master the meaning of this most important document. You must read with an open mind in order to nurture, care for and *foster* your citizenship. Do I make myself clear, succinct and *comprehensible*?"

The three of us fall over the tables laughing when all of a sudden we hear somebody in the background. Simone is instantly silent and we turn around to see Josh standing at the door, a wide grin on his face.

"Josh! Where'd you come from?!" I ask.

"I was coming in to pick up a book. Didn't want to interrupt Simone's performance. Bloody awesome impersonation, Sim."

She looks down at her hands, a horrified expression on her reddening face. "Thanks," she mutters, turning away quickly as she pretends to be packing up her books.

Josh doesn't seem to notice her embarrassment. "Man, you had him spot on! He *so* does that triple word thing. You got talent!"

Simone looks up for a seond and smiles shyly, quickly

turning her eyes away from his grinning face.

"Later," he says, casually waving a hand and walking out.

Eileen and I turn to Simone with wide-eyed expressions.

"He called me Sim. . ."

"I know!" I cry. "How cute was that!"

"What a spunk!" Eileen says. "He's *so* sweet! I reckon he's got the hots for you, *Sim*."

Simone looks at us in mortification. "Are you kidding? As if he'd even look twice! He was just being . . . nice . . . how embarrassing . . . oh my God he saw me up there jumping around like an idiot . . . my arms were probably all wobbly and . . . ugh." She looks down at her body in disgust and shakes her head. Eileen and I go ballistic.

"Oh for God's sake, Simone!" Eileen snaps. "You're not fat! Stop acting like you're the size of a Toorak mansion. I've seen the way guys check you out as you walk down the street."

"You think that's my dream? To get *checked out* by guys? Guys would check out a *street lamp* if it had boobs."

"Simone, just chill out," I say. "Give yourself a break will you?"

"Are you trying to imply I need a break and that I should therefore have a Kit-Kat?"

"Yeah, that was it," I say, laughing. "I was implying you're a fat cow and should go hold up a Cadbury store."

"Good, because the last thing I need from either of you is pity."

"Well you don't have it because there's nothing to pity you for," Eileen says, "except your failure to exercise some intelligence and realize that you're not—"

"OK, OK!" she groans. "Point taken! I *love* myself. Happy? I'm just so excited! I'm over the moon because that hunk of a guy just walked in and saw me jumping around like a roast Christmas turkey doing a rap dance!"

"Hmm, a little bit of perspective would be nice round about now." Eileen raises her eyebrows at me. "Wouldn't you agree, Amal?"

"Nah, I disagree."

"Thank you!" Simone says triumphantly.

"I mean, sure Simone, you do look like a stuffed chicken. A Thanksgiving turkey, even. Man, the meat off you could keep Red Rooster in stock for months."

"Why don't you both just go and inject some calories into your poverty-stricken fat cells?"

Eileen and I giggle and Simone sticks her tongue out at us.

I walk to the milk bar on Saturday morning to buy the weekend paper for my parents and the latest edition of *Cosmo*. I'm a real *Cosmo* fanatic. A *Cosmo* quiz guru. According to *Cosmo*, Adam and I are perfectly matched, although June's edition gave us a low score on physical compatibility so I threw that issue out.

All my *Cosmos* are stacked under my bed because my mum hates me reading such "filthy magazines with nothing but sex and skinny girls". She thinks that if I read them I'm going to spend my Saturday nights bouncing away in cars and throwing up my lunch. OK, so last month she busted Simone and me glued to a sealed section on male body parts. Boy was that embarrassing. And man did she go nuts. She sat me down for a massive mother-to-daughter on sex and intimacy and how magazines and movies corrupt the precious relationship between men and women and blah blah blah. It was excruciating. Anyway, if she finds out I'm buying this month's edition (which has an article on what guys *really* like in a girl), I'll be hung out to dry with the washing.

On my way back from the milk bar, with the *Cosmo* stuffed in my coat, I see Mrs Vaselli standing outside watering her roses. She's wearing her all-year-round thick black stockings, pleated skirt, woollen jumper and schoolgirl shoes. She dresses like that in the peak of summer too.

"Hi, Mrs Vaselli," I call out. Another avoiding-a-lecture defence mechanism.

She pauses with the hose mid-air, scowls at me, and turns her back to water another plant. As I turn in to our drive she suddenly storms over to our fence and starts yelling at me.

"You tell newspaper people no trow paper on my grass!"

She stomps away back to her house.

"What a grumpy old fart!" I yell, slamming our front door and storming into the kitchen, where my mum is preparing breakfast.

"What's wrong?" she asks.

"That old grouch is psychotic. I was walking up the driveway and she comes up to the fence and starts yelling at me."

"What did you do?"

"Why are parents *always* *so* quick to assume it's their children who must have done something wrong?"

"Easy. Because I'm your mum and I can assume anything I want to."

"Nice," I mutter. "Her latest big fat whinge is that when our newspapers get delivered in the week, they *sometimes* get thrown on to her lawn. The injustice of it must burn her. Boy, do I wish I had her problems. Newspapers touching her precious grass."

"Don't say that, ya Amal. You have no idea what her problems are."

"Yeah, I do. She's an anal, cranky, miserable woman who wants to take out her bad mood on everybody else."

"Really? Only person I hear that sounds like she's got a bad case of PMS is you."

I flounce out of the room, stomping my feet as hard as I can as I walk up the stairs.

7

Monday morning. And my class has finally decided to confront me about my hijab. I almost want to jump up and down with relief. I can handle an insult or an interrogation. I can't handle going from getting along with everybody (with the obvious exception of Tia and her Mini-Mes) to being a social outcast.

Somehow, in between classes after lunch on Monday everybody suddenly finds the guts to approach me, wanting to know what's going on with my new look.

"Did your parents force you?" Kristy asks, all wide-eyed and appalled.

"My dad told me if I don't wear it he'll marry me off to a sixty-five-year-old camel owner in Egypt."

"No!" She's actually horrified.

"I was invited to the wedding," Eileen adds.

"*Really?*" This is definitely a case of dropped from the cradle.

"Hey! Amal!" Tim Manne calls out. "What's the deal with that thing on your head?"

"I've gone bald."

"Get out!"

"I'm on the Advanced Hair Programme."

For a second his eyes flicker with shock. Then Josh punches him on the shoulder. "Rocked!"

"Like I believed her," Tim says, looking sheepish.

"Doesn't it get hot?" someone asks.

"Can I touch it?"

"Can you swim?"

"Do you wear it in the shower?"

"So is it like nuns? Are you married to Jesus now?"

It's unreal. Everybody's asking me about my decision and seems genuinely interested in hearing what I have to say. They're all huddled around me and I'm having the best time explaining to them how I put it on and when I have to wear it. Then Adam plants himself in front of me and starts joining in with the rest of them and I want to plant a massive kiss on his face except that really would be defeating the purpose of my entire spiritual roadtrip now, wouldn't it?

"So it's your choice then?" he asks.

"Oh yeah!" I answer. "One hundred per cent."

70

"Wow . . . so how come it looks different on you?"

"What do you mean?"

"Like you see some women covering their faces and other women wearing really bright material with that red paint on their hand. Are they all Islamic too?"

"You mean Muslim."

"Huh?"

"What she means," Josh says, "is that the religion is Islam and the followers are Muslim. Like you can't say to somebody you're a Judaism or a Catholicism. Get it?"

"Right." Adam nods his head. "So are they *Muslim*, like you?"

"Yeah they are. But, every girl is going to interpret the hijab differently. It depends on their culture or their fashion sense, you know? There's no one uniform for it."

"I get you," Adam says.

"A lot of Africans wear those really colourful wrap-around dresses and veils," I continue. "Um, stricter women cover their face, but it's not required in Islam. It's their choice to go to that extent."

"Will you ever cover yours?" Adam asks.

"Nah! No way."

"OK . . . cool."

We all keep talking until our Chemistry teacher, Ms Samuels, walks in and announces she's going to test us to see if we studied over the holidays. We get stuck with an impromptu quiz and Kristy passes me a note with exclamation marks and smiley faces all over.

71

I'm really glad your dad didn't go through with the wedding!! :) :)

Sweet of her. But cradle theory confirmed.

"OK, personal question time, Simone," I say during recess as Simone, Eileen and I are sitting outside on the lawn. "What do you think of Josh?"

"Unbelievably *dreamy*!" she moans, taking a bite out of her carrot.

"You make him laugh," Eileen says. "Always a good sign. I reckon he's got the hots for you."

"*Josh?* Having the hots for *me*? There's more chance of Ms Walsh waxing her upper lip than that happening."

"Oh *puh-lease*!" I groan.

"While we're on the subject of saliva-inducing crushes," Simone says, "what's the latest on Adam? Did you see how cool he was when the class was asking you about your veil? Usually he's so quiet and serious."

"I know!" Eileen exclaims. "He seemed really interested."

I give them a lopsided grin. "He is *so* cute."

"Somebody get me a paper bag," Eileen says, "my two best friends have gone beyond corny on me!"

"Don't worry, we'll try to find some crush material for you too," Simone says.

"No thanks. You two took the best. What am I supposed to admire about the rest of the guys in our class? That they can pick their noses? Have farting competitions? Or maybe it's the fact that they can burp the alphabet? Ooh, I'm on fire."

We all laugh and have a whinge about the disgusting habits of the male species in our classroom. Then Simone leans over to me. "OK, my hypothetical question for Amal."

"Fire away."

"Let's say he asks you out. Would you be his girlfriend?"

I lean back on my hands and smile at them. "Nah, you know I don't do the whole boyfriend/girlfriend thing."

"Not even with *Adam*?" Simone asks. "Surely God would understand! I mean he's your high-school crush. *The* crush. The one you'll be talking about for years to come, when you're old and saggy and grey and telling your hubby and kids about your good old school days and how Adam Keane was your oxygen through Year Eleven!"

"That's right, Amal!" Eileen adds. "Are you telling us you wouldn't contemplate bending the rules?"

"Honestly, I think about it all the time. Like I imagine us being a couple and Tia being institutionalized from grief that I got Mr Popular."

"She'd need shock treatment," Simone says, giggling.

"Don't get me wrong, I'm not frigid or anything! Boy do I sometimes wish Adam was my boyfriend, and if he was dating anybody I swear I'd have a hernia and probably start plotting death traps for his girl. But deep down I know I wouldn't cross the line with him, no matter how tempting it would be. OK, OK, you're thinking I qualify for nerdy geek?"

"Big time," Eileen jokes and I hit her on the shoulder.

"But you know I can't in Islam. You know the whole thing about no sex and physical intimacy before marriage."

"Yeah, we know, you've told us," Simone says.

"And it's not just in Islam, you know," I say. "Christianity, Judaism, Hinduism, Buddhism."

"OK, we get it," Eileen groans. "You've told us before. You don't have to keep on trying to prove yourself against other religions for some sort of legitimacy. Sheez."

"Do I do that? Simone?"

Simone nods her head.

"Well, OK then. Just don't think it's because of my parents. If I wanted to have a boyfriend, I could easily get away with it behind my parents' back. They trust me heaps so if I spoke to a guy for ages on the phone every night and said he's *just a friend* they'd believe me, no questions asked. I could get away with telling them I'm going out with my girlfriends and meet up with my *boyfriend* without any problem. But it has nothing to do with them."

"My parents would probably freak out if I told them I was going out with a guy," Eileen says. "They can be pretty strict about things like that. I suppose, though, if he was a good Japanese boy with plenty of culture and the brains of a nuclear scientist they'd welcome him with open arms."

"My mum would be happy if I went out with anyone, period," Simone says. "She's just dying for me to have a boyfriend and be *normal*, at least that's how she puts it."

"So, Amal, are you happy just being friends with Adam, then?" Eileen asks.

"Oh yeah! But this is the tricky part. See, I'm happy just being close friends and drooling over him without anything actually happening. But I want to be his best female friend. Do you get me? I want to know he confides in me and talks to me and looks out for my opinion more than any other girl. That would be the best. The physical stuff I'll imagine!"

They giggle at me for being a nerd on the outside and a devil on the inside. Simone and I are discussing whether Josh should use less hair gel when Eileen hisses at us to shut up as Adam is approaching. Before Simone has time to push her carrots under her bag (she hates people knowing she's on a diet), Adam is in front of us carrying three textbooks, as usual.

"Amal, what's going on with this question about determining a molecular formula for a hydrocarbon?"

"Do you ever *not* study?" I say, as I get up off the ground and have a look at the page he's referring to.

"Yeah, don't you take a break?" Eileen adds. "Food? Sport? Fresh air? It's extremely unhealthy to subject your mind and body to round-the-clock academia."

"I don't have time for breaks."

"That's the whole *point* of a break. When you've got no time, you need a break."

He pauses and looks at her slowly. "You should do a chocolate commercial with that line."

Eileen and Simone look at each other and let out startled laughs.

"So you *do* joke?" Simone says.

"No," he answers, his mouth twitching as he turns to look at the page.

"Oof! This book is heavy! How about you sit down with us? At least we'll be comfortable while you waste my lunch time on chem." I hold my breath for his answer and avoid eye contact with Eileen and Simone.

"OK," he says. "Just as long as Eileen stops with the counsellor advice and Simone offers me a carrot."

"Ugh! I feel like a disgusting slob!" Tia groans, clutching her non-existent stomach and sneaking a look at Simone as we stand around class waiting for our Biology teacher to arrive. "I ate a whole sandwich. I feel so bloated. I could just kill myself from guilt!"

"You don't look fat!" Claire reassures her.

"Yeah, you look gorgeous," Rita gushes.

Tia flips her long, shiny jet-black hair to the side and flashes them a Colgate smile.

"No, honest, girls. Feel this pot. Look." She lifts up her shirt to reveal a stomach as flat as a cutting board. "What do you think, Simone?"

Simone looks horrified and stands with her mouth gaping open, her eyes fixed on Tia's stomach. The absence of even one millimetre of fat has taken the wind out of her.

"You're right, Tia," I say in a sickly-sweet tone. She darts a lethal look at me, her eyes narrowing as they scan me up and down.

"*Excuse* me?"

"You've put on weight. You should watch your figure. Have you been eating a lot of salt lately? Your face is all puffed up. My pregnant aunt has a good water-retention remedy. Would you like me to get the name for you?"

She sneers at me and I turn away to take a seat.

Later in class, she gets me back.

"I just don't know what I'd do without my long hair!" she says to Claire and Rita, loud enough for us to hear. "I mean, what's a woman without hair? You have to have a model's face to get away with covering up. Don't you think so?"

They nod like obedient puppies and I let out an exaggerated sigh.

"I just don't know what I'd do without a brain, Simone!" I say. "I mean, what's a person without one?"

"Coffee at the Lounge Room, tonight?" Simone whispers to Eileen and me during History on Friday.

Eileen's on. I don't know whether to go. The Lounge Room is a trendy café on Burke Road: long coffee tables centred between big suede lounge chairs and sofas, dim lamps and television screens with MTV and *Friends* reruns. It was our hang-out joint in the mid-year break. Where we'd go to goss and eat strawberry tart and talk school and parents and top five chick flicks and the rest. Because I'd rather eat decomposed meat than be thought of as a chicken, I fake a big smile and tell them I'm all for it.

*

I chicken out.

I'm ashamed to admit it but after dinner I ring Simone and Eileen and tell them I can't make it because we have visitors. They believe me. And why wouldn't they? I'm supposed to be pious and God-fearing. Not a lying, hypocritical, pathetic coward. I'm lying on my bed listening to Craig David's "I'm walking away". On repeat.

What's happened to me? Haven't I decided to wear the hijab because I feel proud of who I am? Suddenly I'm too chicken to go to a café? I don't recognize myself. I'm the one who put her head out the school bus window last year and yelled at a group of boys who threw a can of Coke at our "wog" school bus. It was me who stood up during a Year Nine interschool debate and told the audience that my team didn't appreciate the other team's whispers about competing against "terrorists". When we were at the medical clinic and the secretary asked Leila if she could cope with filling out a form in English, it was me who pointed out that Leila's never set foot out of Australia and can manage an A+ average in Eng Lit, and then some.

So if that's all me, then who's this girl who's making up excuses to avoid going out to a café?

"I'm starving!" Simone moans on our way home on the school bus.

"I think I have an apple in my bag," I say. "Do you want it?"

"Thanks, I'll pass. I'm so sick of fruit and vegetables. Aren't you hungry, Amal?"

"Nah, I had a big sandwich at lunch."

"I don't get the skinny world!"

I nudge her in the side. "Don't be silly."

"But you skinny people eat two slices of bread filled with rabbit food at midday, and you're all 'I'm about to explode' until dinner. I'm *always* hungry. Honestly, Amal." Her voice goes down to a whisper. "Don't laugh. But sometimes I can be eating my lunch and thinking about what I'm going to have for dinner!"

"That's normal," I say.

"Won't Allah punish you for lying?"

I jab her again.

We sit in silence for a while, staring out the window. After some time Simone turns to me: "My mum and I had a massive fight last night."

"What happened?"

"She's been hassling me to join the gym with her. She's going through a Pilates craze. She's constantly on my back about losing weight and how she was a size six when she was my age and how she can't believe I've turned out like this. Am I really that bad, Amal?"

"What is she on about? You're only about one size bigger than me and Eileen and you've got certain *assets* most girls would kill for!"

"My mum says that they're the *only* thing going for me and that I need to work on making the rest of my body more attractive."

"She wouldn't say that!"

"She's said worse, believe me. She says it's because she *loves and cares for me* – spew – that it's only for my own good – spew."

"Simone, you're gorgeous. You're a natural blonde, just about the most sought-after hair colour in the world, you've got amazing eyes, you never have a pimple *and* you fill out a shirt. So your ribcage isn't on display – big deal."

"Amal, best friends are supposed to say things like that. It's like compliments from parents — well, not mine — they don't count. I mean, we wouldn't be best friends if you thought I was ugly and boring, would we? How you feel about me has nothing to do with how other people see me. I'm always going to be fat Simone. Like Tia said the other day, I probably spend more on Big Macs than she does on her annual gym membership."

"Bullshit she said that! The BITCH!"

Simone shrugs her shoulders. "Yeah, well, it's probably true... Sometimes I start a diet and then I open a *Cosmo* or a *Cleo* and there are these articles about pregnant superstars losing thirty kilos in two or three months and here I am struggling to lose a kilo. So I give up and demolish a Mars bar. Or I see all these model shoots of gorgeous beach babes with their bones poking into my hand when I turn the pages and I think, what's the point? Even if I lost ten kilos and was in my weight–height ratio, people would still consider me fat. I wish I could become anorexic. How sick is that, huh? But I don't have the self-control to live off a lettuce leaf a day. And I've tried the whole bulimia thing but I can't even throw up. I'm just pathetic! Abnormal!"

"You know what? Who cares what normal is, Simone. Let's protest. From now on we're the anti-normal, anti-average, anti-standard. You can eat when you want to, I'll wear what I want, and we'll die with a packet of chips in our hand and a tablecloth on our head."

*

"So, can you make it for coffee *tonight*?" Eileen asks me on the telephone the following Thursday.

I can't bear to sit through another night manicuring my nails with Craig David, so I say yes.

My dad drops me off and I beg him to turn down his *Greatest Hits of Jerusalem* album when we turn the corner into Burke Road.

"You used to love this music when you were young," he says, pinching my cheek.

"Dad! Far out, I'm like sixteen. Get over it."

Instead he starts to sing a song about meeting his secret darling love under a tree in the olive groves.

"Just remember," he says as I get out of the car, "before Kylie, Ricky Martin and these blond boys singing like parrots, you were singing songs about olive groves and mountains too."

I roll my eyes at him.

"Have fun, ya Amal. And don't be late. It's a school night. You get dropped off not one second later than ten thirty or else I dial triple zero. Not your mobile. TRIPLE ZERO."

Like I'm really going to be kidnapped when most people are looking at me and wondering whether I've got an AK-47 assault rifle inside my jean jacket.

Simone and Eileen are waiting for me in the front of the café. We say hi and wait in line. There's a big crowd tonight. Panic sets in. A deep flush begins on my neck. At least my veil hides it. Who gets this worked up over a café? During the mid-year holidays Simone, Eileen and I would hang out here, laughing with Pedro, the old Italian owner, or chatting with Ray, the spunky waiter. Now my hands are sweaty, I'm worrying about whether my scarf matches my jeans and I'm convinced my make-up has smudged.

"Hey?" Eileen says forcefully, interrupting my panic attack and grabbing my arm in support. "Relax."

"Yeah, I know," I say with a nervous laugh.

"Shit," Simone says. "Everyone's so skinny. Look at those three girls standing over there. They look like they've had a good binge today. Three peas and half a capsicum." She fiddles self-consciously with her top, pulling it down and adjusting her trousers.

"They look like they need World Vision support. One dollar a day. Let's sponsor them." But I'm also fiddling self-consciously with my top, wondering if I look OK, if I can get away with a veil among all these cool people.

"You both look like you're about to jump out of a plane without a parachute," Eileen says, standing in front of us. "Both of you relax. These people are nothing in the scale of your lives. You're both gorgeous and look hot and I'm dying for a slice of mud cake so quit the panic attacks and let's get a table."

"Ooh yum, mud cake." Simone instantly brightens up.

"I'm fine, I'm fine," I say. "I'm just imagining them all naked."

"Isn't that a sin?" Eileen says as we make our way to the entrance.

"I'm sure God will consider this an exception." I look

around the café as we wait to be ushered to a table. Maybe it was stupid of me to come. I look so out of place. I mean, I've worked on the whole trendy clothes and accessories thing, but you add a hijab and you might as well be wearing a kilt. I can see some people narrowing their eyes as they look up from their conversations and take notice of me.

Imagine them naked. Imagine them naked.

Ray is suddenly before us, looking me directly in the eye. Somehow I don't think God will consider him an exception.

"Amal?" he ventures.

You'd think I'd grown a toe on my nose. I've got two options. Weak, spineless, passive twit. Or over-the-top, confident, Priscilla Queen-style hello.

"Hi, Ray!" I squeal with exaggerated warmth. "*How are you?*"

He looks confused. He should too. My voice is so high-pitched I'm in danger of breaking the windows.

"Can't complain."

"That's great! So what's new?"

"Nothing."

"Me either! Same old."

Eileen and Simone put him out of his misery and ask for a lounge table.

"I'll check if there's one available," he says with relief. "Follow me."

We follow him, and I keep my head high, avoiding eye contact with the people staring at me as we walk across the floor. We sit at a lounge table and Ray takes our order. He seems very formal, no joking around, no conversation, just "Would you like syrup with that?" and then he abruptly leaves to place our order.

"Amal!" Eileen says, doubling over with laughter. "You spun him out. He's probably wondering what cult you joined!"

"Better than the one he did. What's he gone and done to his goatee? He looks like he shaved in the dark."

"Strawberry tarts and *skinny* hot chocolates," Simone interrupts, snorting. "*Really* cancels out our calorie intake."

We talk for ages. About everything: school, guys, politics, our parents, what we want to do when we finish, whether Catherine Zeta-Jones has had surgery.

When I'm home in bed later that night, it occurs to me that all it's taken is a couple of good friends and a lot of chocolate to make me forget I'm the "girl who wears hijab". So I take Craig David's album out of my CD player and go to bed listening to Destiny's Child "I'm a Survivor" instead.

"I need new clothes," I wail to Yasmeen on the phone. I can almost sense her eyes lighting up on the other end.

"Done," she says, in her let's-get-down-to-business-and-talk-shopping tone. "Bridge Road, Chapel Street and the city. Tomorrow. Meet at Bridge at ten. Work our way from there. Wear comfy shoes. Work out what colour scarves you've got so we can mix and match. Also, bags. Have to match your bags to your veil. Tell you what, write a list of all your scarf and bag colours. Shoes if you want as well, but I recommend a triple S be conducted separately, to give it the full attention it deserves."

"What on earth's a triple S?"

"Duh. Shoe shopping spree."

"You need help."

"No, my dear, you do. And we're going to help you transform your look. I'll tell Leila. Get plenty of rest tonight. See you tomorrow."

Our shopping spree is cancelled because Leila's mum woke up this morning and decided to lose all her brain cells and get by purely on liquid membrane.

Leila's been crying on speaker phone to my mum and me all morning. Her mum is refusing to let her go out with us because: a) there's housework to do; b) they have visitors this evening, one of whom is apparently single and "eligible"; and c) she's a "disgrace", wanting to go out and about in the streets with her scarf on.

My mum is furious but is doing her best to calm Leila down. I'm just about ready to report Leila's mum to immigration.

Grounds for deportation: stupidity.

Alternative country: none. No nationality deserves her. Send her to Mars.

"I don't get it!" I wail after we hang up the phone.

"Neither do I, darling," she says with a heavy sigh.

"How can someone so idiotic produce somebody like Leila?"

"Don't be rude, Amal. Gulchin is older than you and you should talk with respect."

"Get serious! She doesn't deserve it." I pace around the living room in a rage. "A *disgrace*," I mimic. "Oh how *scandalous*. Leila goes shopping. Ooh, she's got a first-class ticket to hell now."

"Come here," my mum says gently, opening her arms to me. I sigh, dropping myself down on the couch and nuzzling my head in her chest. She draws me closer and gives me a hug.

"Amal, it's naïve to think that because somebody is ignorant they are a *bad* person. I feel so much for Leila because I know that she understands that she can be all she wants to be, not in spite of Islam, but because of it."

"It's her mum's stupid fault."

"Amal, Gulchin's just trying to bring up Leila in the only way she knows how. She married young. She never had the opportunity to gain an education. She can't read. She can't write. Her world has always been about raising her children and looking after her home. There's nothing wrong with that, if that's what she chooses."

"Yeah, but she's forcing it on Leila!"

"Which is wrong. But try to expand your mind and think about things from other people's perspectives. Everything is relative. If you want to understand a problem you look at its cause. You don't look at its manifestation."

"How is that supposed to make Leila feel better?"

She sighs, playing with my hair. "God knows. . . Sometimes,

Amal, people are paralysed by their traditions and customs. It's all they know, so you can't judge them for following and believing what they know."

"Come off it, Mum! Any moron would realize that she's following her village's culture, not Islam. So for her to go around and tell the world it's Islam when it's the exact opposite is so dumb!"

"Yes, I know that. But from *her* point of view I believe she thinks she is simply trying to protect Leila."

"Protect her from *what*? It's a crappy shopping spree!"

"Everybody's scared of what they don't know, Amal."

I tilt my head back and roll my eyes at my mum. She gives me an exasperated look in return.

"You still have a lot to learn, darling," she says.

"Oh *puh-lease* don't give me that line, Mum!" She smiles and hugs me even tighter.

I don't care about understanding Leila's mum. I'm not interested in all that psychology crap. As far as I'm concerned, if you want to think you're going to heaven because you reckon guys should go to school and get to do what they want but girls have to stay home till they're ready to be married, then piss off. I don't care why you don't know any better. When you have a kid who knows more about your religion than you do and is smart enough to be anything she wants, then in my book you lose your right to excuses.

"So what happened with the man of your mum's dreams?" I ask Leila.

She's at my place for dinner tonight. On her mum's condition that we don't leave the house or ring boys.

"He was actually really cute."

"You serious?"

"Yeah. Cute, funny, perfect English, just finished Medicine at the American University of Beirut."

"Oh, so he qualifies for 'Suitable Marriage Prospects'."

"Pretty much." We roll our eyes.

"She just doesn't get it," Leila says softly.

"I know, Leila," I reassure her, squeezing her hand.

"I'm sixteen for God's sake! I'm not in some village in the mountains where there's nothing else to do *but* get married. She thinks that because I want to be a lawyer, I'm never going to get married. Hey, remember that time she wanted to pull me out of Hidaya? At the end of Year Ten?"

"How could I forget? Mr Aziz spoke with your parents, didn't he?"

"He came over to my house and spent the whole night banging his head against the wall trying to change her mind. It worked though. He was such a cool principal."

"Why do you think she's like this? I don't get it."

"Who knows?"

"Well . . . what were your grandparents like?"

"Poor. They could only afford to send one of the kids to school. My eldest uncle got to go and the rest of my uncles and aunts missed out."

"When did your mum get married?"

"I think she was about sixteen. They came here after she

had Hakan. Why the hell should I live out her pathetic life?"

"It's so crap."

"I mean, which way do you turn? According to my mum, the normal thing is to get married; according to everybody else out there, the normal thing is to get drunk, lose your virginity to somebody you speak to once at a party, and become 'liberated' or, like, whatever."

I shrug my shoulders.

"And what makes me freak out the most is that *everything* I do which she goes crazy about, she brings back to her backward interpretation of Islam. *You want career — you bad Muslim girl! You no want to marry — how you be good wife? You wear hijab, but you talk to boys at school.* She thinks being a lawyer is an evil, twisted ambition. Thinks I want to make money from lying." We roll our eyes and groan.

"Do I look like a bimbo to you?" she continues. "I didn't wear the hijab because *she* wanted me to. I'm going by what *I* feel is right and what *I* know about my faith. Like I'd really follow something that locked me in the house to cook and clean.

"Do you know my mum hasn't even read the Koran? She goes on what her mum told her and what her mum's mum told her. That's her *scripture*." She gives me a grim smile. "It's like talking to somebody from another planet. She's the one offending Islam," she whispers. "Not me."

My dad's discovered Internet jokes and email forwards. He's become obsessed.

I'm shovelling down my cereal, trying to finish breakfast before my bus arrives. He walks in, gives me a kiss good morning, and starts making himself some toast. My mum has already left for work.

"Ask me if I'm going to work this morning." He grins at me.

"Huh?" I manage through a mouthful of cornflakes.

"Ask me if I'm going to work."

"Is this a trick question?"

"No! Just ask me."

"OK. . . Dad, are you going to work today?"

He stands up, excited. "I might as well work. I'm in a bad mood anyway."

He's about to collapse with laughter, then sees me looking at him like he's grown a third ear.

"Don't you get it?"

"You got Uncle Tariq's Garfield forward, didn't you?"

"Yeah I did! It's brilliant. Did you ever have one of those days where you only had one nerve left . . . and someone got on it?"

"Yeah," I say, putting my bowl in the sink. "But it was a morning." He grins at me and goes to ruffle my hair.

"Dad! You wrecked my scarf!" I run to the hallway mirror in a panic and am on a rescue mission of the front curve.

"Looks like you had two nerves." He laughs, taking a bite out of his toast.

Every month we have Forum, when the SRC (the Student Representative Council) reps chair a Year Eleven meeting and we all have a whinge and discuss important stuff that's going on at school.

Our school captain is a Year Twelve girl called Lara. Paul, who's in Year Eleven, is vice. Paul's pretty popular and good-natured. He's into his sports, gets good marks, generally gets along with everybody. Lara, on the other hand, is unbelievably pompous and seems to think that her SRC captaincy equates to a position in the House of Representatives. She also has a habit of singling people out to "share their views" with the rest of the group whenever a topic comes up for discussion, which doesn't sit well with the shy, quiet types who sit as far back as possible to avoid her asking them what they think about putting Ambi-pur plugs in the gym locker rooms.

At Forum today she announces that the DAV (Debaters' Association of Victoria) interschool debating competition starts up in two months and they're beginning to work out which teams will represent Year Eleven.

The DAV is a State-based debating competition where schools registered with the association debate against each other. There are five debates all up and the competition is open from Year Seven to Year Twelve and held once a month at selected school campuses across Melbourne. The topics are set by the association and they can range from whether chewing gum should be banned from school to whether fish have memories to whether America should have invaded Iraq. A notice has been posted on the board in our home room for anybody interested in putting their name down.

In my PHE (Pre Hijab Era) I would have raced to put my name down on the list. But now I'm not so sure.

Afterwards Adam approaches me as I'm gathering my books.

"Do you debate?" he asks.

"A little. I was on the Year Nine team at my other school. How about you?"

"Yeah. So are you putting your name down?"

"Maybe. I have to think about it."

"Why?"

"Just . . . because."

"Because why?"

"It's a bit more complicated for me."

"Why?"

"Because . . . well, you know. . ." I feel a blush creeping from my neck to my cheeks and I beg it to stop, to drain away.

He looks confused. "Nah. What are you on about?"

I cough and try to explain. "My . . . hijab."

He scratches his head. "Nope. Sorry. You've lost me. Is it a sin to debate or something?"

I burst out laughing. "No! Of course not!"

"What then?"

"Well, I'm kind of . . . nervous."

"You? Nervous? Man, you've got more bloody balls than any girl I've ever known!"

"You've known some weird girls then," I say, raising an eyebrow at him.

"OK, guts. You've got more *guts* than any girl I've ever known. What the hell are you scared about?"

He thinks I'm gutsy! Woo hoo!

"You know what those debates are like. I don't know if I'm ready to get up in front of an audience made up of other rich private schools. They'll just stare at me and not listen to a word I say as they try to get over their shock that I know English."

"So?"

"What do you mean, *so*?"

94

"Why do you care?"

"Because I just do."

"OK, then prove them wrong. If anybody can, it's you."

"Is that what you think?"

"No. It's what I *know*."

Somebody get me an asthma pump. And I don't even have asthma.

"Do you know what you want to do at uni?" Eileen asks me later that night when I'm over at her house for a study session.

"Not really. Maybe something to do with science; maybe become a lollipop lady. Who knows? I can't work it out yet. It's too stressful. What about you?"

"My parents want me to do economics and commerce."

"Do you want to?"

"Yuk. I want to do something creative. Like graphics, or art, or fashion design."

"They'd have a fit, right?"

"Oh yes, they will be so disappointed if I don't pursue a more '*respectable* profession', as they put it, such as medicine or pharmacy or optometry. My ambitions are just an arty-farty waste of time and money. Amal, some people, like you, will probably have to fight the world to get where they want. Other people, like me, will have to fight their families. Sheez, I don't know which is worse."

"You'll persuade them," I say. "You're so strong and ... stable."

"What do you mean?"

"Sometimes the thought of taking off my hijab crosses my mind. I guess because it's still new to me. How inconsistent is that?"

"Don't be silly. There are times I freak out about exams and uni and all that stuff. And there are times I'm ready to take on my parents, the vegetable and animal kingdom, the solar system, the entire universe. No one can be gutsy all the time. Imagine how obnoxious and snotty they'd be."

Eileen has a point. I've been strong and defiant in some situations and an absolute wuss in others. Like the time I took the day off school to avoid playing in a final basketball match that I was freaking out about. On the other hand, I remember attending a Grade Six camp dance wearing a dress when everybody else was wearing jeans and runners.

All the girls had planned to dress up and then somehow the plans changed without me knowing. I'd fought with my mum to buy me a dress and shoes and even though she'd warned me that nobody would wear a dress at a farm camp, I insisted and she spent about one hundred dollars on an outfit. I felt so guilty that I'd made her fork out all that money that I decided to wear the dress anyway. I'll never forget everybody laughing at me when I walked in to the barn with my heels and polka-dot black-and-white dress. There was hay on the floor, a Spice Girls track booming and denim in every corner. It's one of those humiliating memories which will be forever etched in my mind.

But the point is, maybe people have to go through a lion

and mouse syndrome at different points in their life. One thing seems certain. If I survived a polka-dot dress experience on a primary school camp then something tells me that I've got it in me to survive wearing the hijab.

On Sunday morning my dad and I are dumped with a list of Mum's neurotic cleaning chores so that she can concentrate on cooking a banquet for tonight's dinner with her younger brother, Uncle Joe, and his family. This time my dad's stuck putting our DVDs and video tapes in alphabetical order. But he draws the line at organizing them in categories.

Afterwards, I help Mum out in the kitchen. Peeling veggies, rolling the vine leaves and doing whatever other support-staff work she needs me to.

Whenever someone's invited to our house, my mum cooks as if she's feeding the entire southern hemisphere. There are no discount percentages on fat content, no carb-free sauces, and don't even dare to suggest salad dressing with a low GI index. My mum is into making an impression when she cooks and her diet regime is therefore non-existent whenever we have visitors.

Uncle Joe and Aunt Mandy crack me up. Big time. Uncle Joe is the complete opposite of my mum. He was born Ismail and my Aunt Mandy was born Aysha. I'm still trying to figure out where Joe and Mandy came from.

They're not into Islam or Arabic culture like we are. They're more into changing their names, peroxiding their hair and acting like they were born in Wagga Wagga and not

Jerusalem. They're always freaking out about us being "fanatics". For example, in Ramadan, we're "mad" to fast. When it's prayer time, they ask us why we bother. When we buy halal food, we're "too extreme". I remember the time we went to a buffet dinner and my mum asked the chef if the pork was carved on the same cutting board as the lamb. Uncle Joe just about had convulsions, and went aggro at my mum for being so "embarrassing". So my mum laughed in his face, walked up to the manager and told her that her brother, the man with the heavy gold chains eating the potato salad, was wondering if it was possible for them to start to use a separate cutting board as a courtesy to those who don't eat pork. The manager immediately walked up to Uncle Joe and started sucking up to him, saying sorry about ten times in the space of one minute. Uncle Joe was livid.

My cousins are Samantha, who's in her second year at uni, and George, who's nine and quite possibly the most irritating human being in the world. As soon as he walks into our house tonight he rolls back his eyelids, sticks his tongue out at me and then yells out that Samantha had the runs on Tuesday. There has to be a scientific research centre that will agree to conduct a study on this kid.

Samantha and I are pretty close. I only see her at family things, as she spends almost every weekend hanging out with her boyfriend, Martin. I've met him a couple of times. He's a real spunk. Seriously, ten out of ten. They're crazy about each other. Although her parents may be really laid-back about religion and culture they'd never accept

Samantha having a boyfriend. So whenever Samantha's out with Martin, her parents are fed a story about her being over at a friend's house for a study session.

Because we're all just family I'm not wearing my hijab when they come over. So, up until dinner, I'm still the relative with flowing locks and "normal" looks.

My mother has gone all out tonight. She's cooked a Palestinian dish called *mansaf*, basically rice mixed with pieces of chicken and pine nuts, dressed with a hot yoghurt soup. It's in a plate that has the circumference of a semi-trailer tyre. She's also made a massive bowl of *fatoosh*, salad topped with pieces of bread dipped in olive oil, with side dishes of pickled cucumber, radish and chillies, minced meat pastries and *warak aneb*, which are vine leaves stuffed with spicy rice. Everybody's digging in when my mum announces that I've decided to wear hijab.

"But why?" my aunt wails.

"Yes, Jamila, why would you go and make her do that?" Uncle Joe shouts. "Isn't it enough you wear it, so you have to force your daughter to as well?"

"*What?* Nobody made me! It was entirely *my* decision."

"Jamila!" my uncle hisses in a tone which makes it obvious he's ignored me.

"Oh, Ismail, just shoosh," my mother says, rolling her eyes at him and helping herself to another serving of food.

"Dad's name is *Joe,* Aunty!" George cuts in, hitting his fork on the table in protest.

"Oh shut up, will you?" Samantha groans.

"Maa! Samantha swore at me!"

"Samantha, don't be rude to your brother."

"Uncle Joe, I said it was *my* choice! Oh put a sock in it, George!"

"But Amal, honey," my aunt says in a sickeningly patronizing tone, "why would you go and hide your hair? You've got such gorgeous hair."

"Well, Aunt Mandy, to be perfectly honest with you, I'm losing my hair. The doctor said that my hair follicles can't withstand excessive sun exposure, and if I don't cover up I'll be bald at my Year Twelve graduation ceremony."

My dad snorts with laughter. My aunt and uncle don't look amused. George sticks his tongue out at me and I go cross-eyed at him. After dinner Samantha and I lock ourselves up in my bedroom and sit on the window ledge. Samantha smokes, so we've got the incense candles burning, the Listerine handy, a can of air freshener, and the window wide open. Samantha's also wearing gloves so her hands don't smell. We've pretty much perfected the after-dinner routine.

Samantha inhales and quickly sticks her head out the window, directing her exhaled smoke into the open air. "Want a drag?"

"Nah."

"You sure?"

"Nah, I'm right. Anyway, Mum and Dad would smell it on me even if I had a bath in disinfectant."

"I think my parents know I smoke."

100

"Yeah. I just reckon they're in denial."

"Big time. . . So tell me Miss *I'm-In-Love*, what is it about Adam?" She takes a last drag and closes the window, spraying her body with perfume and my room with air freshener. We jump on to my bed and lie down.

"He's a great kisser."

"WHAT? *You kissed?*" She jumps up on the bed and I collapse into a fit of laughter.

"Ha ha, very funny. Sheez, you gave me a heart attack. For a second there I thought you'd broken your code of *drool don't touch!*"

"Yeah, all the time. Recess, lunch, after school."

"There's more chance of Mum admitting she's a fake blonde than of you doing that."

We lie on our sides and face each other.

"So what is it about him then?"

"I don't know. I can't define it." I lean my head back against the bedhead. "He's really smart and ambitious and cute, and there are lots of guys like that but one day I just felt this connection and after that . . . I don't know, I started to notice stuff about him."

"Like?"

"Like . . . the time I was waiting for the bus after school and I saw him walking across the quadrangle. One of the girls from Prep was running and stacked it on the ground. Adam helped her up, dusted the asphalt off her knees, had her laughing in a second. It was so different to how he usually is, you know, all macho and stuff in class and with the guys."

Samantha cocks her head to the side and grins at me. "That is without doubt the corniest thing you have *ever* said! GAG!"

"Tell me about it!" I groan. "Man, I feel corny all the time! He says hi to me and I'm gliding for the rest of the day. It's disgusting! But he's just *so* cute."

"Yeah, yeah. I get you. Martin and I are there too. Hey! You're not going to believe what happened last weekend!"

"What?"

"I got busted."

"For what?"

"I got home after four. No big deal. But Mum and Dad were waiting for me, like you see in the movies. Sitting on the couch, legs crossed, all pissed off and geared up for an argument. I walk in and first thing I want to do is laugh because Dad's wearing this black satin robe with love hearts on it."

"Oh my God, that's gross."

She shudders. "Don't remind me."

"So what happened?"

"Some idiot told Mum they'd seen me at a bar with a guy. She freaked out. They told her they'd seen us with our hands all over each other. It must have been an X-rated description because she went all *I'm too ashamed to repeat the details!* It was *so* embarrassing, Amal. Guess who told her?"

"Who?"

"Remember Rahul? The guy I dumped in the first year because he kept making me pay for everything and borrowed money off me to buy me a birthday present! The one whose dad is Indian and his mum is Egyptian. My mum knows his mum. Come on, you know the one!"

"Tight-arse Rahul? The one whose breath stunk? Every time we all went out he'd forgotten his wallet in the car or was waiting for a pay cheque from work!"

"Yeah, that idiot. Apparently he was at the same bar, saw us there, *rang* his mum and casually mentioned it to her! Within bloody seconds she's squawking it to my mum on the phone!"

"No way! What did your parents say?"

"They went mental."

"Were they pissed off about the whole bar scene?"

"Nah. They know I drink. That's not a problem to them. It was me being with Martin. They think we're sleeping together. God knows how detailed Rahul's mum got with my mum. She's such a bitch!

"Then, imagine this. Dad springs the cultural theory on me! He kept going on about how it's not part of our culture. I couldn't handle it from there. I mean, he can't just use the culture argument whenever it suits him. For two decades we get the 'we must be assimilated' crap lecture and then in a minute we've suddenly got *Arabic roots* and *cultural expectations.*"

"Uncle Joe actually said that?"

"Would you believe it? This is coming from the man who thinks the word 'foreign' is the f-word of our times. All our lives George and me get it rammed down our throats that

103

we're to forget our culture and live as Aussies, whatever that means. But then when I do something that he doesn't like, he does a three-sixty turn."

"I can't believe it."

She groans. "I'm still in shock. Anyway, change the topic. Hey, I noticed after dinner Dad cornered you into a big pep talk about following in his footsteps and going into IT. Man, he doesn't stop talking about how the whole family's counting on you getting top marks and making the family proud."

"Like my parents' pep talks aren't enough to handle," I say.

"He raves on about how smart you are and your debating awards and how you'd never settle for *only* an Arts degree like me."

I guess Samantha didn't hear Uncle Joe telling me that he thinks that I've got no hope of a future if I continue to wear the hijab. According to his theory, in today's climate Muslims are better off retreating and concealing their identity not only because they need to assimilate but also to get ahead in society.

Boy does that give me the creepy crawlies. OK, I know I said that I had it in me to "survive" but when an adult questions your ability you suddenly get butterflies. Is Uncle Joe right? Sure, I sometimes feel a strong temptation to retreat and to withdraw to the safety of anonymity. With the flick of a safety pin my hijab will fall off my head and I'll look like an unhyphenated Aussie.

But as Uncle Joe cautioned me about "blending in with

the crowd", some weird sensation started raging through me. I don't know what it was. Defiance? Anger? Pride? I can't define it. Whether I choose to be an astronaut, a pilot, a lollipop lady, a scientist or a Tupperware party host, this piece of material is coming with me. Whether Uncle Joe likes it, or not.

10

"Remember our first days in Australia?" my mum asks Aunt Cassandra, looking at Yasmeen and me with a twinkle in her eyes as we sit around our rumpus room on Friday night after a family dinner. My dad and Uncle Tariq are on the terrace, playing chess. Uncle Tariq's got his water pipe (he takes it along with him everywhere he goes) and is smoking apple-flavoured tobacco. I begged him for a try but my dad told me it wouldn't taste the same posthumously.

Aunt Cassandra and Uncle Tariq aren't related to me but in Arabic culture most adults who are family friends are addressed as uncles and aunts. Their children are "cousins". It makes for a pretty large extended "family".

"Of course I remember," Aunt Cassandra says.

"You wouldn't have experienced this, Cassandra," my mum says, "but oh the problems I had with English! We felt so disabled. I remember going to the supermarket and asking for a kilo of mashed meat. The boy could not understand what I was saying and called somebody over to help. I kept insisting I wanted mashed meat. When they finally realized I meant minced, they couldn't stop laughing at me. I felt so embarrassed." We all laugh.

"Yes, it's funny now. But then we were young and new and people looked at us as though we were aliens. And some people were so impatient with us and our language barrier."

"I had people not understand my English accent," Aunt Cassandra says.

"That's because it is hard to understand sometimes, Mum!" Yasmeen says.

"That's because you have selective hearing. When I'm offering you pocket money you can understand me perfectly, but if I'm asking you to make your bed I'm suddenly incomprehensible!" Aunt Cassandra grins at us.

"Anyway, I remember people being very rude and calling me a bloody pom and telling me I was speaking gibberish. The fact that I was also wearing the veil — well, a beanie — and married to a Pakistani caused a lot of eyebrow-raising too."

My mum shakes her head.

"Oh, we had our fun too. Kissed in public and made people uncomfortable."

"Eww!" Yasmeen cries.

"Sometimes it could be very funny," my mum tells us. "I'll never forget when Mohamed took me for a barbeque at a park when we were engaged. He came running to me in a panic, shocked that there were people eating dogs, and they were eating them hot. I didn't realize what he meant until I saw a family standing over a barbeque, talking about cooking hot dogs. We were horrified. When we later learnt what they were, we were in hysterics."

We can't stop laughing and my mum rubs her eyes as tears of laughter run down her face.

"We cursed this wretched country where people ate dogs, and we wondered whether cats were meals too!"

"I had to get used to curry!" Aunt Cassandra says. "I became so adapted to hot, spicy food that I started carrying little chilli sachets in my handbag for those times I ate takeaway food. Imagine this English girl, who grew up eating bangers and mash, suddenly whipping up spicy sambusas and roti bread and adding chilli to her hot chips!"

"It took time, didn't it, Cassandra?" my mum says. "Your dad, Amal, he used to tell me, if somebody teases you, just start swearing at them in Arabic. At least you'll get the frustration out."

Aunt Cassandra grins. "Exactly what I used to do. Whenever somebody gave me a hard time I'd whip out an Urdu swear word and they had no idea what I was saying."

"Mum!" I say. "How could Dad *encourage you* to swear, he has convulsions if I say—"

Mum gives me a stern look. "He didn't think it was rude because they wouldn't understand what we were saying."

"And times were different then," Aunt Cassandra adds.

"Exactly," my mum says. "I was cursing people's moustaches!"

"*Moustaches?*" Aunt Cassandra asks incredulously.

"Standard Arabic curse. God damn you and your moustache."

"Because that would make you aggro, hey Yasmeen?" I snort. "Ooh! I'm so insulted."

"You were hatched here, you wouldn't get it," my mum says.

But I find it hilarious. I mean, insulting somebody because of his facial hair? It must be a lost in translation thing. Another Arabic curse that cracks me up is the one my parents use whenever they go aggro at me. Instead of cursing me, they curse themselves! When Dad yells out "God damn your father" I'm absolutely chicken pox itching to tell him that he really is missing the point. Mum once went for the "God damn your mother" curse because I'd thrown a mega tantrum at her for dumping all my *Cosmo* magazines in the bin. When I pointed out to her that she was really cursing herself, she flipped. I got the lecture on respecting parents, talking back, insolence, and I had to hear all about how she spoke to her parents and how they spoke to their parents. Boy was I exhausted by the time she finished.

"Anyway," my mum continues, "I used to swear at them and then I'd go home and pray to God to forgive me because I'd damned their relatives!"

"See, girls," Aunt Cassandra says, "we were young once and we had our own challenges adapting our lives to a new country. If we can do it, you will have no problem because you were born here. You can cope with whatever obstacle comes your way."

"Exactly," my mum says.

"Yeah but *you* got to swear!" Yasmeen says.

"That's right," I add. "We've been deprived of your number one secret weapon."

Our mothers look at us, grin, and then tell us, Aunt Cassandra in Urdu and my mum in Arabic, to grow up.

During the week I catch the train to Leila's house. Yasmeen is there when I arrive. Every time the three of us get together, we hug and scream hello like we haven't seen each other in months.

Almost immediately Leila's mum insists we eat "a snack" and starts shovelling food down our throats.

"Amal, you have not eat any sheekon," she scolds me.

"This is my second piece, Aunty." (Leila's mum is another quasi aunt.)

"You no like my sheekon," she moans.

"It's delicious, honest."

"Then have more piece." She serves another helping on to my plate, adding rice and salad because I don't think this woman would wake up tomorrow if I ate chicken without rice and salad.

"Yasmeen, you want bread?" Before Yasmeen answers,

Leila's mum puts a round of pide bread on Yasmeen's plate. Yasmeen and I look at each other in exasperation and Leila wails to her mum to stop feeding us like we've just broken the forty-hour famine.

"Amal is good girl," Leila's mum says, darting a look at Yasmeen. "She wear hijab. She good girl."

Yasmeen ignores the stares and continues eating.

"It's only a piece of material, Aunty," I say through gritted teeth. "What's in your heart is what counts."

I could have been speaking in Spanish. She puts another spoon of salad on my plate, pats my shoulder and says: "Why you no wear it too, Yasmeen? Be good girl like Amal."

"I'm allergic," Yasmeen says as she takes a bite of food.

"Pah! No excuse. More reward for you. Don't you want to be good girl and go to heaven?"

"Mama!" Leila cries. "Stop with the bogus preaching will you! Leave Yasmeen alone, for crying out loud."

"Don't you yell at me, Leila! You so rude. So rude sometime. Ya Allah! Please bless my daughter and make her good girl. Don't punish her. I forgive her, Allah. She make me cry every night. Give me migraine. Oh, big migraine. But I forgive her. No punish her please." She sneaks a look at Leila, but she's washing down her food with Coke, flipping through the TV guide.

Her mum walks off into the lounge room, still moaning about a migraine.

Soon after, the kitchen door is thrown open and Leila's brother, Sam, who was born Hakan but has been calling himself Sam since high school, comes in.

"Hey," he mutters, nodding at us as he opens the fridge.

"Hi," we say, our conversation ending abruptly.

"What's to eat, Leila? I'm starving. Make me a plate."

"It's on the stove in front of you. There's chicken and rice and salad."

He slowly turns to look at her. "Don't give me attitude and don't think you're too good because your friends are here. I *said* make me a plate. I'm going to get changed. Leave my plate in the oven. And where's my blue shirt? Mum better have ironed it. I've gotta be in the city in an hour."

He gives her a threatening look and storms out upstairs.

"Jerk," Leila mutters, getting up to serve out a plate for him, her face pink with embarrassment. "Shit-faced pig. Ya Allah, I don't know how I'm related to this idiotic family."

We don't say anything, only sit at the table, awkwardly playing with our food.

"I'll give him all the leg pieces because he loves the breast," Leila whispers. "I'll hide the rest in the back of the fridge. He's too lazy to look there anyway. And he doesn't need the tomatoes and cucumbers in the salad. I'll just pick them out like so and leave him with the lettuce. Hurry up and drink that Coke, girls. We don't want to leave any now, do we?" She turns to us and grins. "I can get my own back, don't worry!"

Five minutes later we're in Leila's room, clutching our stomachs and groaning about how we ate like buffaloes.

"She would have cried if you refused another helping," Leila tells us. "It's her one pleasure in life, feeding people.

Thank God I've got good genes or I'd be arriving at school in a truck."

Yasmeen sits in a beanbag and starts playing DJ with Leila's stereo.

"Leila!" Leila's mum calls out.

"Yes, Mama?"

"Come vacuum."

"Can't Hakan do it?" Leila cries back limply.

"Eh?" she snaps, storming in to the bedroom. "Why your brother do it when he have sister?"

"Because the last time I saw, he wasn't a quadriplegic and it'd be nice to know he does something around here apart from farting and channel surfing!" Leila's fuming, her eyes popping out with anger. Yasmeen and I dart looks at each other. It's always uncomfortable sitting in somebody's home while they do battle in the family war zone.

"Don't talk big English to me. Don't think I no understand what you say . . . you fart too."

We all burst out laughing and Leila's mum raises her eyebrows at Leila.

"Vacuum. *Now.*" She walks out and Leila punches her pillow.

"See what I have to put up with?"

"A farting brother?" Yasmeen says, giving her a hug.

We laugh, knowing that there's not much to say except to reassure her it will all be OK, even though we're not so sure of that ourselves.

11

In school the next day, at lunch time I go to the girls' toilets to do my *wuduh* before prayer. As I'm washing my feet Tia walks in with Rita Mason. I ignore them.

"What are you doing?" Tia asks me in a mocking tone.

"What does it look like?"

"I don't know. You're not walking in the desert, you know. We do have shoes in this country."

I ignore her. "I'm washing for *prayer*."

"Oh! Looks a bit complicated. You actually wash your *feet*, just so you can, ah, what was it, pray?"

I stand up to my full height, one sock off, one sock on. Very dignified.

"That's right. See, Tia, I wash my feet five times a day. So that means that at any given time of the day, my feet are cleaner than your face."

"*Touchy!*" she snarls, storming off with Rita.

"Are you putting your name down for debating?" I ask Simone as we walk to the school gates to wait for the bus.

"Uh-uh." Simone shakes her head. "Way too stressful. We've got enough work as it is. And getting up in front of all those people? Ew, gives me the creeps. Especially rebuttal. I hate when you've got, like, five minutes to come up with a way to knock their arguments. I'm too busy panicking about whether my hands will shake or my voice will crack."

"Oh come on! You're brilliant at English and Legal Studies."

"No way," she says, looking flustered.

"Why?"

"Dunno. Too embarrassed. Everybody staring at the fat chick with a rebuttal argument."

"Simone!" I growl. "Don't say that about yourself! It's all in your head. Nobody's thinking that. You've got to learn to love yourself!"

Simone pretends to choke. "Amal, get over yourself. You're not Oprah."

"Well then stop with the 'I look like Roseanne' routine."

"And you're not Dr Phil either. Why don't you try for the debating? You've got the big mouth for it anyway!"

"Thanks, Simone. Really convincing argument." We laugh and she jabs me in my side. Then she suddenly stops clowning and hisses to me: "*Josh's* coming our way. . . Oh my God, is my hair OK? Do I look OK?"

"Course you do!" I say quickly. We pretend to be engrossed in conversation and act surprised to see him when he approaches us.

"Hey girls!" he says cheerfully.

"Hi, Josh," we say in unison.

"TGI Friday, hey?"

"Tell me about it." Simone shifts her bag on to her other shoulder. "This week has just dragged."

"This weekend is going to drag for me," he groans.

"Why?" I ask.

"My sister's wedding."

"Cool," Simone says. "Should be fun."

"You think? I'm going to be kissed by a bunch of ageing relatives with bad breath and opinions on what colour socks I should wear with my suit."

"That *is* bad," I say.

"And I'm going to get *so* harassed about school and exams. What TER score I'm hoping for, which unis I can get in to and all that crap." He rolls his eyes. "And my grandma is going to push her nannies' club on to me."

I shudder. "I hate when the oldies gang up on you."

"I know! I get people from my parents' stupid *yacht club* ganging up on me!" Simone cries. "Asking me in their fake British accents whether I want to follow in my mum's footsteps. Like I really want to be a rich housewife who drives a four-wheel drive to the supermarket and spends the day doing Pilates or maxing out a credit card on green organza napkins because Sarah Murdoch or some other high-profile supermodel thinks it's *so hip darling*."

Josh bursts out laughing and Simone blushes slightly.

"Why have they got fake accents?" I ask incredulously.

"Holiday in London. They come back thinking they've developed a sexy Beckham voice. *Losers!*"

I notice the way Josh's eyes light up as he looks at Simone. She's positively glowing.

"So what's the nannies' club going to do to you?" I ask.

"For sure they'll interrogate me about what I think of all the female guests. Do I have a girlfriend? What's my type? Do I like long or short hair? Orthodox or secular? Does she have to keep Sabbath?"

"So do they arrange a girlfriend for you?" Simone asks.

"No! No way!" he says quickly. "They've tried but there's no way. They don't know my type anyway." I could swear he looks her in the eye when he says this and my heart skips a beat for her. I want to walk away and leave them to talk but before I can make up an excuse to do the bolt Simone breaks the silence. I can tell she's embarrassed and unsure of herself.

"So who's your sister marrying?" she asks him.

He appears distracted but then he shakes his head and smiles. "Don't even ask."

"Why?" I ask. "You don't like him?"

"He's just *really* religious." He stops and looks at me sheepishly. "Sorry, I didn't mean to have a go at you."

117

I smile at him. "Don't be silly. So is he an orthodox Jew?"

"Man, he's *ultra* orthodox. And my family are secular Jews. Tamara's always been really relaxed about religion but now she's *really* strict."

"How d'you mean?" Simone asks.

"Since they got engaged, she gets really aggro when we don't follow Sabbath."

"Observant Jews won't do anything that's considered work on the Sabbath," I explain to Simone.

"That's right – so her fiancé doesn't use any electricity. He doesn't turn on light switches or the TV and stuff. Doesn't drive, write, shave, carry anything. Doesn't tear toilet paper even!"

"Yeah, I've heard of that," Simone says.

"He cuts a roll of toilet paper the day before and has it ready for the next day. Tamara's been trying to follow it too. She sits in front of the TV on Thursday night and tears the toilet paper and piles it up and Dad cracks these jokes which just make her go crazy."

"Yeah, I guess she would if she's the only one in her family practising her religion," I say. "Is she going to wear the wig?"

"The sheital, you mean," Simone corrects me.

"Wow!" Josh says. "How come you know that?"

"Simone knows heaps about other religions," I boast. "Don't you, Simone?"

She coughs and sneaks a stern look at me. "Er . . . I try. She has to wear it once she gets married, right?"

118

"Yeah," Josh says. "Solomon, that's her fiancé, really wants her to."

"Somebody's waving to you over there," Simone says. "In that car." He turns around to look and then picks his bag up from the floor.

"My cousin. He's a big shit-stirrer too. The whole family's going to be talking now." He grins at me. "We've got a family dinner tonight for Tamara. It will *definitely* be interesting."

"Why would your family be *talking*?" I ask.

"Yeah? What's so interesting?" Simone adds.

"It's *talking with a Muslim girl* kind of interesting," he says. I glance over to his cousin, who has a puzzled frown on his face.

"Add Palestinian," Simone says.

"Do you want me to wave?" I ask.

"Yeah, Amal, actually, please do." Josh walks towards the car and as I wave at him I meet his cousin's open-mouthed stare. I smile cheerfully but his cousin dodges my gaze, turning his head to look out the window. Josh stops in front of the door and is about to get in when he runs back to us.

"Hey Simone, did you get those notes on that Orwell book, *Nineteen Eighty-Four*, in English today?"

"Er ... yeah. . ." she stammers. "I did. Do you need them?"

"I took them down but boy was Mr Pearse racing through it, so I didn't get it all. Do you reckon I can go over them with you on Monday at recess? We've got that test coming up and I'm so screwed. My notes are *so* bad."

"Yeah ... sure ... no problem."

"Cool." He races off and gets into the car, slapping his cousin good-naturedly on the back as he rolls down his window.

"Hey girls!" he calls out.

"Yeah?"

"We'll continue our discussion about Israel's secret operations in the West Bank on Monday, and you can finish leaking info about the PLO! Have a great weekend!"

We erupt into a giggling fit as we notice the furious scowl spreading across Josh's cousin's face. He slams his foot on the accelerator and screeches off.

Simone and I look at each other then start jumping up and down and squealing with delight like two kids in front of an ice cream shop.

12

It just kind of happens. Adam and Josh become part of our little group. Not every recess or every lunch time. But when they're not in the library or playing sport with the guys, they sometimes sit with us. I emphasize the word sometimes because there is no routine or predictability to it. Therefore, whenever the lunch bell rings I need a Panadol because a million thoughts rush through my head. Three of those million are as follows:

1. (The bell rings.) Is Adam going to join us? Is Adam going to join us? Is Adam going to join us? What is the purpose of living if Adam is not going to join us?

2. (The bell rings.) Do I have time to put some lipgloss on, curl my eyelashes and make it to the oval, and if I do the aforementioned, do I risk him already having gone to the oval, not seeing me there and walking off?

3. (The bell rings.) What if I'm eating my sandwich and he happens to join us right at the moment I'm taking a huge chunk out of it? What if there's food stuck in my teeth? (Yesterday Simone, Eileen and I decided that we'd use code to help each other out. If we say "Big Brother" it means that there's an urgent need for you to pick your teeth. If we say the word "Survivor" it means that you are safe.)

On second thoughts, perhaps I need more than one Panadol.

Eileen is away sick today so at lunch time Simone and I are sitting by ourselves under a tree next to the football oval. Our attention is absorbed in a magazine article about "overcoming your body hang-ups" and how "flabby arms should be no obstacle to loving the inner you". As further reinforcement of this tabloid wisdom, the article features a model in a size six bikini with about as much flab as a foetus. Suddenly Adam and Josh approach us from across the oval and Simone immediately hisses "Big Brother". I do some pretty impressive quick-pick-teeth action and flash her a huge smile. She nods reassuringly at me and my heart resumes its normal beat. Josh and Adam then plant themselves down next to us and Simone and I put the magazine aside.

"Hey, can I have a look?" Josh asks Simone.

"Are you serious? It's a *Cosmo*."

"Yeah, so? My sister used to have them all over the house." Simone passes him the magazine and he opens it.

"Adam, man, check this chick out." Adam leans over the page and I glance at Simone who is suddenly looking uncomfortable and shy.

"Yeah, she's hot!" Adam says.

"Bull crap!" Josh cries. "She looks like she's about to snap in two. Mate, you could be sneezing in another suburb and she'd fall flat from the impact."

It's funny how a person's body can ignore internal messages. I'm pretty sure Simone is silently ordering her mouth to stay neutral but it is stubbornly ignoring her and widening into a massive grin.

"Do they have any of those quizzes?" Josh asks.

"Yeah," Simone says, "but this edition is about whether you're a social butterfly or a wallflower."

"OK, ask me the questions and let's check out what score I get."

"Man, what are you doing?" Adam asks, punching Josh in the arm.

"Getting in touch with my feminine side," he says in a high-pitched tone, batting his eyelashes flirtatiously at Adam.

"Let's see how you score then!" Simone says, opening the magazine. "OK, Josh, question one: your high heels are giving you excruciating blisters. Do you a) sit down; b) go home;

c) continue partying – nothing's going to stop you from getting on the dance floor!"

"You asked for it!" Adam says. He comes and sits next to me, leaving Simone and Josh close together, poring over the magazine.

"So Adam," I say, trying to sound calm and wishing I'd had time for the lipgloss. "What's the *real* deal with your mission to become the next Einstein? I mean, I know you want to get into med, but you've taken it up a notch, don't you think?"

He looks at me and shrugs. "Don't give me the analysing treatment, Amal. There isn't a deep and dark secret driving my ambition."

"Come on. Almost every recess or lunch you haven't managed a conversation without mentioning molecules and electrons. You should find yourself a reason pretty soon or you're stuck with 'nerd'."

He rolls his eyes at me. "Why is it that guys cop the nerd label when they study hard but girls don't?"

"Nerd is nothing. We've got eating disorders, looks, body mass index, hairstyles and dress sense to deal with. We're beating you guys by a mile."

He leans back on his hands. "What do you want to know? That I'm following family tradition? That I nearly drowned when I was a kid and was inspired to live to save lives?"

I snort in disbelief.

"I guess I've just always known what I want to be."

"Lucky you. I still don't know. Do your parents give you the career advice sessions every night? At my place we don't

124

get through one dinner without lectures about how my future is in my hands and this one decision will affect the course of my life."

"So your parents sit you down and give you long lectures about rising above people's low expectations and climbing to the top peak of the mountain and all that crap?"

"Pretty much."

He grins, shaking his head. "Boy, that's intense. I've escaped all of that."

"Lucky you!"

"My dad and his partner don't have time to lecture me, so I'm spared all that crap."

"You mean both your dad *and* your mum leave you alone?"

"Charlene isn't my mum."

"Where's your mum?" As soon as the words come out of my mouth I realize how nosy I sound and want to grab them back.

He doesn't seem to mind and continues. "She left us when I was seven. She lives in Holland now with her boyfriend."

"Oh."

"We're not close. She's got kids and I get a postcard on my birthday."

"Right. . . Do you get along with Charlene?"

"Yeah, it's cool. They've been together for ages."

I can't believe we're having this intimate conversation and that I'm so relaxed about it. I have to admit that a part of me is freaking out about the fact that I'm sitting on the grass with Adam talking as though we've been best friends for ages. Add the whole sexy aura thing happening on his side of the lawn and I could really do with a tranquillizer. But I have to say that given the circumstances, I'm performing pretty well.

"So you're the only child?" I ask.

"Yep."

"Me too."

"Would you want a sister or brother?"

"Would have loved either. But Mum couldn't have another baby."

"Charlene doesn't want kids because she hates nappies and doesn't want her hips to explode. She's not really the mothering type anyway. She'll be in her office working into the night for ever. Like my dad. They're perfect for each other, really."

"Do you get along with your dad?"

"I guess . . . I'm not *close* to either of them. At least he doesn't interfere with anything. He doesn't nag me with all that bull crap about the 'wrong crowd', and studying hard and stuff."

"You serious?"

"Yeah, he knows I've tried the drug scene and wasn't up for it, blah blah blah, so I guess he kind of trusts I can bring myself up alone."

My eyes bulge out. "He knows you've tried?"

"Last year. I was smoking pot with some mates at home and he walked in."

"I would have been ten feet under by the time the joint burned through."

"Nah. He was OK. Did the whole *Son, I know you're experimenting. We've all been there before. But don't go overboard, son.* Then he had a meeting to go to and the topic was never mentioned again."

I shake my head in disbelief. "My parents used to smoke and once my dad caught me stealing a cigarette from his packet and lighting up in the bathroom. He made me smoke half the packet until I was going to vomit myself into the next week. Pretty sadistic but I've never touched one since and he actually quit about a month later. As for drugs? It gives me shivers to even think how they'd react."

"Do your parents stick their noses in your life a lot?"

"Hmm ... yeah, I guess. I mean, compared to you, you probably think I'm on a leash! But I've never felt, strangled or anything. It's ... I don't know ... I feel independent and I know I've got the choice to be whoever I want to be. There are rules and limits, but I don't feel deprived. Don't tell them that, of course."

He laughs and nods.

"But take drugs or go to a nightclub or get pissed on the weekend with my mates. That all obviously comes with a death certificate warranty. But I'm not into all of that anyway. Do I sound boring and tame? Probably, hey?"

I smile shyly and he smiles back.

"Not at all. I mean, yeah, you're weird by teenage standards. But weird in a good way. I mean, it's your life, your

127

liver, your brain cells. It's weird not to respect *choice*. Whether you're choosing to get pissed or go sober, or get high on weed or chocolate, everybody's gotta make their own choices."

"I guess."

The bell rings and we all get up and walk to class. Well, the guys walk. I believe Simone and I float.

13

Dinner tonight is at Yasmeen's house and Yasmeen, Aunt Cassandra and I are sitting around the lounge room munching on fish and chips. Yasmeen's brother, Omar, is glued to the PlayStation and hasn't managed to string two words together since I arrived.

Leila, of course, wasn't allowed to come. Her mum doesn't approve of Cassandra because Cassandra volunteers at St John Ambulance on weekends and wears "hippie" clothes. This refers to Cassandra's passion for interesting costume jewellery, dyed skirts and bloodstones. Her hijab is a beanie. She's got a short bob so it easily fits in underneath.

Whenever I'm at Yasmeen's house I love hanging out with her mum. She's so cool and fun and easy to talk to.

I lie.

It's because of her British accent. I'm a sucker for pom accents, and when she pronounces Arabic words with a pom high note on the end, I'm in seventh heaven. It's just gorgeous. She is forever saying *Inshallah*, God willing, or *Mashallah*, God be praised, even when it doesn't quite fit.

I'm telling Aunt Cassandra about what it's like at school wearing the hijab and she's giving me a pep talk.

"Hang in there. Just be an individual and bollocks to the rest of them, *Inshallah*!"

She cracks me up.

"You can get through it. I should know. When—"

"*I became a Muslim*," Yasmeen mocks. Cassandra throws a cushion at her.

"My parents thought I'd been brainwashed by black magic voodoo! You see, my parents are extremely wealthy and move in 'high society', as they like to call it. My father was a banker and his father was a banker, and his father's father. When I announced to them that I'd enrolled in social studies and not medicine, they were hysterical. The nose ring, spiky hair, feminism and antiwar protests just about put my mother into hospital."

"You had a nose ring?" I'm bewildered.

"It was a requirement in my anti-everything circles. Armpit hair too."

"Eww!" Yasmeen scrunches her face up in disgust.

"Oh that phase only lasted about three or four months. My mother was taking antidepressants and going to church

130

every day praying for my enlightenment. My father couldn't look at me without a sherry in his hand. So I took pity and booked in for a wax. Plus," she pauses, "it was getting rather itchy."

"Mum!" Yasmeen wails. "That's *so* gross!"

"It was the Sixties, Yasmeen. The Beatles, free love, revolution. Go exchange a *Dolly* for a history book, darling. . . Anyway, Amal, when I announced to my parents that I'd converted, and I brought Abdel-Tariq home, they disowned me."

"That's horrible!" I exclaim.

"In hindsight I can understand the shock they must have felt. I'd been dabbling into different faiths for a while before that and my rejection of Christianity had already hurt them deeply. My parents are very staunch, decent, upright Christians. But I was rebelling. I couldn't understand how my parents could be so pious and yet be so racist. Africans, Asians, Arabs, Jews, anybody not of Anglo blood was, in their eyes, inferior. It was an unconscious prejudice but it infuriated me. So I became an atheist."

"You never told us that!" Yasmeen cries indignantly. "You told us you became an agnostic."

"That was later, darling."

"Oh."

"My atheism lasted one year. I was so unhappy though. I felt so empty. There were no answers, no deeper meanings to my life. Then one day at uni I learnt that a student had been killed in a hit-and-run. To me it was inconceivable that the monster who had left her to die on the side of the road would never be held accountable. Atheism just didn't make sense to me. I couldn't reconcile it with my instincts about justice. So I became an agnostic."

I stare at her, fascinated. She mixes pom with Arabic, has decorated her house with paintings and canvasses with Allah and Prophet Mohamed written in calligraphy, and seems to have dipped into just about every movement and trend.

As I look from Cassandra to Yasmeen to Omar, who has been absorbed in his PlayStation and hasn't said one word, I can't help but wonder how odd it is that some people think there is a "Muslim appearance". When I first started at McCleans Grammar, I remember one of the teachers did a double-take when she saw my name on the roll: "But you've got fair hair and coloured eyes!"

I wonder, then, what some people say when they learn that Cassandra's surname is Khan. When they see her blue eyes, pale skin, freckles, blonde eyelashes and light eyebrows underneath her beanie. When they see her arms linked wlth a dark, balding Pakistani. When they're introduced to her freckle-faced, dark-eyed, white daughter and chocolate-skinned son.

14

Adam doesn't stop nagging me about putting my name down for the debating team. Friday is the last day before the list will be taken down and the teams formed.

"Adam, get over it will you?" I say in a harassed tone, as he walks beside Eileen and me on our way to class.

"If you sign up you only have to participate in one debate. It's not like you'll be debating in all the rounds."

"What's your obsession with me being on the team?"

"The only people who have signed up who can actually put a decent performance on are Josh, Kishion and Tracy. Otherwise, we're stuck with Tia and Claire. Now I know Claire's just doing it because Tia is, and I have it on good authority that Tia's only signed up because she's got the hots for Josh and thinks this will bring them closer together. We need you on board so you can be a smart-arse to good effect for once."

"I'm still thinking about it."

"You're such a chicken."

"I am not!"

"Yes you are." He starts making annoying chicken noises.

"Grow up, Adam!" I howl, walking off. He follows us, clucking like a demented chook and making me laugh and groan with frustration.

"Flirt," Eileen says when we're finally alone.

"Flirt? Me? I wasn't flirting."

"You're loving it," she says, grinning at me. "He's practically grovelling and you're all *oh I couldn't possibly*."

I stop dead in my tracks. "Don't tell me that I'm making it obvious that I like him."

"Relax. It's not that. But with the chemistry between you both and your no-boyfriend policy, you might find yourself in dangerous territory."

"Don't be silly. I've got it all under control."

After school, when home room is empty, I march up to the noticeboard and sign up. And then I spend the bus ride home thinking of how I can convince Adam that I haven't fallen for the oldest trick in the book.

Adam approaches me the next morning.

"You signed up?" He grins.

"Don't flatter yourself," I say. "I hate Tia."

He gives me a sceptical look and I tell him to go learn a formula.

On Saturday I'm at my desk at home and I get this craving for a mango, strawberry and pistachio gelato from Lygon Street. So I call Simone and Eileen, but Eileen's shopping with her mum and Simone's got things on. So I call Yasmeen. I get Yasmeen going about the mango and strawberry and my dad has dropped me off at her house within half an hour. Then I call Leila's mum and pull off a story about needing Leila's opinion about what scarves to buy from a Muslim women's clothing store in Coburg. I plead with her that I'm still inexperienced and need Leila's expert advice and what better support than from my Muslim sister? Her mum laps it up and tells us to take Yasmeen along and try to convince her too.

"We're evil!" I groan as the three of us board a tram. "We lied! *And* we used religion!"

"White lie," Leila says, shrugging her shoulders. "Let's not think about it. There are plenty of other things Mum tries to make me feel guilty about."

"Yeah! Let's have fun!" Yasmeen throws her arms around the two of us. "Hey girls, is my hair OK?"

"Yes, Yasmeen."

"Any frizz?"

"No, Yasmeen."

"Is it straight?"

"We can smell the iron aid from here, Yasmeen."

135

"You would too – I spent two hours on the ironing board last night," she says.

"How about my scarf?" I ask.

"It's fine," Leila says.

"Is the front curve OK? I mean, are there any dents in the shape? Is it too tight? Are my cheeks squashed up so my face looks fat?" I take a mirror out and scrutinize my veil.

"It's perfect," Yasmeen says. "Quit panicking."

"You have hair static."

"What? Where? Give me the mirror!"

I smirk at her and she hits me. "Very funny, Amal."

It's a crisp August Melbourne day and I've got this strange sense of confidence as I'm on my way to my first trip to Lygon Street wearing hijab.

We've boarded a Sydney Road to City tram and are wedged between an old man dressed in a brown-tweed suit and red tie, and a couple of guys comparing mobile phone tones. I love trams. Everybody seems so authentic and natural. You kind of get to share a short time-out in between the chaos of everybody's day. And I especially love Sydney Road trams. Watching the street life with the old women with their baggy pantyhose and heaving breasts, clutching their trolley bags filled with discount plastic figurines and two-for-the-price-of-one sock sales. The eyebrow rings, the hijabs, the nuns, the three-piece suits worn by ancient men, the gossiping school kids, the pokie addicts, the families dragging wailing children behind them, laughing kids pressing pedestrian lights and running away.

136

We step off the tram at Royal Parade so that we can cut through Melbourne University on our way to Lygon Street. We walk through the grounds, impressing each other with our big statements about the "moral ineptitude" of an exam-based education system, growing big heads over our vocabulary and acting like idiots.

Yasmeen challenges Leila and me to a race through the lawns, and I manage to slow her down by yelling out that there's a cute guy staring at her from behind a tree. Then Leila and I spend five minutes convincing her that her hair hasn't frizzed from her twenty-metre sprint. Then we have to find a toilet so she can apply a serum to her hair. We end up spending fifteen minutes in the toilets, reading all the graffiti on the back of the cubicle doors, fascinated by the university standard of scribbling as compared to our high-school poetry (*Tia gives it to the footy team* and *Claire woz not here*). Yasmeen wants to write our names on the back of the door with her eyeliner pencil but I go all ethical on her and tell her it's wrong to graffiti. So she tries to persuade us to write *I'm a Muslim and I'm not oppressed*, and I pretend to vomit over the toilet seat, which gives us a reality check that we've voluntarily hung out in a block of toilets for quarter of an hour.

By the time we arrive at Lygon Street, we're swapping cubicle insults and arguing about whether *Big Brother* is better than *Survivor*.

And then we smell pizza and it's all over from there. We take one look at each other, nod in perfect harmony, take a seat at Café Roma and order a pizza with the lot, minus ham, pepperoni, salami and bacon. It turns out gelato was a negotiable craving, after all.

"That's not the lot," the waiter says flirtatiously.

"We're rather fussy about our pizzas," Leila says.

"I'll say." He grins, winking at us as he walks back to the kitchen.

"What a hottie!" Yasmeen exclaims.

"He plucks his eyebrows," I say solemnly.

"No he doesn't!" Leila cries.

"Yes he does."

"No way!"

"Yes way."

"I'm telling you they're natural."

"I'm telling you they're not. When he comes up again pay attention: he's got in-growns and he has a part in the middle the width of the Tullamarine Freeway."

Fifteen minutes later, our food arrives.

"Ladies, one pizza ... apparently with the lot." As the waiter catwalks away, I raise my eyebrows questioningly.

"Definitely a plucker," Leila sighs and Yasmeen nods.

We dig in to our pizza with the lot minus the lot, then we order dessert.

"This is nice," Leila sighs as we lick our gelatos.

"What is?" Yasmeen asks.

"This. *Hanging out.* Chilling like normal teenagers, you know? What's so bad about this? I don't get what my mum's dumb problem is."

"Pretty obvious," I say.

"Oh yeah? What?"

"She thinks you're going to try to pick up. And judging from the way you keep perving on that waiter, I'd say your mum has a point!"

She kicks me lightly under the table. "He's all yours."

"Oh *really*, and why the sudden change of heart?" Yasmeen says.

"Oh, you know how it is." She shrugs her shoulders. "It wouldn't work out between us. We'd constantly be fighting over the eyebrow plucker."

15

It's now two months since the start of term, and it feels like the teachers are on a mission to make VCE the worst two years of our life. The Victoria Certificate of Education is a complete nightmare and I've been up studying every night. I've got Stalin, the formula for glue, and Pythagoras in my head. It's an ugly combo.

It seems like our two-hour class of Biology with Mr Jefferson will never end. When the bell finally rings we all jump up and shove our things away, desperate for fresh air and normal conversation. After I put my stuff in my locker I grab my prayer mat and walk towards Mr Pearse's office. I cross paths with Adam on my way and stop to talk to him.

"Where are you going?" he asks.

"To pray."

"Cool. Where?"

I eye him suspiciously. "Mr Pearse organized a room for me."

"Wow! So you actually pray every day, here at school? It's not sarcastic, Amal. You can drop the eyebrows a notch."

I give him a half-smile. "Yeah, I pray every day here."

"Is it hard? To keep up, I mean?"

"Sometimes it is. I get lazy too, you know. But it's kind . . . kind of like a time-out. You know when — actually don't worry."

"What?"

"Nothing."

"I hate that what/nothing game. Just say it. I won't laugh. Jesus Christ, you take things seriously!"

"You shouldn't take Christ's name in vain like that," I say solemnly.

"*What?* Now you're defending *Jesus*?"

"I wouldn't be considered a Muslim if I didn't believe in Jesus Christ."

He backs away a little, looking flustered but excited. "Are you serious? So you believe in the Trinity and stuff, like me? Come on, sit down for a sec. I want to talk about this. This is *weird.* Can you pray in ten?"

"Yeah . . . I guess."

We walk over to a nearby bench. My prayer carpet is folded in my lap and I'm playing with the tassels on the end of it.

"So you and I, we believe in the same thing after all?"

"Well . . . not exactly. See, we don't believe Jesus was God, or the son of God. We believe he was one of the mightiest *prophets* of God, and performed miracles with God's permission, like healing the blind, curing the lepers."

"Really? So Muslims actually believe in that too?"

"Yeah. I went to a Catholic school you know. In primary."

"You *didn't*? No way!" His eyes widen and his mouth is confused between grinning and laughing out loud.

"Yep."

"This is freaking me out, Amal. So what were you saying about prayer?"

I lean back against the bench and stare at him. "OK. Imagine you're playing one of your basketball matches."

"Done."

"You're running up and down the court, doing your lay-ups, shooting hoops, smashing your body into exhaustion. You've got nothing on your mind except the game. Nothing is distracting you from it. But when it's time-out, you get this three or four minutes of calm. You get to drink your slurpie, catch your breath, rethink your strategy, who's getting in your way, who's working with you, who you could work with more. How much you owe your coach. What was that tip he gave you? What did he say was the best way to get a goal? Right?"

"Yep."

"That's how prayer is for me. It sounds corny, I know. But it's kind of . . . like that. Except there are five slurpie breaks a day, and one of them is so early it makes your teeth sting."

He laughs and leans back, folding his arms across his chest.

"You spin me out . . . I've never met anybody like you."

I don't say anything and continue playing with the prayer carpet.

"You know, you shouldn't pay any attention to Tia," he says. "She's just a bitch. Rich, spoilt brat, obsessed with her looks. Fits the profile kind of story."

"Racist?"

"Yeah, that too. But, well, you can't really blame her. It's what she hears at home. I know 'cause my dad knows her dad. They're not friends but they used to bump into each other at the golf club. That was ages ago but even then her dad would see somebody Asian or dark-skinned and he'd hail them over assuming they were a waiter or something. They don't really mix with anybody outside their circle. You're probably the first Muslim—"

"Yes, yes, I'm aware of that," I groan. "*The first Muslim she's ever met*. It makes me sound like an alien. Oh, it was my first encounter with a Muslim! Wow! I even had my camera! Can't wait to ring the National Museum. I'm sure they'll be interested in putting on an exhibition!"

"OK, OK, I get the sarcasm. You need to *relax*."

"I'd be less hyper if people would stop making up crappy excuses."

"It's not an excuse! I didn't mean it like that. It's just, it's obvious. You judge people on experience."

"Get out of here, Adam! You don't judge *people*. We're not a plural, or some big bloc, all acting and feeling and saying the same things. You judge individuals. Anyway, it goes both

143

ways. I've got family friends who think all Anglos are drunk wife-bashers slumped in front of Springer with a stubby in their hands."

"Are you serious?"

"Yes. Dead serious. Should I make an excuse for them? *Oh, they're allowed to think that. After all they've never really had a conversation with a sober Anglo*. If it sounds so ridiculous for your background, then why doesn't it for ours?"

He runs his fingers through his hair and shakes his head. "You are absolutely the most exhausting *individual* I've ever encountered."

"Shall I do a Tia for you?" I flip my head to the side so the tails of my hijab lift to my other shoulder, and he cracks up laughing. After a few seconds of silence he looks at me with a serious face.

"Hey. . .?"

"Yeah?"

"You know when you first walked in with the veil?"

I'm telling you my lungs start to do step aerobics. I try to breathe evenly and nod my head, too nervous to answer.

"It was weird. I thought . . . well a lot of people, we all thought you'd been forced by your parents. But a couple of us soon threw that idea out 'cause we thought, well, if you'd been forced you wouldn't seem so, I dunno, into it."

"Huh?"

"You just seemed to walk around like it meant something to you or you liked it. I dunno how to explain it."

I keep nodding.

"So then we thought you'd become, like, some fanatic. Like what you see on TV, you know?"

"Mmm."

"But you're not."

"Duh."

"Thanks."

"No problem." I stand up to walk off.

"Hey, Amal!" he calls out.

"Yeah?"

"There was something else that crossed my mind when I first saw you with the veil."

"And what was that?"

"You made for a pretty good-looking fanatic!" He grins at me and then gets up and walks away so quickly that he doesn't catch my mouth stretch out in a smile so wide I'm in danger of damaging my facial muscles.

16

I have a sleepover at my house on Saturday night with Eileen and Simone. Leila's here too; she's not allowed to sleep over but my mum managed to convince her mum to at least let her stay for dinner. Yasmeen has some family thing on so she can't make it and is spewing big time. We're in my bedroom pigging out on pizza. Luckily, criss-crossing my two sets of friends has never proven to be a disaster as everybody gets along.

"So I get this massive lecture from my mum this morning," Leila says.

"About?" I ask.

"How I'm never going to settle down unless I'm more open-minded about her match-making. Boy, she drives me up the wall. She's telling me this huge sob story about how much effort she takes to find guys she knows I'll be attracted to and have things in common with."

"She tries to set you up?" Simone asks.

"Yeah, all the time. About once every two months some new dude comes over for dinner. I'm coincidentally all dolled up. Like anybody really walks around the house with make-up and heels. Sometimes I deliberately wear no make-up and the daggiest clothes. Mum goes off at me."

"Would she force you to get married?" Eileen asks. "I don't mean to be rude, but that just sucks."

"No! There's no way she would force me. She just constantly pressurizes me about being so into my studies and not thinking about settling down. It's weird because my female cousins in Turkey are all at university and their parents, as in my aunts and uncles, would have a fit if the girls wanted to get married before they finished their degrees. It's like Mum came here all those years ago with the traditions of her village and got stuck in a time warp, while all her brothers and sisters progressed."

"I understand exactly what you mean," Eileen says. "My parents emigrated from Japan about twenty years ago and they're still going on about the traditions and cultural norms they were following when they left, all those years back."

"So your family's traditional too?" Leila asks.

"We all speak Japanese at home and my parents made me learn Japanese dance when I was in primary school when all my friends were doing ballet or playing basketball. And my mum wears the *kimono* on special occasions."

"What's that?" I ask.

"It's Japanese traditional dress. What was weird was that when we went for a holiday over there a couple of years ago my aunts, who are older than my mum, were wearing more fashionable *kimonos* than her! They were really into the latest fashion and styles and there's my mum with her taste from twenty years ago."

"I can so identify with that," Leila says. "My mum insists on wearing floral-print scarves with lace trimmings. My cousins gave her so much grief about them over in Turkey. They're all wearing these gorgeous silk and satin materials with funky patterns and there's my mum wearing what can pass off as a doily."

"That's slack," Simone says, giggling.

"Seriously, my mum is in desperate need of a Fab Five rescue."

"My mum wears pantyhose with open-toe shoes and draws in her eyebrows," Eileen says. "They're always smudged and crooked by the end of the day. Beat that."

"Is it because your mum is religious?" Simone asks Leila. "Amal drums it into our head that all those Taliban-type traditions aren't Islamic but it gets confusing sometimes."

"It depends on what you mean by religious," Leila answers. "Mum's following her own customs more than Islam. She doesn't really have an in-depth understanding about the religion, you know? Whereas my relatives in Turkey are all educated about Islam. The girls pray and some of them wear the veil and they go to university and work, because they know that it's their right to do that in Islam. Mum's more into following social customs."

"Is that why she wants you to settle down and get married?" Simone asks.

"I suppose. I know she's doing it because she loves me and in her own head what she wants for me is the right thing. But it's just so frustrating! Especially her pep talks before a guy comes over!" She stands up and starts to impersonate her mum. "Leila, you are beautifuls and smarts. You can cook the vine leave and pide breads. Don't let the man inside the lounge room make you feels you don't deserves the best. But Leila, oh my daughter, please don't talk smarts like you did the last times so he gets scared. Last times you told the man you believes all men are lazy and can irons the shirt if they try. Oh! No good, Leila!"

We all burst out laughing and Leila laughs along with us.

"So there you have it," she says, plonking herself back on to the beanbag. "My mum, the matchmaker."

"I'll never have that problem," Simone says matter-of-factly.

"What? Getting set up?" Leila asks, taking a bite of her slice of pizza. "Wannapieshe?"

"No, I've got this salad Amal's mum made. The lettuce is especially appetizing." Simone ordered pizza with us and then backed out when she looked up her pocket calorie counter. My mum made herself and Simone a big crispy salad with fetta cheese and savoy crackers instead.

"So what's the deal with your parents?" Eileen asks Simone.

"Well, there's no danger of my parents inviting people over and trying to get me to go out with their perfectly eligible sons. They're always telling me I'll never find a boyfriend until I lose weight."

"Oh come off it, Simone!" Eileen cries. "No way!"

"Mum has her figure even after having my sister, Liz, and me. She is constantly complaining about how I'll end up lonely and single if I'm not thinner and find myself a boyfriend. She seems to be embarrassed by me."

We all stare back at Simone, horrified.

"When my sister and her boyfriend are over from Adelaide, I get this huge debriefing session from my mum. See, Liz's boyfriend is really popular and apparently he's got a lot of friends. So Mum always sits me down weeks before we know they're coming and tries to persuade me to diet so I lose weight and impress him enough for him to set me up with one of his friends."

We cry out reassuring words and compliments but it's obvious that they don't mean much in the end. She shrugs us off and continues picking at her salad. So we throw the pizza to the side, put on the radio and pull Simone off the bed.

"Come on!" I cry. "Let's practise Tai Box moves. The ones we learnt in aerobics last year!"

Once the music gets started we spill over each other laughing as we perform our uncoordinated jabs and hook turns. Simone is yelling out names of people we should picture in our minds as we perform our uppercuts. Except she doesn't really move on from Tia, Claire and Rita. And then Aretha Franklin's song "Respect" starts playing and we're dancing like we're at a Grade Six slumber party, singing like we're the final act at the ARIAs.

Simone starts singing at the top of her lungs.

"RESPECT! Tia needs to find out what it means to me! That snob! I hope she becomes a FAT*TY*. Ow! Yeah! A little respect!"

I'm sitting in home room on Monday morning fuming over a newspaper article about crime and "people of Middle Eastern appearance" when Tia walks up to my desk.

"Hey Amal, did you watch that interview with those girls who were raped by those Lebo Muslims? You must feel *so* ashamed."

"Why?"

"Don't you have any *feelings*?"

"The only thing I'm feeling right now is that artificial intelligence beats real stupidity."

"*Funny*," she says sarcastically and walks away.

Tuesday morning. I'm at my desk in home room, fuming over an article about terror suspects and "people of Middle Eastern appearance" when Tia walks up to my desk again.

"Hey Amal, how's it going?" she asks in a sickly sweet voice. "Did you catch that doco on those Muslim fundamentalists last night? You're Arab aren't you? It must feel awful knowing you come from such a violent culture."

"You know, Tia, I came across a book the other day. The shortest book in world history. It was called *My Thoughts* by Tia Tamos."

For a moment she looks at me in mock-stunned silence, then she flips her hair and walks away.

Wednesday morning. I'm at my desk in home room, reading an article about Jennifer Lopez's exercise regime, when Adam is suddenly in front of my desk, smiling down cheerfully at me.

"Hey Amal, what's up?"

"Nothing much," I answer.

"There was a mad doco last night on September 11. Man, they were showing how these guys were all religious and holy and shit. Spin out! Did you see it?"

I've had it. I try to think of daffodil meadows. The moment the ugly stepsisters realize Cinderella's got the prince. Sunsets at the beach, the instant you take a bite of food after a day of fasting in Ramadan, and why people just won't give me a break. Do they think I'm a walking ambassador, that because I'm wearing hijab I'm watching every single documentary about Islam?

I take a deep breath. "Look, Adam, sorry to disappoint you but just because I'm Muslim doesn't mean I'm a walking TV guide for every 'let's deal with the Muslim dilemma' documentary churned out."

"Huh?"

"And why can't you and other people get that you can't be very holy if you're going around blowing people to smithereens?"

"Sorry," he says. "I didn't mean to offend you. I just thought you might have seen it. I'll let you chill." He walks off and I bite my lip, feeling instantly guilty for lashing out at him. I jump up and run after him into the locker area.

"Hey," I say.

He turns around and stares at me. "Yeah?"

"Look, Adam," I say, "I'm sorry for losing my temper at you but try to see it from my perspective."

"Which is?"

"It's just ... overwhelming. Do you have any idea how it feels to be me, a *Muslim*, today? I mean, just turn on the television, open a newspaper. There will be some feature article analysing, deconstructing, whipping up some theory about Islam and Muslims. Another chance to make *sense* of this *phenomenon* called 'the Muslim'. It feels like you're drowning in it all. And Tia has been having a go at me all week about it, so when you asked it was just wrong timing, you know? That's why I lashed out."

He runs his fingers through his hair. "OK, fine. I understand where you're coming from. But you have to stop assuming I'm judging you. Look, maybe at first when you put your scarf on I went through all these different theories, but that's all changed. Right now I'm judging you by whether you make me laugh and how smart you are and how annoying you can be when you have your smart-arse lines and go through your feminism moods and the way you're so gutsy and stand up for yourself. All the other stuff means jack-all to me. So get it straight, OK? I like you because you're a good friend. Not because you're some interesting horticultural specimen."

I give him a funny look. "You mean *anthropological*?"

We stare at each other and then break out into sheepish grins.

17

It's the first anniversary of September 11. I wake up this morning to the screeching buzz of my alarm clock and want to throw it across my room. I'm so tired. I listen to tributes all morning as I get ready for school. Another bad hijab day means a long session in front of the mirror.

I remember when it happened. My whole family stayed up all night watching the scenes on television. It was horrific. All I could think about was how a powerful country like America, with people just like those who work down Bourke or Collins Street could be hit like that. I kept thinking about those people. Mucking around at work. Probably reading a funny email. Having a whinge about their boss around the coffee machine. Telling their partners when they'd be home for dinner. I know it sounds awful, but I felt confused. Because for some reason their deaths were more shocking and disgusting and numbing than all the deaths you normally read about and see on the news. You know how it is, you turn on the six o'clock news and there are people starving and countries bleeding and people dying for the right to freedom from occupation and dictatorship and what do you do? You tut-tut and sigh. Most times I flip over to *The Simpsons*. That's what got me all confused and upset. Because I couldn't stop bawling, watching the towers come down. It was a terrible thing to happen. And a terrible thing to realize that I don't sit through the night crying when such horrors happen all the time.

I'm running late and miss my usual bus. When the next bus arrives I buy my ticket from a grumpy-looking driver who gives me a morning scowl as he hands me my change. The bus is full so I take a seat in the front row, diagonal to the driver, next to an elderly lady clutching an oversized canvas bag in one hand and a walking stick in the other. She's drawn over her eyebrows in a line of thick black eyeliner. She's wearing bright-pink lipstick. She's got beautiful, high cheekbones that turn into small apricots when she smiles at me as I squeeze myself on to the seat, careful not to hit her feet with my bulky school backpack.

"Morning, dear," she says in a cheerful, grandmotherly tone of voice.

"Good morning," I say, smiling back at her.

"That's a lovely shawl, dear."

"Thank you," I say, touched by the compliment.

"I was a young girl once too you know," she says. "And I used to work in a lovely clothes factory. Some covered girls worked there too. And some of them used to wear shawls just as you do. Oh my, the different patterns and colours and styles . . . and of course we girls would be green with envy at lunch time because they used to bring such delicious, exotic lunches with them." She chuckles as she remembers.

"We'd bring our boring ham, cheese and tomato sandwiches and, my goodness, they'd bring vine leaves stuffed with meat and rice or little fried *koftas*, they called them. Mmm. And always so sharing!" she exclaims.

As we talk, I suddenly become aware that the volume of the radio has been raised so that it blares out through the bus. A voice on the early-morning talkback shouts words of outrage about "Muslims being violent", and how "they're all trouble", and how "Australians are under threat of being attacked by these Koran-wielding people who want to sabotage our way of life and our values". My face goes bright red, and my stomach turns as the bus driver eyeballs me through the reflection of the mirror, looking at me as though I am a living proof of everything being said. I feel almost faint with embarrassment as the angry voice blasts through the bus for everyone to hear.

The bus driver keeps watching me, and my face burns with shame. Shame that I have let him get to me.

I thought I was prepared for this. But here I am now,

fighting back tears. The old lady beside me glances at me and I look away, focusing on a speck on the bus floor. When we stop at a traffic light she suddenly stands halfway up out of her seat.

"Bus driver!" she yells, trying to get his attention over the noise. He looks up in the mirror and pretends not to hear.

"Mister! Driver!"

"Yeah?" he answers impatiently.

"Would you please turn that nonsense *down*! We can't hear ourselves talk with that rubbish on full blast!"

He looks at her in annoyance and roughly turns the volume down. I feel like giving her a big hug. I smile at her shyly and she pats my hand.

"I'm sixty-seven years old. And, dear, in my sixty-seven years I've never let politics tell me how to treat people."

We sit in silence and she soon begins gathering her things ready for her stop. I let her out and as she steps off the bus she looks back at me and smiles. I wave goodbye.

Sometimes it's easy to lose faith in people. And sometimes one act of kindness is all it takes to give you hope again.

18

It's my parents' twenty-six-year wedding anniversary tonight. Last month I overheard them tossing up the idea of celebrating with a week in Bali but my mum was worried about me coping because of my studies and my dad was worried that if they left me with Uncle Joe and his family they'd return to find me with two counts of murder to my name (three, depending on George's mood, but Samantha would probably earn first degree on that count).

The last time I stayed over, Uncle Joe ordered pizza with extra ham and gave me funny looks when I asked if I could make a peanut-butter sandwich instead. Aunt Mandy spent dinner trying to persuade me to convince my parents to ban speaking any Arabic in the house because it would interfere with my English skills.

So, out of fear for my uncle and aunt's safety, my parents' romantic island holiday has been replaced with diamond earrings and dinner at a waterfront restaurant in South Bank.

I know about the earrings because my dad asked me to find out discreetly from my mum what she wanted. Like that was really a dose of detective work when my mum had Tiffany brochures in her glove box, her bedside-table drawer and posted on the fridge. I know about the dinner because all day he has been stressing about whether the restaurant will be diet-friendly.

He brought home a dozen roses and a box of carob chocolates. My mum was more excited about the fact that he thought to buy carob. She offered him one but he was adamant that his darling should keep the entire pack to herself.

"Come out for dinner with us," my mum says as I lie on her bed watching her apply her make-up.

"Like I really want to sit and watch you and Dad flirt with each other." I shudder, making gagging noises.

She throws a cotton bud at me and I can't help but notice how beautiful she looks tonight. She's picked out a cream, embroidered veil, with tiny roses weaved through in pale-pink and apricot silk. Her outfit is a long flowing cream top and a matching skirt with layers of chiffon.

"You look gorgeous," I tell her.

"Thanks *habibti*. What do you say I torture your dad a little?" She has a mischievous look in her eye. "Ask him if my bottom looks big in this?"

"That's *cruel*! That'll push him over the edge after what he's been through picking a restaurant."

"You're such a softie on him. By the way," she adds in a casual tone, "I had a chat with Mrs Vaselli this afternoon."

"Oh yeah? Did she put the evil eye on you?"

"Don't be rude. I feel so sorry for her. Poor lady. No one visits her. And it's her birthday today. She told me she hasn't seen her son for years. She's cooped up in that house all alone."

"Poor lady, my arse—*enal*." She can give pretty good death stares, my mum.

"What do I always tell you Islam says?"

"Increase your children's pocket money and achieve eternal bliss?'

"Paradise. . ."

". . .lies at the feet of mothers," I groan, completing a saying of Prophet Mohamed.

"That's right. Now go and give her the shawl I got her for her birthday and I might just let you touch my toes!"

She laughs hysterically and I cross my eyes.

"I can't go in!" I wail. "She hates me."

"That's nonsense. She's too old to hate. Get to that age and you don't have the energy."

"That's not true. She's got more time to draw on all her years' conserves of energy. Trust me, she *hates*."

161

"Well if she does, all the more reason to cheer her up. No excuse."

"Well, how about this then? The other day I was standing across the road and her door was open and I could see a cross in her hallway. It was the size of the entire wall. They must have used a whole forest to carve it. There are crosses everywhere. She's ultra Greek Orthodox. I simply can't go in." It was a cheap shot, but I was desperate.

"That's the most ridiculous excuse you've ever concocted. We go to friends' weddings in churches and you went to a Catholic school – I don't care if she offers you holy bread. You will go and you will be gracious and polite and kind, and if she's cranky, you will give her that winning smile of yours and ask her if she'd like you to make her a cup of tea. Understood?"

I make a face at her and she sticks her tongue out.

She really can be immature at times.

Mrs Vaselli lives in a massive old yellow Federation house. Her gardener keeps her front yard immaculate. One time he forgot to trim the hedges and she yelled out Greek swear words at him until he went back and finished the job.

I ring the front door bell and count to three. If she doesn't answer by three, I'm out of here. No way will I stay longer than three. But then I get to ten, and then fifteen, and it's on seventeen that she opens the door.

"What you want?" she snaps suspiciously, sticking her head round the door.

"Hi, Mrs Vaselli. It's Amal. From next door."

"Ahh. Ze smoker."

I don't even bother. I lift up the present so she can see. "Er . . . happy birthday."

"How you know it my birzday?"

"Mum told me. It's from her."

"Huh! Zat mum of yours. A big busybody. Always try talk to me."

I hold back a scowl and study her black shoes instead. They're so shiny I can almost see her moustache in the reflection.

She opens the door and turns her back to me, walking into the house. I stand at the entrance wondering what episode of *Seinfeld* I'm missing.

"Well?" she yells, turning back to look at me. "What you wait for?"

I follow her inside, past a large dining and living room, and into the kitchen. Her house is spotless and clinical. There are no photos. No proof of her memories. Nothing to show people where she's been, who she's hugged and posed next to.

She sits in a large wicker rocking chair and directs me to sit at the kitchen table, next to her. I pass her the present and take a seat. She frowns at me as she unfolds the wrapping paper.

"Why so much sticky?" she complains as she struggles with the ribbons and tape.

"My mum likes to wrap presents."

She finally gets the parcel open and takes the shawl out. It's a cashmere knit, swirls of turquoise and green and emerald, with royal-blue tassels. She holds it up in front of her and stares at it.

"Huh," she grunts, folding and putting it back in the paper. "My favourite colour red."

I look up at the ceiling and count to ten.

She rocks in her chair, a flat expression on her face. I tap my fingers on the table, trying not to hear my mum's voice in my head.

After a few moments she turns her head and looks me up and down. "Don't you get hot in zat?"

"Sometimes. But I don't wear black on a hot day. I'll wear light colours. And I don't get burnt this way either. Anyway, it's winter now."

"You too young to looking like your husband dead."

I grit my teeth.

"Your dad? He hitting you wiz ze belt if you no wearing it?"

I burst out laughing. "Of course not!"

"Huh!" She looks at me sceptically. "You wasting your time anyway." She glances at me from under her eyelashes as she picks the lint off her skirt.

"How am I wasting my time?"

"Why troubling to look like widow when you no having salvation through Jesus Christ anyway."

I wriggle myself in my seat, trying to hold my temper.

"Would you like a cup of tea?" I snap, remembering my mum's words.

She looks up in surprise. "No. But you do, ozerwise you no asking. Did your mum no teaching you manner?"

"Actually, no, she didn't. She brought me up like a jungle girl."

Her eyes narrow at me and I look at her defiantly.

"Kettle is on bench. Cup in cupboard under oven. Don't use good china set. For guest only. Use za mug. I taking no sugar, no milk. Don't fill za cup. And use same tea bag for boze cup."

I grit my teeth as I fill the kettle and switch it on. She's yelling out orders to me, about wiping any spills and not peeping through the other cupboards. It's all I can do to keep from exploding. I whisper every Arabic swear word I know under my breath.

And then I see her china tea set, stacked neatly in the cupboard. A white set with lavender lilies painted around the edges. The saucers are in one pile, the cups upside down and spread out in a diagonal pattern. There's a doily on top of the cake plate, and a cake knife sits delicately across it. I don't think she's used it in years. There's something so lonely and redundant about it. And all of a sudden this feeling comes over me. I don't care what she says. I don't care if she demands I convert, or calls my dad a criminal, or accuses my mum of child abuse. She has a useless china tea set and she can say anything she wants. And so I make her a cup of tea and put it on the coffee table next to her.

"So, got any biscuits, Mrs Vaselli?" I ask, flashing a wide grin at her.

She looks up at me roughly and eyeballs me, suspicious of my tone. And then she slowly lifts herself upright in the chair and, in a gruff voice, tells me to look in the left-hand side of the pantry, and suggests that while I'm there, I should try a piece of her fruitcake too.

At breakfast the next morning my mum shows me the earrings my dad surprised her with at dinner.

"They're gorgeous," I gush. "So did you like the restaurant?"

She looks at my dad and bursts out laughing.

"What's so funny?" I ask.

"The restaurant was lovely. A magical night."

"So what's funny?"

"Well. . ." My dad takes a sip of his coffee. "We hadn't even left the car park before she tells me she could do with a kebab."

"*You didn't*?" I ask incredulously. "You ate a *kebab*."

"With the lot."

"The lot?"

"I even had a fried falafel on the side."

"And then we get home and she asks me if her bottom looks big!" My dad rolls his eyes in bewilderment and shakes his head.

I look at my mum.

"I couldn't resist," she whispers, winking at me.

19

After lunch we're sitting at our desks waiting for Mr Piper, who's running late for class. I'm scribbling my signature over and over again in the January entries of my diary. And then I get bored and start working out my mathematical love equations with Usher and Adam.

"Hey Amal," Tia calls out, swinging on her chair as she turns to face me.

"Yeah?" Like I'm really in the mood.

"There's this article in *Marie Claire* about Muslim girls getting circumcised in Nigeria." She says circumcised loud enough for the boys to hear, knowing, of course, that they'd abort a Nintendo game to hear any part of the conversation now. Simone and Eileen are giving Tia filthy stares, but Claire and Rita are looking back at them with big smirks on their faces.

"So are you, you know, whole down there?" She bursts out laughing, and I hear some people giggling. My eyes pass over Adam. He's sitting at his desk, a look of shock on his face.

My neck is bright red. Flushed so hot that I can almost feel my necklace melt down my body. I don't know what to say. If I start explaining how it's culture not religion, she knows she's got to me, that I've dignified her with a response. But the thought of ignoring her makes me want to throw up. The humiliation of everybody looking at me, wondering if I've gone through with it, makes me almost giddy with sickness. I hate her. How dare she? I hate her so much my eyes feel blistered and I want to evaporate back to Hidaya, back to bed, away from this classroom of people staring at me, waiting for an answer.

"So?" She's looking at me with an arrogant smirk on her face, dangling her legs from the chair. "Or is it *private*? I'm sorry, I shouldn't have embarrassed you like this. I guess whether you're still intact is something you'd want to keep to yourself."

And then suddenly Simone is standing up, hands on her hips, a wild look in her eyes.

"Why don't you just shut your face, you stupid ugly bitch!"

The class is divided between those gasping for air from the shock, and those doubled over in laughter. Tia's face kind of collapses and then twists into a raging fury.

"Oooh! The fat girl finds her voice, does she? Has it been hiding under all your rolls?"

There's so much hatred in the air it's almost suffocating. Simone looks like she's about to jump on Tia and flatten her and Tia is looking back at her with repulsion. Some of the guys are heckling them on, yelling out, "Cat fight! Cat fight!"

And then Josh stands up. "Tia, get a life and shut up," he calls out.

Some of the class laugh, some of them start gossiping. Tia is sitting down with a mortified, angry pout. Simone is sitting at her desk in a happy trance. Adam looks at me but I don't meet his eyes, and he looks away. Eileen touches my arm but I shake her off. I don't want contact. I don't want anybody. I feel like I've eaten something rotten and I want to vomit. I can hear some girls whispering about circumcision and what it is. And I have to hold on to my chair so tightly that my palms feel bruised, just to keep myself from running out.

The next few days nobody mentions the topic again. Whether or not they're wondering is another thing. Simone and Eileen try to make me laugh but I'm not in the mood for fighting myself. Instead, I give in and enjoy an obscene dose of self-pity, dreaming up comeback lines in my head and being thoroughly miserable and selfish. It's so bad that I'm horrible enough to forget to thank Simone and Josh.

My parents think I'm under VCE stress from homework and assignments. It's the most adaptable excuse for any mood during VCE. My mum asks me to wash the dishes and I go all stress symptomatic on her and the next thing I know I'm lying in bed and my dad is bringing in a cup of Milo with skinny milk and asking me if I want Mum to make me low-fat muffins.

Towards the end of the week, after I've avoided Adam from sheer humiliation, he walks up to me at lunch time.

"Are you OK?" he asks nervously.

"Course I am." There's an awkward silence and I stare at the ground. I'm still feeling so embarrassed I can't look him in the eye.

"Tia's just having a go at you because you look different, because you're religious. I think she's freaked out about it and in her typical bitchy way sees you as the perfect target. . . It *is* freaky in a way."

"What is?"

"You being all religious and holy and stuff."

"Gee, thanks."

"Don't get pissed off, I'm only trying to explain how it is."

"So if I got pissed every weekend I'd be normal, but because I take about ten minutes out of my day to pray and wear a piece of material on my head, I'm this freak of nature?"

"Well, yeah." He gives me a goofy grin.

"It's not funny."

"Oh come on, you know I'm kidding. I like teasing you. You lose your temper so quickly. I don't really think you're a freak."

"You used to."

"Yeah, well, that was only for a couple of days. Now I think you're a smart-arsed big mouth with bloody female mood swings—"

"You're so unbelievably sexist!"

"Well, it's true!"

"Give me a break!"

"It's not my problem if you're in denial about the facts of life. Girls are schizo."

"I swear to God, Adam, you give me one more mental chauvinistic comment and I'll tell everybody you have a crush on Sandra Sully."

"Hey! That's low!"

I grin at him and fold my arms over my chest.

"Quit the macho sexist bull crap and I'll protect your rep."

"All right, all right... Anyway, it's not a *crush*. How dramatic can you get? There's just something about her..." He laughs.

"Yeah, well, that does it to a person ... every time."

20

I spend the two-week midterm break doing my holiday homework, which is killing me. The only thing getting me through it is the long telephone and MSN chat sessions with Adam. We talk about anything and everything. Like the time we discovered we liked the same movies and that we're both *Law and Order* addicts. Or the time we spent hours talking about our favourite music and what annoys us about our families and where we see ourselves after high school. It feels like it can't get any better.

As happy as Simone and Eileen are for me, Eileen's been sending me regular text messages cautioning me to take things easy if I don't want Adam to think I'm in the middle of a red-hot crush on him. She knows me well enough to predict my admission to the intensive care unit at the Royal Melbourne Hospital with a diagnosis of EMS (Extreme Mortification Syndrome) if Adam finds out. For somebody who's not very religious, she sure does act like my personal portable Sheikh. In the space of the holidays alone I've received the following messages from her:

Monday: IF U DON'T WANT HIM 2 KNOW, THEN DON'T LET YOUR FEELINGS SHOW.

Tuesday (morning): IF U FLIRT EXPECT 2 GET HURT.

Tuesday (late): ACTUALLY, U CAN FLIRT. JUST DON'T MAKE HIM FEEL LIKE HE'S THE ONLY 1 U FLIRT WITH.

Tuesday (very late): FLIRT WITH EVERY1?? IGNORE ME. UR NOT PARIS HILTON. JUST HAVE YOUR FUN & DO WHAT U FEEL IS RIGHT☺

Tonight Adam and I are watching some forensic/police/law show while we're on the phone, making comments throughout the programme, when my mum comes over and gives me a big, sloppy loud kiss on the cheek.

"Ma! I'm on the phone!"

"So I can't kiss my baby?"

"Jeez, Ma! At least wait until I get off the phone."

"Don't be so ungrateful, ya Amal. Say hi to whoever."

"OK I will."

"So say it."

"Hi."

"Who is it?"

"It's Adam."

"Oh . . . well, say hi. Your dad and me are going out to Uncle Joe's. Want to come?"

"No."

"I didn't think so. We won't be long."

"Don't shorten your visit on my account."

She looks at me knowingly. "How generous of you, Amal."

She ruffles my hair, I yell at her to leave me alone, and she disappears with my dad.

"I take it that was your mum?" Adam asks.

"Yeah, sorry about that. Talk about having no phone etiquette. She always has parallel conversations with me when I'm on the phone."

"Is she always so affectionate?"

"No. She hardly kisses me. That was so out of the blue."

"Amal, you don't have to lie because you think I might start crying in a corner because my mum's not here."

I mumble a sorry and he chuckles. "I think I have accepted the fact that I have a mother who walked out on her son. I can handle the fact there are happy families out there."

"Sorry . . . anyway, happiness is relative. Some days you'll have better days with your dad and Charlene, and my family will be in a bad mood, fighting over who left the milk out."

"Charlene's pretty neat. She doesn't pretend to be replacing my mum, which is good. Anyway, we don't really see each other that often. Like I told you, they're always working."

"My parents can work long hours some days too. I mean, their surgeries close at a set time but there's paperwork and sometimes they fill in for other doctors."

"But you guys are always doing stuff together. You're like the bloody Brady Bunch or something. I mean, you eat dinner together, you shop with your mum, you all go out for dinner or the movies. Didn't you tell me the other day you sat around and watched DVDs together?"

"Weird, hey?"

"Big time. I couldn't imagine doing that with Dad and Charlene. We'd have nothing to talk about."

"Tell me something up front and personal."

"Huh?"

"You know, deep and meaningful, spin-the-bottle type confession."

"What do you want? OK, um . . . I feel – you chicks like that word don't you—"

"I hate it when you say chicks! What is it about the female gender that even vaguely resembles a fur ball that chirps and eats worms?"

"Bad boys bad boys whatcha gonna do? Whatcha gonna do when they come for you? Cool song, hey. Seen the sequel?"

"Original kicked butt. So. . .?"

"OK, sometimes I *feel* like it could have been Dad that left. Does that satisfy your morbid curiosity?"

"Look, if we're going to be friends I'm going to have to know more about you than your obsession with sports, and Angelina Jolie."

"Angelina . . . ahh . . . don't make me drool."

"So why do you feel that way about your dad?"

175

"Hmm, let's see . . . because we're on parallel train tracks all the time. Occasionally we'll cross. Like when he's rushing out to work and I'm getting ready for school. Or when he goes all guilt-trip on me and gives me a pep talk when I'm studying."

"Are you angry with him?"

"Most days."

"Are you angry with her . . . your mum?"

"Every day."

"Why were you singing *Bad Boys*?"

"Because it's on at eight thirty tonight."

"Want to watch it together over the phone and analyse Will Smith's ears and acting ability?"

"Now *that's* a conversation I can enjoy getting into."

We're invited to Uncle Joe's house for dinner tonight. It's Aunt Mandy's birthday. She's turning "forty-three", although I've worked out the maths and she's dreaming if she thinks she had Samantha when she was twenty. When I point this out to my parents in the car on our way they tell me to stop being disrespectful, but I catch them glancing at each other, stifling laughs.

When we arrive Samantha opens the front door and kisses us hello.

"Full-on religious look now, hey?" she says playfully, looking me up and down. It's the first time I've come to their house wearing hijab as a "full-timer".

"Yeah, because a jean jacket and cargos are really Koranic

injunctions." She punches me playfully on the shoulder and laughs.

George approaches me and scowls. "Your face looks fatter in a scarf."

"Shut up, you dork." Samantha aims a kick at him. He sticks his tongue out at us and runs out before we can attack him. Aunt Mandy walks down the staircase in stilettos and tight Capri pants, her peroxide hair reflecting the spotlights in the ceiling. Uncle Joe follows, his gold chains hanging down his shirt, tufts of black curly hair finding their way through the gaps between his shirt buttons. He's wearing flip-flops and jeans. He's fifty years old and uses more New Wave Gel than the guys at school.

"Happy birthday," I say as Aunt Mandy comes over and kisses me hello.

"Thanks, darling," she says. "You look so ... *different* wearing that thing, Amal. A lot older. . ."

I fight back the temptation to remind her that she was born a brunette and her ankles are too thick for stilettos.

"Don't sound so disappointed in her, Mandy," my mum says, coming to my rescue. I want to give her a massive hug. "And I think Amal looks lovely."

Aunt Mandy gives my mum a fake smile. "Oh, of course she does," she coos. "Would you like to take if off now, Amal, sweetie?"

"Nah, I can't be bothered. My hair's a mess. Bad hair day. I'll just leave it on."

"Hmm, OK, it's up to you."

Samantha grabs my arm and pulls me towards the stairs. But Aunt Mandy insists we join them in the lounge room for a drink before dinner is served. "You're young ladies now. You should join the adults."

Samantha makes a retching sound and we reluctantly shuffle behind our parents.

The lounge room is decorated with little stuffed toys, koalas and kangaroos wearing T-shirts in the colours of the Australian flag. There's a holder on the coffee table that's filled with toothpicks with miniature flags stuck to their ends. The coasters are green and gold with the words *Sydney 2000* written on them. I've never dared to ask where the Crocodile Dundee beanbag came from. I have a sneaking suspicion it's handmade. I don't think any free market would have the nerve to sell something so lame. The hands-down most hideous item in the room is the large oval mirror on top of the artificial fireplace with the metal frame. Every last inch of it is filled with magnets with messages such as, *I'm a too right Aussie sheila* or *Strewth, let's have a shrimp on the barbie*. The room is like a holy shrine for those craving fairdinkumness and identity salvation.

After a short time of small talk, the doorbell rings. Uncle Joe answers it and ushers in a man who scans the room flashing us an enormous and sincere smile.

"This is Alan," Uncle Joe says pompously. "He's head of the department."

"Just call me Joe's *boss*," Alan jokes good-naturedly. Uncle Joe roars with laughter, and Alan looks at him with a tinge of

179

amusement, obviously aware that his joke was lame and that Uncle Joe is kissing butt big time.

As soon as Alan takes a seat, Aunt Mandy's doting begins.

"Would you like a drink before dinner?" she asks.

"Yeah, *mate*, want a VB?" Uncle Joe interrupts in a let's-try-an-ocker-accent. "You'll probably cark it if you don't get the grog in soon, hey mate?" He roars with laughter, slapping his hand on his knee. Samantha and I lock eyes and try not to gag.

"Oh, of course," Aunt Mandy gushes. "I'll get you a beer, Alan."

"No thanks. Have you got any soda water?"

Uncle Joe and Aunt Mandy look puzzled. Samantha lets out a titter and slams her hand over her mouth.

There's nothing weird about the fact that Alan's sitting with us at a family get-together when none of us have ever met him. It's part of the whole Joe and Mandy campaign to show off how Aussie they are.

Once it was their neighbour, Tim, a forty-five-year-old bachelor who had nothing to contribute to the conversation apart from endlessly blowing his nose because of the chilli in the food. The next time it was Uncle Joe's work colleague, Matthew, who spent the night talking CD-roms and Java scripts with my dad and uncle. Another time it was Aunt Mandy's gym buddy, Penny, who sat at the table counting calories and looking ill when my dad started carving the fat off the lamb roast.

The first few times, we just assumed Uncle Joe was being

friendly, you know, introducing us to his friends and acquaintances. It all started to make sense when, during one dinner, he started raving about how "broad-minded" his family is for socializing with people "outside the Arabic community".

Every time after that, it would be the same.

"We live in Australia," he'd say. "So we should assimilate and act like Australians. How can we be accepted and fit in if we're still thinking about Palestine and talking Arabic? Multiculturalism is a joke. We need to mix more. Make friends outside our own community. Look at my family. We're not stuck in Palestinian or Egyptian or Turkish ghettos. We're part of the wider community. Our friends, our colleagues, they're all average Australians, not wogs."

Matthew, Penny, Tim or whichever Anglo Uncle Joe delegated to grace our company with their superior presence would nod politely.

Samantha and I usually roll our eyes at each other and ignore everybody. As for my parents? Well, with fifty-two years of Aussieness between them, they generally don't swallow Uncle Joe's performances and would be more likely to belly dance in Bourke Street mall in pink tutus then seek approval as Australians.

Tonight's no exception. As we take our seats at the dining table, Aunt Mandy and my mum bring out the dishes. My mum's shooting looks at me to come and help but I pretend I don't notice and continue gossiping with Samantha.

When it comes to cooking, Aunt Mandy's a star. Tonight

181

she's cooked *makloba*, a spicy rice dish with pieces of marinated lamb and fried cauliflower and eggplant. The spicy smells mingle with the scent of hot baked pastries of minced chicken and garlic. Next to the *makloba* is a huge plate of sliced potatoes and chicken breast swimming in bubbling hot cream, garnished with tarragon leaves and fried pine nuts. Beside that is a pyramid of tomatoes and zucchinis stuffed with rice cooked in tomato paste and minced meat. The food's piping hot and the aromas tease our noses and stomachs until Aunt Mandy brings out the garden salad and insists that we dig in.

It's going smoothly. My dad, Uncle Joe and Alan are talking football. Probably the one thing that my dad and uncle have in common. Aunt Mandy's talking recipes with my mum, and Samantha and I are trying to decide whether Hugh Grant is cute or quirky.

But then, halfway through dinner, as I'm beginning to hope that we'll get through the meal without being tortured with lectures about citizenship, Alan takes a bite of *makloba* and I want to run for cover.

"I love Middle Eastern food," he says, smiling at us. "It's so delicious, I could live on it! This meal is superb, Mandy, thanks very much."

"Thank you!" Aunt Mandy says, beaming.

Alan takes another bite, unaware of the silence that has overcome his host.

Uncle Joe takes a sip of water and then clears his throat. "Mandy knows how to cook all kinds of recipes. Not just

Middle Eastern food. She knows Spanish, Chinese, French. She's a very *well-rounded* Australian."

Alan doesn't know what to make of Uncle Joe's outburst and smiles awkwardly. "Yes . . . I'm sure she is. . ."

"Mandy is, mate. A fairdinkum cook who knows all kinds of recipes."

"Come off it, Dad!" Samantha groans. "You sound like the Crocodile Hunter guy!"

"See, Alan, how my daughter talks to her old man? No respect."

"Dad called himself old!" George yells in delight.

"Old man is what *we* say about *you*," Samantha says. "You're not supposed to say it! You're just insulting yourself."

Uncle Joe looks embarrassed and a blush creeps over his neck. He darts a glance at Alan who, thankfully, is gracious enough to pretend not to have heard and mercifully changes the topic back to sport. My dad and Alan go off into their own world and Uncle Joe pretends to be occupied with the task of refilling everybody's glass.

"Bloody hell, when's he ever going to get over the slang?" Samantha whispers to me.

"When he realizes that flip-flops and a Bonds singlet aren't going to make him more Aussie."

"In other words, I'm doomed to hear him say *fairdinkum*, *crikey* and *mate* for the rest of my life!"

"Too right, Samantha, you beaut sheila." We look at each other, groan and erupt into giggles.

This Friday evening I'm at Leila's house watching a Ben Stiller comedy. We're sprawled on the couch, stuffing our faces with chips and Tim Tams and laughing over the movie when Hakan walks in. He nods at me and grunts a hello.

"What time did you get home last night?" Leila asks him.

"What the hell is it to you?"

"Dad woke up this morning and found the front door left wide open. He freaked out! Anybody could have come in the house. We could have been robbed. Attacked. We're on a main road, for God's sake!"

He chuckles. "Hear that, Amal? I've got a frigging paranoid

family. They start hallucinating about robbers because a door's left open. Bloody wogs think so stupid."

I ignore him, not wanting to interfere, and pretend to be watching the movie as they argue in front of me.

"You left the door wide open! Were you off your face again?"

"Got a problem with that?"

"What was it this time? Drugs? Alcohol? You're so predictable."

"I enjoy life. Not like this crap family, stuck in the Dark Ages. Bloody villagers."

"At least Mum and Dad aren't alcoholic weed-heads like you!"

"Why don't you frigging stop trying to show off in front of your friend? Trying to act like the Queen of Sheepa."

"It's *Sheba*," Leila says, rolling her eyes. "Jeez, why don't you go read a book?"

"Shut your face."

I adjust my position on the couch and start biting my nails. This is getting really uncomfortable.

"So I guess they haven't told you off about it yet? You're in big trouble. Mum and Dad are going to chuck a fit at you!"

"*Me*? Huh! Like those old wogs have the guts to tell me off. You think I'm going to listen to *them*?"

"You're so full of it."

"Watch your mouth, you bitch, got it?"

"Don't you dare call me a bitch!"

"*Ooh!* Leila's upset! What's she going to do? Run to

185

Mummy? Sweet talk Daddy? What are they going to do? Tell me off? Huh! Like they would! Man, you're warped. I'll say and do what I want and nobody's going to stop me!"

He storms out of the room and Leila stares at the coffee table, her breath heavy and angry. "Sorry you had to see that."

"Don't be silly. It's *me*. Family fights. Way normal."

"I swear, Amal, I hate him. I absolutely hate him. How can a sister hate her brother? He's my blood brother but if he left home now I wouldn't feel one single atom of sadness."

"Don't beat yourself up about him. He's all show. Just macho and full of himself."

"But what he said was so true. Mum and Dad probably won't tell him off. Mum has this almost reverential fear of him. Her first child. Her only son. I know she cries about what he does and I've heard her and Dad talking about how to control him and pull him into line, but they won't do anything about it."

"What about your dad?"

"Sometimes he has a go at Hakan. Like when Hakan gets home really late or when he's all doped up and has a hangover. When he's like that, Dad orders him to get out of the house and Hakan storms out and shouts he's leaving for good and then Mum breaks down and fights with my dad for losing her son and blah blah blah. So then Dad gets fed up because Mum gets hysterical that Hakan might not return. So now he lies low, for Mum's sake. If Hakan left, Mum would never forgive Dad and Dad's just too attached to Mum to make her angry at him like that. It's all a big mess. . . Let's just not talk about it."

She snuggles up next to me and places her head on my shoulder.

"Amal?"

"Yeah?"

"Can you rewind the movie to the start? I missed the whole thing and I can't even remember what I've watched!"

I rewind the movie and we watch the comedy in silence.

23

On Saturday night I stay up late and watch *Erin Brockovich* on TV. It makes me feel kind of emotional and do-gooder, so on Sunday morning I tell my mum I want to visit Mrs Vaselli and she chokes on her breakfast.

"Has my daughter seen the light? Can this be real?"

"Maa, don't make a big fuss. Do we have anything to take over?"

"Want to make her something?"

I'm not exactly in the mood for getting all domestic but she looks so excited that I smile and say yes. Fifteen minutes later we're caked in flour and butter, rolling out biscuits filled with fresh dates and cinnamon.

It takes us about two hours. When the biscuits are cooled,

we arrange them on a platter and my mum hands them over, beaming at me.

"I'm proud of you, Amal."

"Maa! Stop acting like I've turned into Mother Teresa."

I manage to escape my mum's You'll-be-rewarded-for-your-kindness-to-the-elderly speech and knock on Mrs Vaselli's front door, feeling idiotically nervous. It takes her a couple of minutes until she opens the door a fraction and sticks her head out.

"Hi, Mrs Vaselli. I . . . thought I'd come over for a visit. Mum and I made you fresh biscuits." I hold them up for her to see and she peers out at me suspiciously. We've been living next to her for over a year now and she still looks at me like there's a record of assault-and-battery-of-the-elderly convictions hanging over my head.

"*Visit?*"

"Er . . . yeah." I notice the edges of a shawl wrapped around her shoulders, and immediately recognize it as the one my mum bought her. I try not to grin as she looks out at me, hiding herself behind the door.

"One minute."

She closes the door and returns shortly afterwards, leaving me to follow her down the hallway. No sign of the shawl now. As I enter her house, I take a closer look around. I don't know why I expect it to smell mouldy and damp. It's what you always read about in books. Poor little old ladies in damp, stale houses, filled with mothballs and dusty photographs. But her house smells of talcum powder and scones. As I walk through the corridor, stickybeaking around me as I go, I notice a blue tassel dangling out of a cupboard in the hallway, and I bite my lip to stop myself from saying something.

She sits down on her rocking chair and I put the biscuits on the kitchen bench.

"So," I say, facing her, "would you like to try them?"

"Hmm . . . I guessing you want tea too? You not have tea at your house? You have to coming annoying me for it?" I grin sheepishly at her and nod. She does the sign of the cross and shakes her head. "Do I looking like supermarket? Wanting tea and coming here to finish mine." I ignore her because I can see a twitch in the corner of her mouth and her brow has loosened up.

"Well? What you wait for?" she says gruffly. "Don't pretend you no know where everyzing is."

I leap up from my chair, chatting away as I make the tea and set the biscuits out.

"I just made za scone."

"Really? Yum. I love scones."

"Of course you do. You love anyzing zat *free* . . . zey in ze pantry, in a box. You can try one if you want."

I smile at her and she looks back at me. But she doesn't scowl or frown and it makes me feel good. I put out the scones and take a seat, talking to her about school and Adam and Tia and Simone and Eileen. She doesn't say much, just listens and nods when she thinks I can't see her. And it's strangely comforting. So I tell her everything.

190

And for once she doesn't snap at me. Her wrinkled hands are wrapped around her mug of tea, the crumbs of three biscuits down the front of her dress, as she rocks back and forth, giving me her full attention.

"Zis Adam boy. He good boy?"

"Huh?"

"You very stupid. Your scarf too tight maybe and squash your brain. He maybe liking you."

I can feel my cheeks burning. My body is so annoying. You'd think after living with me for sixteen years it would owe me some loyalty.

"Your face red. You liking him and he liking you?"

I cough. "Yeah right."

"Eh?"

"Um . . . we're just friends."

"Pah! No such thing. Boy and girl. Friend. Boy zink of one zing only."

I shake my head and laugh at her.

"You always laugh. Laugh over anything. Silly . . . zis biscuit . . . it . . . OK. Your mum make?"

"I helped her."

"Huh! So you knowing how cook?"

"Not really. Just basic things."

"Zey making you into good wife so you get married and have kids?"

"No! I'm only sixteen! My parents would shoot me if I even mentioned marriage now!"

She leans back in her chair and gazes up at the ceiling.

"You know, I marrying at fourteen."

"*What?* Fourteen?"

"Yes. But we no . . . being husband and wife *really* . . . until I sixteen. You understanding?"

"Wow. How old was your husband when you got married?"

"Twenty-six. We were cousin. I live in village in Athens. He live in next village. He come my house and ask my papa if we marry. I was school zen. My papa he come to me and he say, you want marry? And I say yes because I wanting to wear make-up and high heel."

"*That's* why you agreed?"

"I wanting to be old. Like woman. You understanding?"

"I guess."

"And my mama she fight with my papa and me and say I too young. Because if I go she have no one talk to when she home. I have no brozer and my sister die when she two."

"So when did you come to Australia? Did you come straightaway?"

"Yes. I marry and I go to what zey say *luck country*. I cry and cry when I saying goodbye to my parent and my friend. I no want marry and I want go home but my husband he was good to me. Always good to me. I, how to say, vomate all way on za ship. First time on water. I come Melbourne. I see sky dark and sad. People look me and my husband and zey smile but bad smile not good smile. You understanding?"

"Yes, I understand."

"No talking to anybody. We no speak ze English. We using

192

hand to talk and zey laugh. In Greece, we talk. We hug. We know everyone. Here, we know nozing. No one. When we arrive we live in small house and my husband he work in factory. He work, work, work. I alone at home all day. No speak ze English. No speak to people. Only house and clean and cook. No friend. No family. I cry all time. I cook, I cry. I wash, I cry. He leave work, I cry. He come home, I cry. He come home and he tell me he no wanting me make him lunch because zey laugh at him. He vanting white bread, zey say tost. Very stupid bread. No taste or shape. He wanting tost with this Veg—Veg—"

"Vegemite?"

"Yes!" She makes the sign of the cross. "Oof! Like eat salt."

I laugh and it's the first time she laughs with me. Her eyes dance around making a stage debut amongst her wrinkles, and her heavy chest heaves up and down.

"I crying for all night. Because all I knowing to do good is make him good Greek lunch. Zat what I am. And he take from me. And I feel . . . I feel I nozing in day. All I do is pray to Jesus to make easy for me. So I now making him white tost and this Vegmate, and I hating Australia and white people and zere stupid food and I want Greece and my parent."

"What about kids?" I ask her.

She makes the sign of the cross again. "You asking za questions all za time."

And she frowns at me, but it's only small and it's so obviously forced that I grin widely back at her.

"My babies zey die in my stomach."

"You had miscarriages?"

"Yes. My husband, you know, he get sick of factory. So we say why not open ze shop and sell ze fish and chip."

I chuckle and she gives me a suspicious look. "Why so funny?"

"Oh, nothing. I just remembered when kids at school used to find out I was Arabic they'd assume my parents owned a newsagent's or 7-Eleven."

"I knowing many Greeks owning fish and chip shop. We making best fish and chip. Zen no McDonald's and zese food fast shopping. I working wiz my husband in shop all day. We no have people working for us. We open shop, we cut potatoes, we cooking, we cleaning, we doing everyzing, every day. Zen I coming home to clean my house. Seven day a week we work. On Sunday we closing za shop but my husband he doing work paper.

"So I be pregnant and I working. And I writing my mama in Greece and she writing but take long time to have letter. And she telling me to take rest but I working because we no affording za workers and I no having family to help us. My husband he good. He temper man but he look after me. But what can do? We must working zen. And I one day frying za chips for customer in shop and I feel want make toilet. You understanding?"

"Yes, Mrs Vaselli."

"We having many people in za shop zen. Busy. And zen man come. How to say? Spec—spec—spectatating za shop?"

"An *inspector*?"

"Yes. Zat. And my husband he so nerves. He scared zey maybe close us down because zen hard to, how to say, communion wiz people, you knowing my mean? Hard to talk with za people zen because we no speak ze good English. And he worry maybe say somezing and man no understanding and close down. And man he talk hard to my husband. He like . . . like sandpaper, you understanding? His words like sandpapering on my husband. So I going toilet quick because I feel I maybe doing accidental and I go and, Amal, I seeing blood in toilet and on my underwear! It bad and I want to scream, because I want my mama. I nineteen and I wanting my mama because I seeing blood in toilet and I knowing no blood when I pregnant. You understanding my mean?"

I nod frantically, my eyes transfixed on hers.

"And Amal, you knowing what I tinking? I tinking if I go inside and telling my husband he maybe scream and man close down shop tinking we crazy people. . . I no telling him zen!" Her eyes are open in horror as she sinks into her memories. "I wait to telling him! I putting tissue down zere and I wiping my face because I no stop za crying. And I go and fry chips, Amal! My baby die and I frying chips! And my husband he looking so scared when za man talking to him and I say Jesus please help us Jesus. Give me za strength Jesus."

My eyes are watery as I listen to her, my hands clasped tightly together.

"When we closing za shop I telling him. He sitting drinking

tea after we cleaning. He look so tired and worry. And I telling him and he smash ze drink on to ze wall and screaming and crying. I so scared. But he no screaming at me. He screaming at zis country and he screaming at lonely and no family and me wizout my mama and I crying and he quick take me hospital and I feel I going funeral not hospital because zey tell me my baby die and I dying wiz my baby too."

We sit in silence for a while. And then she heaves a sigh and closes her eyes, leaning back against her chair. And then with her eyes still closed she continues: "I having tree more babies dying in me. Each time I feeling like I no woman. My husband he wanting baby so much. And I wanting baby so much. But we no understanding zings zen. I still working and doctor telling me somezing wrong in me. So we no have za sheeldron for years."

"But you do have a son, don't you?"

Her eyes darken and she sits up abruptly, slamming her mug down on the table.

"None business!" she snaps, her eyes fixed on the floor. I don't say anything and sit still, waiting for her to say something. But she doesn't. It's like she's forgotten I am here.

"Mrs Vaselli?" I venture nervously. "Are you all right?" Such a stupid, obvious question.

She doesn't answer. So I get up and pack the dishes away, wipe the bench, clingfilm the biscuits and straighten my chair behind the table.

"It was nice having tea with you, Mrs Vaselli. Thanks for the scones."

"Go to drawer in hall." She's still looking at the floor.

I look at her in surprise. "Oh, OK, sure. What do you want?"

"My cigarette."

I just about do a belly dance on the table. "*Huh?*"

"Right drawer. Ashtray next it."

Five minutes later Mrs Vaselli is lighting up a Marlboro and is ensconced in a haze of nicotine smoke.

When she gets to her second cigarette, I can't contain myself any longer. China tea set, Vegemite sandwiches or lonely old woman, I've got issues to clear up with her.

"You *smoke*?" I say angrily. "After you told me off about the cigarette packs?"

She doesn't even bother to lift her eyes to look at me. "I trow mine in bin. You maybe on my grass."

"I *don't* smoke!"

"You good girl zen. Smoking for girl, it look like street woman. No nice."

I read an entire passage from the Koran in my mind to restrain myself from throwing her cigarette packet across the room.

"So why didn't you smoke the other time? Why did you hide it?"

"Because. . ."

"Because why?"

I'm standing up now, my hands on my hips in a defiant body pout. She avoids my glare, puts her cigarette down in the ashtray and sighs uncomfortably.

"I . . . no . . . I no want your mum say I bad lady. Zen . . . zen she no let you come."

She finally looks at me. I never noticed that her eyes have flickers of grey and hazelnut in them. Or that her wrinkles are like a confused map from a street directory, roads and boulevards intersecting in strange patterns. I wonder which line represents her loves. Which ones represent her joys, her laughs, her intimacies, her sorrows. How does it feel to lose your babies alone like that? What does it feel like, I wonder, to be over seventy years old and to have buried the man you woke up beside almost every morning of your life?

24

The following month, I go out rollerblading at St Kilda beach with Adam, Josh, Eileen and Simone on Saturday. It's October and the weather has warmed up and we can do more outdoor things together. My dad has agreed to drop me off in front of Luna Park. It takes him the entire stretch of Punt Road to get through his Golden Rules of Visiting St Kilda.

First he warns me not to use the toilets in McDonald's. Then it's about touching syringes, which he must think is my weekend pastime. Then it's drinking anything but bottled water, avoiding waiting for my friends on any street corner or kerbs, and making sure we comply with pedestrian footpath etiquette and rollerblade to the right. There's a little bit about talking to strangers, checking for foreign objects if we decide to sit in the sand, and dogs dribbling saliva on us. By the time we reach Luna Park I'm begging him to relax. So he gives me a harassed sigh and I cop the Who's-been-living-longer? lecture.

When I join the others the first thing we do is argue about who's going to win the World Cup soccer over coffee and chocolate éclairs at a cake shop on Acland Street. Then we decide to walk over to St Kilda esplanade and burn the calories off with an hour of rollerblading. On the way, we pass through the park in front of Luna Park.

"Who's up for the roller coaster?" Josh asks with a mischievous grin.

Eileen, Simone and I look at each other, our eyes gleaming in excitement. The next thing we know, we're waiting in line.

"Front row or back?" Adam asks.

"Front," Simone says. "It's scarier because you can see the dips."

"Nah!" I cry. "The back is better. It's bumpier. The carriage lifts up on all the dips and drops."

We decide to go with the back end of the ride. Eileen moves in to sit beside me, leaving Simone available for Josh to sit next to. Simone hops in and Josh follows quickly after her. Adam sits behind Eileen and me and keeps poking his head between us, trying to scare us before the ride begins.

"Did you hear about how it went off the track three years ago and those people were thrown off and they had to close the ride down? Guts and entrails everywhere."

"Ooh, we're shivering with fear," I say.

"You chicks will be screaming your heads off the second the ride starts."

We both turn around and hit him.

A guy called Gary hops on to the ride and takes his position in the middle carriage, manoeuvring the controls.

"Hi guys," he says, grinning at us. "Ready to have some fun?"

"Yeah!" we shout. It's like we're ten years old again.

"You scared?"

"No!"

The ride starts. It's obvious Gary regrets ever letting us on board as Simone, Eileen and I just about bust everybody's eardrums with our tonsil work. I can hear Adam yelling, "Typical chicks!" Even while we're on an amusement park ride Eileen and I don't give up the chance to advocate for equal opportunity and scream out to him to shut up with his macho sexism, but we can't really convey our thesis effectively given we're being zoomed up and down a track at a speed that is making us wish we'd worn sports bras and gelled our hair down more – or in my case pinned my hijab on tighter.

When the ride ends, we stagger away, clutching our stomachs and regretting the chocolate éclairs.

"You girls are wimps!" Adam cries.

"The three of you just about gave me tinnitus!" Josh says.

Simone bats her eyelashes at him. "Who us? *No!* We were

just exercising our vocal cords. Anyway, speaking of being scared, I noticed you tensing your feet against the floor pretty tightly when we were going down the roller coaster. Wouldn't have been itchy feet, would it?"

She flashes him a flirtatious grin and he smiles back at her. If this were a musical they'd both break out into a corny song and dance now.

The guys then go to the toilet, giving Eileen and me a chance to share a quick debriefing session with Simone.

"Did he hold your hand on the scary parts of the ride?"

"How close were you sitting?"

"Was there any physical contact?"

"Yeah! We were pressed up next to each other. He smells so good! And Josh actually — oh my God — he actually winked at me when we were about to go down one of the tracks!"

"Excellent sign!" Eileen cries. "Flirtatious but slightly subtle."

"Any good convo?"

"Like we could really talk on the ride! But he did say one thing. When we were getting out he looked at me and said: *Your hair's pretty neat. It didn't even get out of place.* Do you think it means anything?"

"He likes your hair!" Eileen cries happily.

"This guy is dropping hints, Simone! First he makes the effort to sit next to you — I saw him step in before Eileen or I could. Definitely a big sign. Secondly, he winks at you! Eyeball action is always a point scorer. And thirdly, he's throwing you a compliment! Since when do guys notice our hair unless there's an ulterior motive?"

"This is unreal! I'm not going to be able to sleep tonight! Hey, they're coming back. Quick! Change the topic. . ."

We have a perfect afternoon. We walk down to the end of the pier and sit on the rocks, letting the waves spray us as we play truth or dare. Except there aren't many dares you can perform when you're stuck on rocks, so we stick to interrogating each other about our crushes, enemies, favourite teachers and worst pick-up lines. We rollerblade along the bike track, humiliating ourselves by falling over each other more times than we can count. We eat hazelnut gelato, get chased by a German shepherd, and don't stop laughing. It's like one of those scenes from a feel-good Hollywood movie. Where everybody is happy and nobody's hair frizzes in the wind. Where it doesn't rain, your shoes stay comfortable all day, and everybody's jokes are funny. It's so good, I even think there's a possibility the chocolate won't go straight to our hips.

On Sunday afternoon I go for a jog around the block and come back feeling really pumped up with energy. I feel so good I decide to visit Mrs Vaselli because I haven't seen her for a couple of weeks.

I arrive and she sits in her rocking chair puffing away. Because it's just Mrs Vaselli and me, I take my hijab off and sit down. She looks at me and she makes the sign of the cross.

"You stupid girl for hide your beautiful hair."

"Thanks," I say sarcastically.

But then she pauses and says something that really touches me. "But your choice in end, I guessing. Oh well. No one should telling no one what to do when come to God. You no have salvation but you laugh a lot. Maybe Jesus let you in."

She says it so solemnly, so sincerely, as she puffs away and stares at the ceiling, that I have this urge to hug her. We talk about general stuff. She keeps avoiding mentioning children so I bring it up because I'm not about to pretend I'm not a major stickybeak.

"Mrs Vaselli, don't you . . . Mum mentioned once that you have a son."

She coughs and splatters on her cigarette and takes a quick sip of water. She gives me the silent treatment again, only this time it lasts for ten minutes.

"You no mind business . . . but you . . . you annoy me wiz your question all time . . . huh! My son, he marry Jehovah's Witness ten year ago. He conversion. I no speak him since." Her lips are pursed together as though the topic is now closed.

I feel as though Muhammad Ali has punched me in the chest. I was expecting death or kidnapping or abandonment. Something uncontrollable, outside her power. Never in a trillion years could I have guessed that she would have deliberately cut herself off from her only kid.

"Where does he live?"

"Tasmania."

"But, but ... you're alone, Mrs Vaselli! Why don't you speak to him? He's your only son! You've got nobody else!"

"Amal!" she yells, her voice bitter. "None business, I tell you. You no understand. He break my heart. Break my heart! Run off wiz zis girl and he conversion! You born Islam. You no fault really. How you know better? But he? After all do for him. He cut his papa heart. We give our life for him. Every day my husband working and money for school and clothe and food and we give him anyzing. He give us back shock. We trying nice Greek girl for him and he marry her and divorcing after fifteen year. No children. She no can have ze children. Cause problem. I say be patient. Have enough. Jesus work way we no know." Her voice is soft now. She's holding her cigarette and the end burns until the ash falls off on to the table, but she doesn't notice. "I no know what happen. He no tell us. One minute zey here for dinner and laughing and joking. Next minute zey divorcing and we never see her again."

I lean over towards her, looking her in the eye. "Do you miss him?"

She looks sadly back at me. "Yes."

"Then can't you forgive him?"

She shakes her head and slowly butts out her cigarette. "See zis ash, Amal? Za cigarette it burns, za ash falls, some bits solid zen zey fall apart, zey disappearing into tiny bits and zey fading away. To making it whole again you needing to go and finding each bit and putting togezer again, yes?"

She glances sidelong at me. "Too many bits, Amal. Zey

205

gone, zey disappeared, zey faded. Zat is it, Amal. I no knowing how to put it all togezer again."

In the evening I'm doing homework on my bed when I get a text message from Adam: WHAT DO U THINK OF SIMONE & JOSH AS A COUPLE?

I leap off the bed in an excited panic attack because something of this magnitude cannot involve a solo response. It requires a well-thought strategy, external contribution and a huge debriefing session with a friend. It would be an act of criminality against Simone to simply message back the first thing that pops into my head. So I call Eileen.

"He wants to know what I think about Simone and Josh! Oh my God, Josh likes Simone! Oh my God! He's going to ask her out. I just know it. Then she'll have a boyfriend. Suck eggs to her mum and dad! Oh my God, he must have set up Adam to ask me! *Eileen!* What do I text back?"

"Calm down, will you. Deep breaths. We can't do this on impulse. We have to think it through – Oh my God! She'll be over the moon! – OK, focus! Let's focus!"

"OK, we're focused."

"Now, we don't want him to think we've been thinking about it. That makes Simone look desperate. At the same time, we don't want him to think it never occurred to us. Because that would turn Josh off."

"So do you reckon Josh is behind the message or is Adam just sharing his own thoughts with me? Because it makes a difference."

"Hmm, well, I reckon the reply should take into account either scenario. How about, *Hmm – that implies thoughtful consideration but not premeditation – they do seem to connect.*"

"Connect is the wrong word. Too *Cleo*. A guy reading it might think it's too serious. *Having a connection*. You marry people you connect with. We don't want to scare him off."

"Good point."

"How about: *Hmm, they do seem to get along*?"

"Yeah! Simple but not too bloated with *Cleo* meaning. Why not throw a question back at him?"

"Brilliant! Put the ball back in his court!"

"Like: *I don't know, what do you think?*"

"Get rid of *I don't know*?"

"Yeah, instead just ask *what do you think*?"

"OK, so all up: *Hmm, they do seem to get along. What do you think?*"

"Perfect. It's positive but not so enthusiastic as to be desperate. Also invites him to dig up more information from his side. OK, send it now."

"Now?"

"Actually no. We've got to think about you too! If you reply instantly, he might read into it. As in, *Oh I can communicate with Amal at the drop of a hat. She's waiting around for my call. It's late on a Sunday night and she's up waiting for me to contact her.*"

"Yeah, but we're not going out. We're friends, so why would he read into it?"

"You're not friends like me or Simone are with him, are you? If it was us, no big deal. If we look desperate or lonely or boring in front of him we couldn't care less. But you still want him to have the best impression of you, don't you?"

"I'm not sending it for another half an hour."

"That's the way. OK, let me know what happens."

After I hang up I listen to music for half an hour, watching the seconds on my watch until I want to throw it down the toilet bowl from frustration. Finally, forty-seven minutes after he sent me the orginal SMS, I text back the agreed message. Seconds later, he replies: GOOD 1. CAN'T TALK NOW, I'M ON THE PHONE. WHAT TOOK U SO BLOODY LONG? TALK 2MORROW.

Typical.

25

Why oh why do guys do that? Bring something up and then ignore it until you want to grab them by their shoulders and scream at them to talk, open up, share! Eileen and I are literally two nanoseconds away from cornering Adam, tackling him to the ground and forcing him to discuss *the message* with us. But, in an act of extreme will power, we don't. Instead, we pretend to have forgotten all about the events that transpired last night and shoot some hoops with Adam and Josh on the basketball court at lunch time. Josh is the one who makes the suggestion and Eileen and I force Simone to play along. Usually Simone is allergic to any form of sport or activity which requires her to move because she thinks it draws attention to her body and makes her look fat and clumsy. Eileen and I hint that if she doesn't play with us Josh will think she's lazy. It's such a low, cheap shot but we have the ends-justify-the-means concept firmly in mind with this project.

It's so much fun. Simone surprises herself and us and turns out to be a really good goal shooter. Josh seems impressed. After her tenth score he says, "So all the times we've been hanging out on our arses on the oval you've been a star basket player and didn't even tell us? We could have been playing some ball!" Simone blushes and grins and of course misses the next couple of goals.

The best part of the entire hour is when I notice Tia, Claire and Rita sitting on one of the benches beside the court. Tia has her arms crossed and looks like she's accidentally eaten a cockroach. Her face is twisted with annoyance and disgust as she looks at Simone and Josh laughing and flirting on the court. I make eye contact with her and flash her a gigantic grin. She raises her eyebrows haughtily at me and turns away.

Sweet.

Disgraceful. Torturous. Sadistic. Not a word all day. Finally, in the evening, Adam calls me at home. Before I have a chance to launch into a lengthy deconstruction of his text message, Adam tells me that his mum called him last night to ask him what size he wears in shirts so she can send him a birthday present. Adam's not impressed.

"At least she sets her goals high. She expects to erase ten years of not being there for me by sending me some polo tops. I'd say that's pretty ambitious thinking."

"Was it out of the blue? Does she usually call you? I remember you said she sends you postcards."

"Since I was about eleven she's being calling me on my birthday and at Christmas. So what's your opinion on world soccer?"

"Would you prefer she ignored you?"

"Why would she think I cared? I have more interest in what's going on in the life of our school lollipop lady than my mum's. So, answer me. Soccer?"

"Cool sport. Maybe she's . . . trying to make amends. Say sorry in her own way. How do you feel about it all?"

"Amal! Are you trying to do a *let's express our feelings* thing here?"

"No."

"Yeah right! Amal, *puh-lease* do not think I am about to let myself be analysed and dissected and no, don't try to interrupt, I'm not being *sexist* and trying to make out that I can't talk about my feelings because I'm a boy but that you can because you're a girl. I'd really rather talk about soccer at the moment."

"But I'm curious. I want to know what happened. Please. I promise I won't give you advice or anything remotely resembling a pep talk."

"Fine. It was ten years ago. I was seven. It was a rainy day. It'd been a good day. In show and tell everybody had to bring

211

family pictures so I brought along some happy shots of me and my parents at the zoo, at the park, feeding ducks and all the usual crap. Dad picked me up from school on his way home from work because Mum apparently couldn't make it. He bought me a McDonald's junior burger meal and I can still remember how it tasted. I got home and it was silent. No Mum waiting for me. No dinner cooking in the kitchen. No *Bold and the Beautiful* or some other dumb-arse soapie blasting on the television. And after that, the silence never went away. . ."

"You are such a liar!"

He roars with laughter. "You asked for it. I bet you've been expecting some corny, tear-jerking crappy story with some Bryan Adams sop song playing in the background."

"Yeah! Something juicy, you know? What you just gave me is the kind of B-grade movie script that never gets a cinematic release and is screened at, like, eleven p.m. on a Saturday night some time in December."

"Don't bag those December late-night movies. I saw my first Sylvester Stallone movie then. . . Hey, I've got something juicy to divulge! But it stays between you and me, eh?"

"Swear on the Koran."

"Deal. I saw a shrink. Can you believe it? A shrink! How tripping is that? Dad and Charlene sent me to see one a couple of years back. Because they thought it'd be so hard for me to adjust to the whole idea of Charlene and they said I needed closure or whatever stupid term they use about my mum pissing off on us."

"What was it like?"

"The shrink kept trying to suggest that I felt guilty about my mum leaving and that I couldn't admit to it. Far out, he couldn't get that I've never felt guilty. Not once. Why should I feel guilty? I was seven! And the shrink kept saying that if I couldn't face up to my guilt I'd find it hard to trust women and have a meaningful relationship. Who was he kidding? It was as simple as me being bloody pissed off and that's never changed. I lasted two sessions."

"Only two?"

"Yeah, he pissed me off. Plus, he picked his nose when he thought I wasn't looking. Lost his credibility for ever."

At the start of semester I wouldn't have been able to imagine having a whole opening up/sharing secrets/D & M session with Adam Keane. But not only are we gossiping on the phone, he's actually confiding in me about his own family secrets.

According to my extensive research based on literary articles in *Dolly*, *Cleo* and *Cosmo*, the number one problem with the male species is their inability to communicate and share their feelings. After tonight I plan to write to all these magazines and inform them that my friendship with Adam Keane has discredited their theories and put the whole Venus/Mars philosophy to shame.

"So you didn't tell me what you think about Josh and Simone," Adam says. "I waited for you to bring it up at school all day but you didn't so I take it you think it's a bad idea?"

"No! Not at all! I was waiting for you to bring it up."

"Why would you do that?"

"Never mind," I sigh.

OK, I might hold off on that letter as I believe Mars and Venus might still have their merits. I might just approach a publisher instead and ask them to invest in a how-to manual for decoding guys' text messages with a prologue written by some psychologist.

"Anyway, did Josh mention, er, is he interested in Simone?"

"Maybe."

"Oh come off it, Adam. Why would you message me then?"

"Well, is Simone interested in Josh?"

"I don't know . . . she's never said anything to me."

Ahem.

"I reckon there's something between them," he says. "But she's so shy. I mean, when she breaks out of her shell she's funny and outgoing and Josh, *in my opinion*, I mean, he *would* be attracted to her at those times."

"Well, so he should be! She's smart and funny and gorgeous and caring and—"

"OK, Amal, I get it. Talk about hard-core marketing."

"Oh yeah? And what about Josh? Haven't you got anything to say about him?"

"Yeah, he's the only guy I know who can beat me at Daytona."

"That it? That's how you promote your friend?"

He chuckles. "I was stirring you. I'm not going to sit here and do a public relations campaign for him. He's your friend too; you know he's a top bloke."

"So be honest then. Is he going to ask her out?"

"How should I know? Even if I did, I know what girls are like. You're going to call Simone and Eileen within one second of hanging up the phone and start attacking our conversation like vultures on a Colonel fillet burger."

"We are not!"

"Oh yeah right! Every tone in my voice, every word and sentence and pause is going to be analysed to death. You're going to delegate lines to each other and come back and brief each other about the meanings."

"You're so full of it!"

"OK, Amal," he says, laughing at me. "I'll let you go now. Be sure to tell them that when I use prepositions in my sentences it means I'm buying time to think up ways to mislead you about Josh."

"Oh just shoosh!"

After I hang up I sit on my hands for fifteen minutes, wondering if I should call Eileen.

Oh stuff it! I think, reaching for the phone. He's probably calling Josh anyhow.

As I go to dial her number my phone beeps an incoming message: MAKE SURE 2 SAY HI 2 THEM 4 ME.

26

On my way to prayer I go to see Mr Pearse for help on an assignment. After we've finished I stand up to leave and he asks me to remain seated. He wants to "talk". Teachers don't talk. They either lecture or advise or recite a rhyme or an analogy. They do not simply "talk".

He leans back in his chair, scratching the bald patch on his head. I wonder if he's married or has children. There's a ring on his finger but you can never be too sure. I've heard some guys wear rings just so they can pick up (*Girlfriend*, Edition no. 56).

"Amal, let's have a chat about how you're coping."

"Er . . . coping with what?"

"School, class, *Tia*." He smiles at me and I shrug my shoulders.

"I'm fine. School work's making me age prematurely, but that's called education."

"Oh, I completely agree."

"I've also started taping myself reading out my essays and I go to sleep listening to an essay on the Cold War, thinking it will sink in. Like I'm some smoking addict listening to a Quit tape."

He chuckles and shakes his head. "Impressive. You're capable of getting top marks in VCE. You can be anything you want to be."

Oh my goodness he's going all To Sir with Love *on me.*

"You think?"

"Of course I do. Why? Don't you?"

"Yeah I guess. . ."

"How are you coping with other things? Have people been giving you a hard time . . . about your veil?"

Don't tell me we're doing the counselling thing!

"No. Everything's fine."

I avoid eye contact and stare down at my shoes. There is no way I'm getting sucked into a one-on-one "tell me how you feel" session.

"If you experience an iota of prejudice I want you to inform me immediately, Amal. Got it?"

"Yep."

"As I said, I have every faith that you will achieve your goals if you work hard and stand up for yourself when challenges arise."

"Thanks, Mr Pearse."

217

"OK, well, you can go now."

"Thanks."

I drop off to sleep that night thinking about what Mr Pearse said to me. About achieving my goals and being anything I want to be. Ever since I wore the hijab I've been feeling pretty scared.

Even if I get the marks I need to get in to the best uni course, assuming I can decide which one I want to do, I probably couldn't find a casual job now. So what about later on? Look, I'm not some whinging conspiracy theory victim who blames red traffic lights and rainy days when you forget your umbrella on "prejudice". But you hear stories, you know? Friends who get top marks in university and then when they get up in front of an interview panel they find the interviewers choking on their bottled water because the candidate is wearing hijab.

I wonder sometimes where I'll get my answers from. At Hidaya we were all going through the same thing. Whenever we felt like a mishmash of identities and started to wonder what our place was here, there was Mr Aziz telling us we didn't need to apologize for our heritage. Sometimes I just don't know what to think and I can't even be bothered trying to work it out. I know one thing though. There's nothing scarier than fearing your future won't live up to all you've dreamed it to be.

"So Mum comes into my room and shows me a photo of this Turkish guy, lives in Adelaide," Leila tells me on the telephone.

"Résumé?"

"Twenty-five, mechanic, looking for sweet, innocent housewife. Willing to move to Melbourne. Prefers brunettes. Mum was quick to assure him that I have brown hair and can cook and clean."

"Excellent press agent."

"Cream of the crop."

"What did you tell her?"

"Told her I had homework and to leave me alone, but that if he needed a lawyer in several years' time, he was welcome to call."

"She must have flipped."

"She has her approaches. Sometimes she has a hernia. Other times she tries to reason with me. *You think you lawyer you get job with hijab? Who take you? Why you want work hard for nothing? They see your hijab and they refuse.*"

"Someone will employ us," I say.

"I wouldn't fight so hard if I didn't believe that *someone* wasn't out there."

I pause and then it hits me. "Me either." And I mean it.

27

In English Mr Pearse announces the teams for the last two debating rounds. So far our Year Eleven teams have won two out of three debates. I'm teamed up with Adam and Josh and our names are down for the last debate, which is at the beginning of November, about a month away. Claire, Rita and Kishion are competing in the fourth round. I peek a glance at Tia. She is pouting angrily at Claire and Rita.

Josh, Adam and I meet up at lunch time to start preparing our debate because we want to get it all out of the way so we're left to kill ourselves over our end-of-year exams when they come up. Josh is eating a gorgonzola and salami sandwich. We need oxygen masks. One kid enters the room, takes a sniff, asks who farted then walks out.

"I learnt my lessons young," I tell Josh, holding up my odourless (and tasteless) cheese and lettuce sandwich.

"I didn't," Adam grins, taking out his lunch. "I've got leftovers from last night."

"Whatigit?" It's interesting how cheese and salami, when mashed together in somebody's wide-open mouth, can produce a rainbow of colours.

"Who cares! You just made me lose my appetite."

Josh swallows his food down in a gulp and grins sheepishly. "Sorry man. I'm just so starving. I tried to eat my chips in class but Mr Piper busted me."

"I've got garlic chicken pizza. It's fatal."

"You guys are gross! There are some things you just avoid eating at school."

We spend ages talking about food, swapping "the most I ever ate" stories until Adam looks at the time. We finally end up discussing the debate and start preparing our speeches. Adam and I get into about fifty-five arguments about the team line-up and theme until Josh tells us to shut up or he'll burp.

Each of us has a practice run and we boss each other around with hints and tips until we've all pretty much established that we think we're top and know what we're on about.

"Hey Adam," I say after the bell rings and we're packing up our things to go to class.

"Yeah?"

"Did you watch that doco last night on SBS about the Taliban?"

Adam looks at me dumbfounded. "Is this a...?" His voice trails off.

"Nope!"

He looks at me suspiciously, and then we break out into these big goofy grins. We don't stop talking all the way to class, swapping ideas and arguments and theories and big, impressive words. We pass each other notes in Maths and Mr Loafer swipes one off our desk and demands to know how our note about the government's asylum-seeker policy has anything to do with our Maths class.

"Er . . . it doesn't add up?" Adam answers, kicking my foot under the table as we try to keep a straight face.

Adam follows me out of last period and walks with me to the bus stop.

"Look," he says after a couple of minutes of chitchat, "I've got this party at my house on Friday night. It's kind of my birthday."

"*Kind of* your birthday? What, you couldn't decide if it is or isn't?"

"Shut up, OK. It's my birthday. Can you . . . can you come?"

I take a deep breath.

"It's complicated. Is it one of those . . . is it one of those parties where everybody gets blind drunk and takes turns throwing up in the pot plants?"

"No! No, it's not. It's just a group of friends coming over. Mainly from school, some from my weekend soccer club.

Food, music. We have to have alcohol, but it's not like one of *those* parties."

Almost every weekend somebody throws a party. I'm usually invited and I've been to a couple but to be honest it's not much fun if you don't drink. When you're sober the jokes aren't as funny and you have to pretend to be in hysterics when everybody is pissing themselves laughing over a leaf on somebody's shoe or something. Simone hates them because finding something to wear is her nightmare and then she spends the night thinking everybody is making fun of her. We dance a little but to be honest we're so self-conscious that we end up doing a little step to the side and back thing, which is about as uncool as you can get. That was all without my hijab. Unless I'm going to a costume party, I don't really think I'm going to fit in very well. But then again, it *is* Adam's party. I mean, I'd walk in dressed as a polar bear for the chance to go to his party.

"Can Simone and Eileen come too?"

"Yeah, sure, of course. I was going to ask them anyway."

"I'll have to check with my parents first."

"Nerd alert!"

I laugh. "Tell me about it. You tell anyone and I'll bring up the SS secret."

So Adam has invited me to his birthday party. Now just how am I supposed to convince my parents about this?

They're not stupid. They know what high-school parties are like and the whole drinking scene is strictly out of bounds. Just as I predicted, my dad gives me a flat-out no, turns his back and continues with his crossword. So I go inside where my mum is sitting reading a Diana conspiracy theory book. I give her a kiss and tell her I love her. The worst possible "yes" extraction method for a cluey parent.

"Spill it out."

"Can't I give you—"

"*Yallah*, I'm reading."

I take a breath. "Can I go to a birthday party Friday night? It's at this guy's house in my class. Eileen and Simone are going too."

"No."

"Why?"

"Because."

"Because why?"

"Because, I said so."

"But *why* do you say so?"

"Because I can say *because* and *I said so* and get away with it and when you have kids you'll do the same thing."

"No, I won't," I say, storming out of the room. "I'm making a conscious plan to be an *explainer* parent. Not a *because* parent."

"If you say so."

I give her a look and go and mope in my room. I make sure to turn the volume up really high and listen to mushy love songs because it allows me to feel even worse than I already do. It eventually works. I hear a creak on the hallway floor and prepare myself. I jump into bed and lie facing the wall, rubbing the mascara on my eyes so I look like a panda.

My mum enters my room and sits down on the edge of the bed.

"I spoke to your father."

I let out a noncommittal grunt in acknowledgment.

"I know you too well, Amal. Your it's-the-end-of-my-life performance is not going to work with me."

I sit up and hook my hands under my knees, resorting to a sulky pout instead.

"Whose party is it?"

"A guy called Adam Keane. Biggest nerd in class. Straight A student."

"The one you talk on the phone with?"

"Yeah."

"As *friends*?"

"Of course!"

"I sincerely hope so. Just be careful that you both understand that. Actions speak louder than words, ya Amal."

"Ma! I know what I'm doing and I know what's right and wrong. We're just good friends. And as if Adam would even think of me in that way. I'm wearing the hijab. He knows I'm not the type to do anything and, anyway, he's way too hot and cool to even consider me!"

"Of course he would. You're gorgeous. But that's besides the point. Is he decent? And please don't patronize me, I want an upfront answer."

"I've never heard anything bad about him, Mum. Honestly."

"So this Adam, he's a good boy?"

"We have very mature discussions about interfaith issues."

Cringe.

"*Really?*"

"Yeah. He's really into understanding my beliefs and stuff."

"Will his parents be there?"

"I'm not sure, Mum. He didn't say."

"Alcohol?"

"No. He's not like that. His parents . . . wouldn't approve."

I can't believe I'm lying to my mum. I'm an absolute hypocrite. Please Allah, I'm so so sorry, just this once let me get away with it. Only this once. Please.

You never feel good when you lie. It doesn't matter how much you want something, if you lie to somebody you love, and they actually, sincerely believe you, you feel like a cockroach that needs some serious Mortein action.

"Wise parents. So Simone and Eileen are going?"

"Yep."

I told them on the bus and by the time we got halfway home they were already discussing what they were going to wear.

"And how will you get there? I think we should drop you off."

Panic floods through me. "Simone's mum offered." She hasn't but I'll make a quick call as soon as my mum leaves the room. "She's going out that night so she doesn't mind. It's on her way. And she said she'll drop us off home too. So you don't have to bother or worry about anything."

226

"We want you home by ten thirty. No later."

"What about eleven?"

"No."

"Oh come on, Mum! Ten thirty is embarrassing! I'll look like a geek! Please! It's hard enough as it is. . ." I bat my eyelashes at her and she rolls her eyes.

"OK."

"Eleven thirty would be more appropriate for Simone's mum though. I don't want to wreck her night."

"If there's any possibility of her night being wrecked, we're more than happy to get in the car and pick you up. Eleven or you will not hear the end of it, Amal. Do I make myself clear?"

"Waterford."

Simone and I meet up for a walk after school.

"So your mum's OK being taxi driver?"

"Oh, yeah, sure! No big deal."

While we're walking Simone asks me to promise that I won't go aggro on her.

"About what?"

"Just promise first."

"I hate those tests. I use them on my *parents* for God's sake." She gives me a desperate, pleading look and I promise.

"OK," she says nervously. "I've . . . I've started . . . look, I've tried every diet, OK? And nothing works. My appetite is just too big for carrots and celery. Even if I go all moderate, like a sandwich for lunch, I still crave something sweet or I just

227

don't feel full up. So I've . . . started smoking."

"*What?*"

"Apparently it's a good appetite suppressant. How do you think Tia keeps her figure? I overheard her telling Claire and Rita that she doesn't eat much, just smokes because it stops her cravings."

"Yeah but my cousin Samantha smokes and pigs out all the time! She has Macas *at least* once a day."

"Is she skinny?"

"Er . . . yeah."

She sighs. "See? It's not fair! That sucks. I'm so sick of seeing everyone in their tight jeans and little tops pigging out on chocolate when I'm eating an apple. Nothing works. I don't give a shit what happens to me. I just want to hate food, so every time I feel like eating I'm going to smoke. I don't give a damn any more."

"You're serious about this?"

"I've made up my mind." Her eyes are narrowed tightly and she looks at me with full conviction. "I know it causes cancer and stinks and stuff, but that's all too hypothetical for me. My weight isn't. And it's all calculated, OK? Part of a plan. One year of smoking to get the weight off, and then I'll quit. It can't honestly affect me for one year!"

"You'll get hooked."

"No I won't. I know what I'm doing."

"You're crazy. It's addictive. It says so on the packet! It's like getting into a car with a big warning sign on the windscreen, 'If you drive this car you will eventually die'. You

228

wouldn't even contemplate touching the car. So why would you get into smoking? Does that sound sane to you?"

Simone looks at me and shrugs. "Amal, give it up. I know what you're saying makes sense but I'm not interested." She takes a lighter and packet of cigarettes out of her bum bag and lights a cigarette.

"It stinks!"

She exhales her cigarette smoke and sighs melo-dramatically. "No, Amal," she says, "being fat is what *stinks*."

I want to shave his eyebrows off and superglue pink feathers in their place. Tia's here. Since when is she part of his circle of friends? She's standing by the pool, a drink in one hand and a cigarette in another, throwing back her hair and laughing with a cute guy she's talking to.

Simone, Eileen and I walk through the crowd. There are lots of other people we don't recognize hanging around, huddled together, dancing, laughing, gossiping and drinking. Everybody's divided up into their status groups. The cool group, the good-looking group, the confident group, the shy group, the sober group, the tipsy group, the spectators, the participators. The school hierarchy is comfortably setting itself up and the three of us are feeling nervous.

"Why is everybody staring?" Eileen asks us.

"It's obvious, isn't it?" Simone and I say in unison. We all stare at each other in surprise and then burst out laughing.

"We are ultra stress heads!" I say.

We walk over to the side of the crowd and Simone lights a cigarette, anxiously looking around as she inhales.

"I can't believe you, Simone!" Eileen exclaims. "You look like a try-hard. Do you actually enjoy it?"

"Hell no! I hate the bloody things. I stink and I'm still learning how to inhale the stuff."

"So why are you doing it then?"

"Can we please not open up that discussion again? Hey, Amal, there's Adam. He's seen us. He's slowly walking through the crowd. He's approaching—"

"*Simone*, I don't need a news report. I can see. Don't make it obvious." My skin starts to feel all goosepimply. Lucky I'm wearing long sleeves or it'd be a dead giveaway. "He looks so good. He shouldn't be allowed to wear a black skivvy. Doesn't he have the most amazing muscles?"

"Doesn't he have a brother?" Eileen asks and we chuckle.

He's beside us in a moment and we all have a bit of a laugh and small talk. Things always start off a little awkward outside of school gates.

"So are you having fun?"

"We just got here," Simone says.

"But the atmosphere's pretty cool," Eileen says.

"How about you, Amal?"

"Great skivvy."

"You like?" he says, cocking his head to the side and looking at me with a cheeky expression.

"I meant the fabric."

"Sure you did."

"Oh, well, you're entitled to one compliment on your birthday, I guess."

Somebody calls out to him and he looks disappointed. "I'll come by soon. Don't go anywhere!"

"Yep."

"Subtle," Eileen says, grinning at me when he has walked away.

I groan and she slings her arm around my shoulder. "Hon, I believe somebody well and truly has a crush on you."

"Nah!"

"Most definitely," Simone says. "The way he looks at you."

"I feel hot. I need a Coke."

We head off to grab drinks and mingle with some people from school. For the next hour we end up sitting on the edge of the pergola studying the crowd and wondering why we bothered to come. Simone is on her fifth cigarette and is telling me how difficult it is to suck her stomach in as she inhales and Eileen's gone to the bathroom to fix her hair.

I'm watching everybody, fascinated by the effect of alcohol on people. The self-conscious or haughty or dignified air they have when they first arrive seems to just burp out of their bodies. There's a girl who, when she arrived, had been looking at the floor as she walked, tugging her top down and avoiding eye contact. She's on a chair now doing a cheerleader routine. A guy who walked in with a scowl on his face is now clowning around in an attempted solo Zorba dance.

"Adam's looking for you," Eileen tells me when she returns.

"Me?"

"Yep."

"Where is he?"

"He's been walking around asking people where you are. You're kind of hidden here, don't you think?"

I grin at her. "That's the idea."

"A bit uncomfortable?"

"*Uncomfortble?*" Simone chuckles. "This whole night is like a permanent atomic wedgie."

Eileen and I laugh, nodding our heads in agreement. Simone suddenly motions at us to look towards the pool area. "Check it out!" She points to a circle of people cheering on Tia, as she stands on a table and slips her top off, throwing it into the crowd. She only has her bra on and is laughing and trying to keep her balance as she dances, winking at people in the crowd and blowing them kisses.

We look at each other wide-eyed, and then collapse into hysterical giggles. Adam appears before us. We smile sheepishly at him and I try to regain my composure, smoothing out my clothes and hijab.

"Hi!" I say, smiling at him.

"Having fun?" he asks.

"Sure," the three of us reply at the same time.

"Can I speak to you alone?" he asks me and I stare back at him in surprise.

"Yeah, OK." I jump off the edge and walk with him through the crowd and inside, where the music is pumping loudly and people are dancing in a frenzy. For a moment I lose my pace with Adam as I squeeze through the crowd. He's already ahead of me, at the French doors at the end of the room. I squash myself through a couple when a guy comes up to me and puts his arms around my shoulders, and I nearly choke on his breath.

"Scarf girl!" he shouts happily. "Helloooo scarf girlll! Tell me, do you have hair? Take off your scarf and belly dance for us!" He laughs in my face and I want to gag, wondering why they don't make it compulsory to serve cool mints with alcohol. "Hey," he whispers in my ear, "the story goes that Adam's planning on getting you in the sack! Woo hoo! Who said you Middle Eastern girls don't have fun?"

My face crumbles into shock and I quickly walk away. I feel numb and dizzy. Then I reach Adam and he grabs my hand, leading me away from the crowd and through the house. He takes me out through a side door, to another courtyard, only this one is quiet and empty of people.

I feel almost panicky, wondering whether I've just heard a drunken joke or if it's true. I sit on a chair, not knowing if I should stay or go. Adam sits on a table, smiling at me.

"I've been looking all over for you."

"Have you?"

"Yep. So? Are you having fun?"

"Me? Yeah, yeah . . . sure I am. Cool party."

"You're such a bad liar. You couldn't spin if your life depended on it."

I crack my knuckles nervously.

"So. . ." My head is going to burst through my scarf and explode into a shattered pulp on the floor. He doesn't say anything, just dangles his legs and stares at me with an intensity that makes me feel giddy. I look away, down at my hands, up again at his face, and then down again. I don't want things to change. I want things to stay as perfect as they are between us. I want to forget about what that guy just told me and for Adam to stop leaning towards me.

His face is inches from mine and as he moves in to kiss me I jolt back.

"I . . . I . . ."

"What's wrong?"

"I'm so sorry, Adam. . . I didn't. . . I mean, I never thought to lead you on. . ."

"What's wrong? I thought you liked me – I thought—"

"Adam, I . . . I don't do that stuff. . ."

"What stuff?"

"Kissing – I mean dating – I mean, you know, physical—"

"*Why not?*"

"Because. . ." I can feel my face blushing, "well, sex before marriage is uh-uh."

"You can't have sex before you get hitched?"

"Yeah."

He coughs. "Who said we were going to have sex, anyway?"

My face is now unbelievably cooked with embarrassment and I fidget uncomfortably in my seat. "I didn't mean it that way. . . Oh my God this is so embarrassing."

"For you or me?"

"I did hear a rumour, though."

"You can't be serious."

"I heard . . . you know, that you wanted to. . ."

"What? Do it with you? Shit, Amal, how bloody naïve are you?!" He runs his fingers through his hair and shakes his head. "If I was going to sleep with you, don't you think you'd have something to say about it? If people are talking about it, what the hell has that got to do with you *and me*? Do you think I'm the type to go around and talk about you?"

"I . . . somebody just told me they'd heard you were going to try to get me in the sack. Look, I know you wouldn't have talked about me, OK? But do you know how cheap it made me feel to hear somebody say that about me?"

"Look, Amal, just because I want to kiss you doesn't mean I'm running an Durex account at the local chemist."

"I should hope not," I say lightly, making an effort to smile at him. But he's silent and stares awkwardly at me. After a few moments he speaks up.

"So you don't date then?"

"Er . . . no."

"I don't get it . . . that means you can never live for the moment. You'll always be repressing yourself."

I shake my head. "I don't see it like that."

"Oh come on. Your parents aren't around to hear you. You can tell the truth."

"It is the truth. It's got nothing to do with them. It's what I believe in."

"So if you meet a guy and you like him and he likes you . . . what happens? You just ignore your feelings?"

"No. But I'm not . . . look, I don't believe in the 'playing the field' and 'try before you buy' philosophies, OK? I don't want physical intimacy with a list of people in my life. I want it with one person. And I want to know it's the same with him too. That's my faith. It's not about guys slutting around and virgin girls waiting patiently at home for a guy to come along. It's . . . look, in my religion we both have to be . . . pure . . . untouched . . . you know? Agh! It's so hard to explain. . . Oh hey! Jessica Simpson kept her virginity before she got married! There you go!"

"Well you *are* repressing yourself." I can tell he's losing his temper and I suppose it's because of the rejection and the confusion but the atmosphere is getting more intense and uncomfortable.

"I'm not repressed. I don't feel left out. I can still care and share with a guy without having to get physical with him."

"How will you know how to find this chick obsession with '*the one*' when you've never even been with a guy? Never even kissed a guy?"

"There's no formula to love! If I got with ten guys, each time will be different and each time I'll be thinking this is a risk. And when I finally meet someone I'm still going to be facing the biggest risk of my life but ten other experiences aren't going to tell me if this guy is the right one. Each person is . . . too unique to be judged by ten others."

"That's crap. You need experience. How will you know if he's the right one if you don't know who the wrong one is?"

"So I have to fall to know how to walk?"

"Yes."

"Well, I don't think so."

He hops off the table, pacing angrily up and down. "So what you're saying then is that we're all sluts and sleazes and you're above that?"

"*What?* No! I didn't say that! Why would you think that? My own cousin has been with her guy for two years now. I love them to death, I'd never think badly about them. What do you think I am? Some bitch who walks around looking down at everybody just because I believe in something different?"

He doesn't say anything, only shrugs his shoulders and grunts.

"Why is it that when I believe in something different, I'm the one apparently judging you? What about you judging me? Why is it so bloody offensive that there are people out there who don't do the whole sex thing before they get married? Or who don't do the whole physical thing? Who gives a shit? Isn't it my business? Or is that just too weird to accept? I'm obviously a bitchy love-me-do because I'm different. Yeah, great logic there, Adam."

We look at each other and then the anger in his face suddenly drops away. And something worse replaces it. Aloofness.

"Hey, whatever you believe in is up to you." His tone is so dry it feels like he's put it in one of those machines Mum uses to dry fruit. Like an apricot whose juices have been sucked out, leaving a shrivelled, dehydrated lump. "I thought we had something more than *friendship*. But I guess we are different. *Too different*." He lets out a bitter laugh.

"You don't understand me after all," I whisper.

He looks at me with hollow eyes and casually shrugs his shoulders. "I think you're right. You don't understand me and I don't understand you. We're even."

I feel like I'm about to suffocate on the tension and I run out of the courtyard and through the house. Tia bumps into me on my way out and stands in front of me, bursting into laughter as she looks me up and down.

"What are *you* doing here?" she asks, her voice an intoxicated mix of smugness and haughty amusement. "Isn't this, like, sinful for you? Won't you burn in hell? Rebelling tonight, are we? And all for *Adam's* sake."

Rage hammers through my head and I am momentarily too overwhelmed with emotions to move or say anything. She takes a sip of her drink and leans towards me conspiratorially.

"Piece of friendly advice: you should take that thing off before you do the dirty with him. It might get in his way."

I push her. She sprawls back on to the floor, her glass smashing next to her.

"You bitch!" she cries. "You could have cut me. How dare you! Why don't you just get out of our country and go back to some desert cave where you belong?"

I stand over her, my heart drumming in my chest. "This is *my* country and if you ever forget it again I'm going to rip your head off!" I turn away and plough through the crowd to find Eileen and Simone.

The thought of seeing Adam on Monday has given me stomach cramps all weekend. I spend all of Saturday and Sunday in bed with my Walkman blasting out mushy love songs which just make me feel sorry for myself.

Should I have seen it coming? Did I lead him on? I remember Eileen warning me but I was having such a good time becoming closer to him that I never considered he would interpret it as an invitation to be anything more than really good friends. OK, really good friends who occasionally flirt. And talk for hours on the phone. And pass notes in class. And share secrets. Oh no. I'm a big fat hypocrite.

Yet a part of me, a teeny weeny part of me, is making a lot

of noise in my head at the moment wondering about what it would have felt like to be kissed by Adam.

It's confusing. Not for one moment do I regret my decision. But even still, I can't stop thinking about his lips and whether they would have been soft and whether it would have been sloppy and squishy or tender and smooth. I wonder do people lose their breath when they kiss? Do they have to come up for air? It looks complicated. Would my nose have bumped into his nose? And how do you know what side to lean on? His head was tilted to the right so I guess I would have had to tilt mine to the left. What would have happened if it tickled and I wanted to sneeze?

I've wondered about these things many times but now, having been so close, I'm wondering even more. Because on one level I really would love to be kissed by Adam and I can imagine it in my head with digital TV precision. I don't know if it's a bad thing to feel this kind of desire for him. I can't help it though. He smelt *so* good. It would have been special.

But I know that what's even more special to me is being true to what I believe in. I want to be with one person in my life. I want to know that the guy I spend the rest of my life with is the first person I share something so intimate and exciting with. OK, I'm only sixteen which means I've got plenty of years to come before that happens. I'm willing to wait though. But it's not a bad wait. It's not the kind of annoying, painful wait you go through in a medical centre or when sitting in an airport lobby waiting for the boarding announcement for your delayed plane.

I suppose it's the fact that I have the personal freedom to go out there and be with someone, to have kissed Adam back but have *chosen* not to, that makes the decision quite simple for me.

I have no idea what to expect at school. Will Adam ignore me? Will we never talk again? Will we hate each other? Will he make fun of me to his mates? Will I become known as the frigid dag?

But then something happens. Something that doesn't come within ten solar planets of what I expect. A group of lunatics rip bombs through a nightclub in Bali on Saturday killing and maiming many Australian tourists.

I go to school not knowing. It's one of those weird chains of events. It's surreal because my parents are major news and documentary addicts. But for some reason this weekend they've both been snowed under with work. They're both out the door on Monday morning before I'm up, so there is no listening to the news over breakfast. I simply wake up, get ready and catch the bus to school. The bus driver doesn't have the radio on, and we don't even make eye contact. I just slip my ticket through the automated machine, take my seat and lean against the window with my Walkman blazing.

When I arrive at school there's an announcement that we're all to file into the auditorium for a senior school assembly. I put my bag in my locker and make my way to the auditorium, wondering whether Eileen and Simone are already there.

I find them in line and hurry up to them. I pass Adam on my way and he looks at me. He holds his head up and ignores me. His coldness slices through me like a knife. I stand next to Simone and Eileen, fighting back tears.

"What's going on?" I ask.

"Didn't you hear?" Eileen whispers in my ear as Ms Walsh walks across the stage and the teachers all start their shushing chants.

"Hear about what?" I whisper back.

"Bali," Simone says.

"Huh?"

They look at me in surprise.

"Terrorists bombed a nightclub in Bali on Saturday. It's horrific."

It's like a sandpit in my throat.

Ms Walsh's voice booms over us: "I know how distressed you'll all be about the weekend bombings in Bali. Please make sure to talk to your teachers and the school counsellor if you need to. I'm sure you'll all have the chance to share your feelings and emotions in class."

It's agonizing. I can't feel only grief. Or horror. Or anger. It's too mixed up. Incongruous, disjointed and completely insane thoughts flash through my mind. Mum and Dad wanting to book for their anniversary. What song was on when the bomb went off? Were there honeymooners? Oh my God, how could honeymooners be killed like that? Did the bombers watch as their inferno turned human life into carcasses? Was I going to be incriminated for their crimes?

244

Was I going to be allowed to share in my country's mourning or would I be blamed? How many Indonesians died? Do people care? Who would look after their children? Did brothers lose sisters? Parents lose children? Children lose their parents? Would a husband or wife or partner be left to watch the death toll on television from Sydney or Darwin, wondering if their other half was alive? It could have been Mum or Dad.

I cry, but it's bizarre because I can't even break down and grieve without wondering about what people are thinking of me. I wince every time Ms Walsh says the word "massacre" with the word "Islamic" as though these barbarians somehow belong to my Muslim community. As though they're the black sheep in the flock, the thorn in our community's side. It gives them this legitimacy, this identity that they don't deserve. These people are aliens to our faith.

After assembly we go to home room. Almost everybody's eyes are red and blotched. A haunting silence fills the classroom. Adam is sitting at his desk, his head in his hands. Mr Pearse goes through the roll in an exhausted voice as we sit limp at our desks.

"Those bloody Islamic terrorists! Has to be them!"

I don't even flinch.

"That's enough!" Mr Pearse says softly, looking anxiously at me. "In these times we have to know how to channel our hurt and anger."

"It's not how to channel it," somebody else calls out, "it's *who* to channel it at."

"I don't want to hear anybody using this as an opportunity for ugly racism or for making other Australians feel less. . ."

My mind blocks out his words. I'm not interested in being defended or protected.

By recess I've had enough. I spend the rest of the day in the sick bay wondering how naïve I was to ever think that I could find my place in my country and be unaffected by the horrors and politics in the world.

I have nowhere else to go and nowhere else I want to go. Once again I don't know where I stand in the country in which I took my first breath of life.

I refuse to go to school the next day. And the day after that.

"Say I've got the chicken pox," I tell my parents, and spend the entire two days in bed.

At first they're cautious, tender, understanding. But then on the second night I overhear them arguing about how to approach me, whether I'll be OK at school.

"Maybe it was a mistake, this hijab," my father sighs.

"Don't be absurd!" my mum shouts. "With or without it she's still an outsider to them. I'm sick of it! I'm sick of the whole thing! She's only sixteen and she has to go through this. What do they want from us?"

"Don't yell. She'll hear you."

"Hear me? She doesn't need *me* to tell her. She lives it every day!" I've never heard my mum so negative, so bitter.

They argue for ages and I want to scream out to them to

shut up. I sink into my mattress and cram the pillow over my head.

After two hard days at school we go to a peace vigil on the weekend. My parents, Uncle Joe's family, Yasmeen and her family, Simone, Eileen and Josh. We stand there in the crowd, holding candles, clutching on to each other, singing prayers and John Lennon songs, swaying together in a gentle, evening breeze that smells of birthday cake candles and tragedy and agonizing incomprehension. It's the first time we don't question each other. The first time we don't all stop and think about our labels and rationalize our participation. Nobody speaks about identity or religion or politics or ideology. We just sway and grieve with the crowd. And something builds up inside me as a priest and a rabbi and a sheikh and a monk stand together on the steps in front of Parliament House and prove to us that our labels mean nothing compared with what we have in common, which is the will and right to live.

I can imagine that there's a lot of hate right now. If it ends up turning people against each other then I'm petrified; I'm sickened to think that we will allow those murderers to end up winning.

30

This is my corny, mushy, soppy moment and boy oh boy am I lapping it up. I'm lying in bed listening to a CD of love ballads which includes Shania Twain's "From This Moment" and yes, I will admit, a couple of Celine Dion songs. It is obvious that I have a serious case of the blues because I'm finding that each line in each song is a perfect description of my life. These songs are suddenly like tarot cards and with each piano and saxophone interlude I'm getting more and more depressed. . .

I miss Adam, and I am going to enjoy this dose of self-pitying misery while I can. I miss talking to him on the phone while we're both watching some cops and lawyers show or a *Big Brother* eviction. I miss his laughing eyes, his curiosity, the vulnerability in his voice when he talks to me about his mum (at least I like to think it's vulnerability, although I suspect there is a hint of detached disinterest). I miss looking out for him in the corridors at school and feeling needed by him when he doesn't understand something in class. I miss the way he shared Simone's carrots and celery without asking her any questions and the way my insides went all mushy and electric when our eyes locked in class. Since the party he hasn't called, he hasn't sent me a text message, he hasn't asked me about school work or met my eyes or sat with us at lunch time or shown the slightest bit of interest in my existence on planet Earth. I hate myself for feeling so disgustingly limp against my emotions because it means I have no control and leave myself as vulnerable as a blindfolded person crossing a freeway on rollerblades.

I'm not dumb. I know I rejected him and that he went off at me because he was trying to save face, and having a go at my beliefs was an easy way to hide the fact that he basically went in for a kiss and I moved away. I mean, in the land of high school, sexual rejection is catastrophic. I just wish Adam would understand that I'm not about to announce to the world that I turned him down. I wish he'd see that it had nothing to do with him. I mean, if I wanted to kiss any guy at school, he'd be number one on my list, no questions asked. If he needs a public relations campaign to help his self-esteem get over it, I'll be first in line to spread the news at school that he's one melt-worthy guy. But instead he's opted for keeping things icy cold with me and it's giving my heart major frostbite.

If that's not bad enough, my mum consoles me by promising me I'm going through a teenage crush, a phase I'll "grow out of". Like I want to hear adult clichés when Adam is flirting with someone else in Biology right in front of my eyes.

Lara approaches me during the week and asks me, in her "I'm such a dynamic school captain" tone of voice, whether I'd be willing to give a speech in our next Forum meeting on the topic of Islam and terrorism.

"It'll be really valuable, Amal. I mean, what those Muslims did in Bali was so horrible, so if you could explain to everybody why they did it and how Islam justifies it, we could all try to understand. What do you think?"

"I think *no*."

"No? Oh, come on, Amal! *Please.* It'll really spice up our next Forum meeting. Everybody's got loads of questions and you're the perfect one to answer them."

"Why? Because I'm Muslim?"

"Yeah, obviously." She gives me a "well, duh" expression. Why do I have to deal with this? I feel like my head is permanently stuck inside an oven. Every time something happens in the world, and the politicians start barking out about Islamic terrorists and the journalists start their flashing headlines, it's as though they're turning up the oven heat dial. My head starts to roast and burn and I need air, coolness, somebody to keep me from exploding.

"You're Christian, right?"

". . .Yeah . . . what's that got to do with anything?"

"OK, well I'll give the speech if you give a speech about the Ku Klux Klan."

"Huh?"

"Yeah, why not? They were really religious, so obviously what they did was textbook Christianity, right? And how about those Israeli soldiers bombing Palestinian homes or shooting kids?"

"Hey, you don't have to—"

"And while we're at it, maybe somebody else could talk about the IRA. Remember we covered a bit of it in Legal Studies last term? I'm just *dying* to understand how the Bible could allow people to throw bombs and still go to church." I can feel a red flush staining my face as I take heavier, angrier breaths. I fold my arms across my chest and stare at Lara's face.

She looks taken aback and coughs self-consciously. "Look, I didn't mean to offend you, OK? I just thought . . . well they're Muslim and stuff and the news is going on about it, so I thought because you're Muslim you could. . ."

I sigh and my anger suddenly evaporates as I sense the sincerity in her voice. "Yeah, but Lara, Muslim is just a label for them. In the end, they're nutcases who exploded bombs and killed people. It's politics. How can any religion preach something so horrific?"

"I guess. . ."

"And if you want me to talk on their behalf and act as

though they're a part of me, what are you telling me you think about *me*?"

"I . . . I . . ."

"Look, just . . . never mind . . . sorry . . . I can't do it."

She shrugs and seems to be struggling to understand. "OK, Amal. . . Hey, again, sorry if I upset you or anything. . . I really didn't mean to." She goes to touch my shoulder and smiles reassuringly at me. I don't know why, but the tenderness and warmth of her smile affects me. It gets right down into my throat, my veins, my capillaries. I smile back at her. In her own way, I feel as though she's turning the oven dial down.

It's Leila's seventeenth birthday on Saturday and Yasmeen and I are organizing a surprise dinner at a restaurant on Chapel Street in Toorak. The only problem is convincing Leila's mum. Yasmeen wants me to make the call. Given Yasmeen is on her Heretics to Convert List, it probably makes sense.

Before I call, Yasmeen's on the phone to me, offering last-minute tips.

"Make sure you emphasize it's a *surprise* party," she warns me. "Otherwise, she'll blame Leila for the idea and go mental at her."

"OK."

"Actually, don't call it a party," she adds. "Say it's a . . . get-together . . . or a gathering."

"This is painful," I groan.

"We have got to do this. For Leila's sake. If she's cooped up at home with her mother on her birthday I reckon there'll be a manslaughter."

"OK, I know, I know. I'll ring now."

When I telephone Leila's house her dad answers.

"Allo?" he says in his thick accent.

"Er . . . hi, Uncle . . . er . . . is Aunty there?"

"Who is it?"

"It's Amal."

"Allo, Amal. How are you?"

"I'm good, thanks. How are you?"

"Good. I get Aunty for you."

After a minute or two she comes to the phone.

"Amal?"

"Hi, Aunty."

"Ahh! Amal! How you are?"

"I'm fine, thanks, Aunty. How are you?"

"Oh, no good. No good, Amal. All I do is clean, clean, clean. And my children? They so messy. Ah! My migraine from these children. They no care about their mum. Leila no help me. Every day in her room, study those books. Every day, books, books, books! Oof. She no help me like I help my mum when I was girl. How she be housewife one day, I no know. I no know. Oof. Make me very angry."

I dig my nails into my palms.

"She reject good man for marriage last month. Can you believe? She think good man come all time? I no understand what these books do to her mind. Ya Allah! If only God show her right path, she stop—"

I interrupt her because if I hear one more word I'm going to vomit my lunch. So I sink my nails deeper into my palms and start to kiss butt.

"Er, Aunty. It's Leila's birthday next Saturday."

"Yes. I know. *Seventeen*. She no get any younger. She getting old and look at her rejecting—"

"The *girls* and I want to organize a *dinner.* A *sit-down* dinner where we *eat* and *talk*. We want to give her presents and buy her dinner so she can sit in a nice place with us and *eat* and *talk*. You'd like that for Leila, wouldn't you?"

I hold my breath, squeezing my eyes closed, desperate for her to agree. This is some major butt-kissing.

"Eh? Where this dinner? Your house?"

I cough and take a deep breath in. "Um, it's at a restaurant. The food is beautiful there. Very nice place. Families and married people go there to eat dinner."

I shudder as I hear myself. I don't think I've ever sounded so thoroughly idiotic.

"Restaurant? You go in day?"

"Er . . . no, it's for dinner."

"Dinner? No, no, NO. Leila no go at night."

"Please, Aunty?" I beg. I've gone straight into third gear The grovelling state. "It's something she'll love. It's a very respectable restaurant and we won't be back late. We promise. She'll be home by ten thirty. Please, Aunty? It's her *birthday.*"

"No. Leila no go out at night. I no want my daughter bring shame on family. Walking streets at night. Like disgrace. You have dinner in house OK. But outside? Impossible. If people saw her! They talk! What shame."

My heart is squashed up in my socks as I agree to change our plans to dinner at my place.

Leila rings me that night.

"We're going to Chapel."

"What? How do you know about it?!"

"Mum spilled it. I can't take this crap any more. I know I'm not doing anything wrong."

"But ... what if ... Leila, what if she finds out? She'll go ballistic!"

"Completely ballistic."

"It's too risky."

"I'm going insane. She's twisting it all around. Driving me crazy. And Dad spends twenty-four/seven at the factory or he's at home on the couch, smoking his Marlboro and watching the Turkish version of *Candid Camera* on satellite. We don't mix with other people. Everybody is a 'bad' influence. I met this woman at the mosque on the weekend. She's a med student. I told her she should come over for a coffee. Mum flipped it. Said it was shameful that a Muslim girl would study medicine and look at male bodies! Can you believe it?

"And my brother, Hakan? He gets to do whatever he likes. He's changed his name to Sam and I'm the one with cultural denial! He got home at four in the morning yesterday and she had food wrapped in foil for him in case he was hungry. Yeah, I'm guessing he would have worked up an appetite considering he'd probably drunk the bar dry. Oh, but mention to her that her son drinks like an alcoholic and she conveniently forgets that's one of the biggest sins. And what about his bimbo girlfriend? He picked her up at some bar and she comes over with half her tits hanging out for the world to see, and my mum lets him get away with it! He doesn't even have enough respect for his family to ask her to put a cardigan on in front of my mum and dad. It's sick. Her idea of telling him off is, *Oh Hakan, find good girl and settle down*. But then she'll laugh when he brags about how his girlfriend's crazy about him. I don't know what that bimbo sees in him. And I know he smokes pot because he comes home high sometimes and my mum thinks he's just had a hard day at work. They all make me sick! I don't understand how I have a genetic connection with them."

"What if she calls my parents?" I ask anxiously.

"I'll tell her to call my mobile because we'll be on the net and using the phone line. I'll tell her we're on an online Turkish match-making chat room trying to find me a potential husband. That'll make her happy."

The next day at school I'm walking through the hallway when I see Adam bouncing a basketball on his way out of the building. He looks at me awkwardly, I look back at him awkwardly and then we both look away awkwardly. Then something really embarrassing happens. He goes to walk to my right, but I think he's going to walk to my left. We do the right/left thing two more times and I'm so mortified I want to melt to the floor quicker than a biscuit dunked in Milo. Then, as he's about to walk out of the door, something comes over me and I yell out for him to wait a minute.

"*What?*" he asks impatiently.

"What is it with you lately?"

"What are you on about?"

"Oh, so it's all in my head, is it? Some *chick* thing, hey?"

"Give me a break, Amal. I don't know what you're on about."

"How about you cut *me* some slack, hey? You've been acting so up yourself lately. I didn't mean to . . . I mean it wasn't about me rejecting you. This is who I am. This is what I believe in. Does that give you the right to ignore me? Why have you been acting like I'm some stranger?"

"I haven't."

"Yes you have."

"Have not."

"Have *so*."

"Amal, do you think I'm going to walk around like a wuss just because you didn't – because of what happened at my party? So I tried to kiss you and you didn't want to because your religion says you can't have a normal relationship with a guy before you find *the one*. That's fine and good luck to you. It's your life. I mean, it was something that just happened in the moment so don't stress, I'm really *very* over it."

258

"Oh. . ."

This is the wrong moment to be speechless. Where is my comeback line? Come on brain.

"Anyway," he says, shuffling his feet impatiently, "the guys are waiting for me out on the court."

"Mmm. . ."

This is just treacherous. My brain has totally betrayed me.

After he leaves I rush to the toilets and lock myself in a cubicle and fight back stupid, pathetic tears. It seems my body is in total traitor mode. My chin realizes I need to stay composed and it does the wobbling thing. My tear ducts know that I can't return to class with red puffy eyes and they insist on going Niagara Falls on me.

As I'm washing my face, Tia and Rita walk in. They see me and their conversation immediately comes to a halt.

"What's wrong?" Rita asks with concern.

Not.

"Yeah." Tia says. "What's up with you?"

I take a deep breath and turn the taps off. "Why don't you both go back to doing what you're good at? Go give somebody an eating disorder, spin some rumours, sacrifice an animal to the devil, but just piss off."

"You know, Amal," Tia says, "you've got the worst temper."

"Yeah, how premenstrual are you?" Rita says.

"Well done," I say. "Another piece of original thought by Rita Mason."

"Maybe we're being insensitive," Tia says. "Did somebody *dump* you, Amal?"

"Yeah," Rita says, giggling, "was *it Adam*?"

"You've all become a little lovey-dovey, haven't you now?" Tia says, smirking. "Adam and you, Josh and Simone. Well, there's something to say for opposites attract. Fat and thin. Hip and daggy. Hey Rita, maybe I should wear a tablecloth on my head and live on Snickers bars and I'll get a man too!"

Rita bursts out laughing and I flash them a knowing smile.

"It must burn you, hey Tia? I mean, there you are chucking up your bottled water, applying your fake tan, conditioning your hair and throwing yourself at Josh and he picks *Simone*."

She crosses her arms and looks at me with narrow, angry eyes. "Let's get one thing straight, I've never been after Josh. If I wanted him, I would have had him."

"You must be joking, right? Tia, you are beyond a cliché. I mean, does it come naturally to you or do you stay up late at night and practise this whole Hollywood-soapie-drama-queen-bitch act?"

Before giving her a chance to respond I walk out. If there's ever been a time when home education sounded appealing, this is it.

32

It's a warm October night and Mrs Vaselli and I are seated outside on her front porch drinking hot chocolate. She's wearing the shawl. It took her a while to appear in front of me with it on. I kept seeing a tassel or two protruding from the hall cupboard every time I visited. One evening I walked up to the cupboard, took the shawl out and put it around her shoulders.

"Should have been black," she said gruffly, trying to salvage some pride.

"Should have been any colour but blue?" I joked knowingly, and she looked at me for a moment and then let out a short, hard laugh.

"Yes, any colour but blue," she said, hugging it closer around her.

"Don't you ever feel like calling him?" I ask her tonight.

"Sometime," she says curtly.

"Won't Jesus be upset with you for lying, Mrs Vaselli?" I wag my finger at her.

"Don't joke to me wis Jesus," she says sternly.

"Don't lie to me about your son."

She sighs and leans back into her chair, playing with the tassels on her shawl.

"He no call me."

"But he must have at first. What happened?"

"I tell him I no want him call me." We look at each other gingerly. She's unsure how much to give out. I'm unsure how much of a right I have to interfere.

"But . . . that's obviously why he doesn't call."

"Huh!" She's not impressed.

"Mrs Vaselli, I know it must hurt you. That he rejected your religion—"

"His religion."

"OK, *his* religion. But everybody . . . you can't cut off from him like this!"

"I know he no have salvation now. How I be happy? How I see him and knowing he going hell? All because zat woman he marry!"

"But . . . but . . . nobody knows where they'll end up. Nobody can play God with other people's destiny."

"I know he choosing wrong religion."

"Yeah but then everybody would be cut off from everybody else if we sorted people out into hell and heaven."

"Huh! You no understanding. When you have child, maybe you understanding. He become other religion and you sit easy?"

I scrunch my face up in thought. "I don't know . . . but don't you miss him? I don't get it. Are you telling me that if your son were to walk up to your front door now you'd slam it in his face?"

"You tinking life like movie. You people born here, you no understanding what life is. You having life easy. You no going through what we went through. You changing your religion and your mama and papa culture like changing clothe. My son he no showing his papa and mama respect . . . you, you tinking, I know, I bad woman. Reject my son and no talk to him. But I am a mama. Yes?"

I nod.

"You asking if my son come door I close in his face?"

"Yeah."

"I am a mama. I . . . I will . . . listen to me. He will never coming door first place! I angry at him and I saying tings and he saying tings. I blaming him for his papa dead. His papa die from heart attack and I blaming my son. And somewhere inside me I still blaming him. And I angry and so sad and pray for him to return to Jesus. But too late. I no call him. After all I do for him he reject. And he no call me . . . he no call me any more . . . so . . . no fixing ze problem, Amal." She looks at me pensively and sighs.

"Look, I know you built your life here from scratch,

without English or your mum and dad or your friends. So I kind of get that maybe loyalty means the world to you. Especially seeing as you only had one son."

"Yes! You understanding now!"

"And you worked really hard and you heard about your parents' death through the mail and you never knew what it felt like to have an extended family around you."

"Yes, exact. My life very, very hard."

"And your husband he worked so hard for you and your son, to build a new life for you here."

"Jesus bless him."

"Well then, what I don't understand is why you're punishing yourself with loneliness when your reward in old age should be your son and his family! I don't get it. Why can't you just call?"

"No!" she cries, throwing her face in her hands and shaking her head. "Why he no call his mama?"

"How will you know unless you call? Maybe he thinks you're going to hang the phone up on him."

"Always stupid answer! Why I listen to you? You a child. You no understanding."

"I think I do understand, Mrs Vaselli... I understand that you left your homeland without even knowing what you were coming to and that you lost your babies without a mum's shoulder to cry on. I understand that you're really religious and your son broke your heart when he converted. I come from a religious family. I can only imagine how my parents would react if I did the same thing."

She looks up at me in surprise.

"But you're alone now... Some people live in agony wishing they had just one minute more with someone they love who's left them. It's in your hands ... you have an only son out there and you can spend the rest of your life reunited with him."

She looks at me intensely and I expect her to slap me or tell me to shut up. But then her body just kind of shrivels. Her frame collapses into a heap and her eyes well up with tears. "I no knowing what to do..." she murmurs, staring at the concrete. "I just no knowing what to do..."

It's so dark out in the garden. All we have on is a single porch light, capturing us in a whirl of shadows and pools of artificial light or evening darkness. The cicadas are partying hard all around us, breaking the silence of our street

I approach her cautiously. I reach out to touch her but shrink back, scared, of what, I don't know. Am I scared her pain will somehow transfer from her skin to mine? I reach out again, and place one hand on her shoulder, sitting on the armrest of my seat. She doesn't stir, just sits shrunken, deflated of energy and rage. She doesn't say anything so I talk.

"My mum's had three miscarriages. I don't even know if I would have had a brother or a sister." She stirs slightly but doesn't speak.

"She told me some people said some really dumb things when they came over and tried to make her feel better. They'd tell her God was saving her from a bad child. How awful is that? Or they would tell her that she never got to know her child so it shouldn't hurt her so much, she'd get over it. How idiotic can people get? Because I know for a fact that it aches inside my mum until today... Maybe you're really upset because you think your son is lost to you. But isn't that, like... Look, don't make him a miscarriage, Mrs Vaselli. Not over religion. Nothing's worth that." We sit in silence. And then I let out a startled laugh.

"I don't know why I'm telling you all this, Mrs Vaselli. Why should I care? I've never even met your son. 'Cause when I think about it, actually, I reckon you're the grumpiest grouch of a neighbour I've ever had." She looks up at me and I almost detect a twitch of a smile.

"You cheeky girl," she says slowly.

"Look, if you don't call him, I think I will, 'cause you are so stubborn! You put my dad to shame! There's this Arabic saying my mum always tells my dad when he's really stubborn. She says his mind is like a shoe."

"A shoe?"

"Yep," I shrug. "Lost in translation, I guess."

She bursts into laughter. She doesn't stop, her chest heaves up and down and she leans over, wiping her eyes and shaking as her lungs gasp for air. I see her and I crack up, and we're sitting on the porch, an old woman with her tasselled shawl, me with my hijab, and we're finding out that we're connected enough to affect each other. And it makes us laugh harder to realize we'd ever doubted it.

33

Survival through high school is all about appendages, specifically, the hand (left or right is irrelevant). Let me explain: whether you overcome ridicule, acne, cellulite, rejection, unrequited lust, bitchiness and the rest of what can make high school awesome fun (*not*) is entirely dependent upon who maintains the upper hand. For example, Tia and I, in our long-standing efforts to destroy each other, are really involved in a struggle to establish who has the upper hand. Some days her comeback lines are infinitely more eloquent than mine and we both know that she's come out on top. Other days I, to put it bluntly, kick arse.

This is what I am thinking as I watch Mr Piper flap his arms about and pace the classroom in his excitement over the Somme offensive in World War I. I really don't understand how teachers manage to conduct themselves in such a deluded state of mind. How can he possibly believe, with any degree of sincerity, that we're interested? Doesn't he realize that he has managed to put Tim, Rachel and Carlos to sleep in the back row? And over to my right we have Tia, Rita and Claire hiding magazines in their textbooks and pretending to be absorbed in Chapter Six.

Well hello, hello. Adam, who is sitting at the desk next to me and has barely made eye contact with me since class started, has suddenly caught my eye and, check this out, rolled his eyes. Not rolled-his-eyes-*at-me* scenario. But rolled-his-eyes-at-teacher-in-united-solidarity-with-fellow-student scenario. I wonder if this is an opportunity for me to gain the upper hand again. Because until now he has undoubtedly had exclusive possession of it. At first, I did, when I rejected him. But after the rejection-due-to-principles-not-aversion-to-Adam incident, Adam's two-week sulk/macho act enabled him to regain the upper hand. I think I might attempt to normalize things again. So I slip Adam the following note, squashed in the lid of my liquid paper pen to avoid Mr Piper's watchful eyes: *Do you think he wears that toupee to bed? Incidentally, what's with the verbal constipation?*

The rest of our literary conversation goes like this:

Adam: *No, he would take it off. Probably put it down for the night in a kennel. PS: Ran out of Mylanta.*

Me: *There's always prune juice.*

Adam: *It would interfere with my consumption of sardine and banana sandwiches.*

Me: *Yummo. . .*

Adam: *I've just noticed that your handwriting is pretty ugly for a girl.*

Me: *Thanks!* ☺ *So, kissed anyone lately? Ha ha* ☺☺

Adam: *Heaven forbid! It's SINFUL! PS: I hate it when people (especially girls) draw stupid smiley faces. There are plenty of words in the thesaurus which express joy. Expand your vocab and stop with the bad art.*

Me:☺☺☺☺

Adam: *Mature.*

Me: *Do you think he realizes that the colour of his toupee doesn't match the colour of the hair fuzz on his ear?*

There are two things I'd like to say about our scholarly exchange. First: that I think things are back to normal between us. Second: that I just got busted by Mr Piper.

"Amal Abdel-Hakim!"

His pronunciation of my surname is commendable.

"Er . . . yes, Mr Piper?"

"Hand me that note at once! I will not tolerate students slacking around in my classroom!"

As any wise student knows, if a teacher intercepts a note-exchanging exercise, you should scrunch the paper up in the hope of smudging the pen and making the words illegible. I scrunch like mad.

It doesn't work. I think the pen is one of those brands that dry upon impact with the paper. Stupid efficient stationery. I hand Mr Piper the note and, in accordance with the first lesson in the Diploma of Education which states that teachers must always revel in humiliating and exposing students, he reads it out loud. Adam is blushing like an overheated solar-power system and gives me a sympathetic look. The rest of the class is sniggering. Simone and Eileen flash me supportive smiles. Mr Piper sighs and rolls his eyes at me.

"Your perception is riveting, Amal," he says in a bored and sarcastic tone, dropping the note down on my desk. "It's comforting to know that there are people in my class who have the maturity and intelligence to make derogatory comments about other people's *external* appearances."

Now what the hell am I supposed to say to that?

"What do you have to say for yourself?"

Bloody mind-reader.

"I'm really sorry, Mr Piper."

"Why?"

"Because it was wrong of me to make fun of you."

"Why?"

"Because it's, er, insensitive and hypocritical of me."

"Why?"

"Because I wouldn't want people to make fun of me either."

"So your remorse is basically based on the fact that you can identify with me? Mere empathy has prompted you to apologize?"

This is one of those trick questions. I'm sure it is.

"Um. . ."

"That's what I thought. Don't let me catch you again or you'll be slapped with a detention."

"Yes, sir."

Tia arrives at school the next morning with a bandage on her arm. Two point five seconds in home room and the whole class is forced to listen to her morbid tale.

"I was assaulted," she sniffs, wiping her nose with a tissue for dramatic effect.

"How?"

"No way!"

"You poor thing, what happened?"

"Well," she says, sitting on her desk and crossing her legs modestly. Not. She's wearing black undies.

"I was at Heat nightclub—"

"But you're not eighteen yet!" Kristy pipes up. Maybe there was a cushion on the floor beside the cradle after all.

"I have my ways," she explains in a smug, coy tone. "I was with my sister and her uni friends."

"Ohh!" Some of the girls and guys are thoroughly impressed.

"So I'm on the podium, dancing with my friends, when this group of *Asians* comes along to dance next to us."

Eileen starts scribbling furiously in her book, channelling all her anger into her pencil, until the lead snaps.

"We knew they were trouble as soon as we saw them. They just had that look, you know."

"What look?" Rita asks.

"*That* look," Tia snaps. "One of them had the nerve to jump up with us on to the podium and started to try to dance real close and dirty with us. We told him to get lost. It was so gross."

"No!" Claire gasps.

"How dare he!" Rita shrieks.

"This is while you're on the podium?" Adam asks sceptically.

"Yes," she snaps. "Harassment can occur anywhere."

"Hmm."

She glares at him and turns to her audience, which has grown from Claire and Rita to some other girls and guys who have a love–hate relationship with her (hate her for her looks and bitchiness but would swoon if she said one nice word to them or gave them the slightest bit of attention).

"There he was with his filthy hands on me and so I slapped him away and then I fell off the podium and hurt my elbow!"

"Oh no!"

"You should sue!"

"Sure it wasn't your heels you tripped over?" Josh mutters to Adam. Tia ignores them.

"Honestly, nightclubs are just infested with trouble-making *gangs* now. I avoid going out to them any more because of the kinds of people who go. It's like an invasion of—" She darts a look at Eileen but doesn't continue, knowing her message has been delivered.

"My dad's right, you know," she continues smugly. "He

predicts Anglo-Australians will be extinct in this country, soon!"

She glances sidelong at us and I demonstrate to the class how quickly the skin can turn from white to volcanic red. I'm about to say something. Eileen is about to say something. Simone and Adam both show signs of saying something. But we don't have to because Josh speaks up instead.

"Well with the number of people you sleep with you should be capable of fixing that dilemma and populating an entire town."

Totally crude. Totally offensive. Totally vulgar.

We can't stop grinning.

34

We're invited to a family friend's wedding on Friday night. My parents know the bride's parents from way back when I was still in nappies. We haven't really kept in contact, but my parents met them at a mutual friend's house several months ago and got an invitation soon after.

There are about four hundred and fifty guests, and it's being held at an enormous reception hall overlooking a lake that looks like a flow of sparkling lemonade. There are four singers performing throughout the night and a ten-piece band. There are ten people in the bridal party.

Apparently it's a small wedding. That's according to some of the guests who love weddings because it gives them a chance to hog all the food while scanning the hall filled with their family and friends in their mission to detect any backstabbing ammunition. We call them the Wedding Gossipers. They're notorious for going on wedding crawls, attending one wedding after another, sucking up (or creating) fresh rumours, then regurgitating them.

Tonight's wedding should make them salivate. The bride is Syrian and the groom is Afghani. Of course, the big mouths are lapping it up, having a field day with their hushed "You didn't hear it from me, but. . ."

The bride, Amina, met Hosnu when he was in the last year of his temporary protection visa. She's a migration agent and they met at the asylum seeker centre she works at. It's all pretty simple from there. They fell in love and got engaged. So the Scandal Scavengers are dribbling with glee: *He's too handsome for her, proving he only married her for the visa; she's turning thirty and was well and truly on the descent down the hill; the bride's family paid for most of the wedding. How shameful, when it's the man's responsibility! But I suppose it's because her parents were just so happy she finally found somebody.*

It all feels a little Bridget Jones, only Amina isn't the type to sit around in her pyjamas singing songs about loneliness over a bucket of butter popcorn and slab of chocolate.

Uncle Abdel-Tariq and Aunt Cassandra also know the bride's family and we're all seated at the same table. Yasmeen and Omar are here too. After listening to Aunt Cassandra and my mum tell us their wedding-day stories for

275

the billionth time, the MC finally announces that the bride and groom are waiting outside the doors of the reception and asks us all to stand. Then the drums and flute start to go wild and the singer begins in an enthralling, intoxicating voice, which makes my heart bounce around inside me with excitement and anticipation. My mum and Aunt Cassandra are beaming, and my dad and Uncle Abdel-Tariq are sticking tissue into their ears, grinning sheepishly. Tissue plugs are an age-old tradition for them whenever they face over-enthusiastic amplifiers at weddings. My mum and Aunt Cassandra are mortified.

A group of people, mainly extended family members and close friends, stand around the entrance, clapping in rhythm with the music as they wait for the doors to open. The drums beat passionately and I can feel them − thumping inside my skin. Then suddenly the doors open and we all gasp as the bride and groom enter, their faces glowing like two lighthouses.

They move slowly down the red carpet as the band plays around them and the singer performs. People start to dance a Syrian form of the *dabke*, where you hold hands and move in a circle, stepping and kicking and twisting your feet in complicated but graceful ways. Every time I go to a non-Palestinian wedding and my mum pushes me on to the dance floor and tells me to stop being so shy, I end up looking like the daggy, confused girl. At Palestinian weddings I'm a pro. It's just that everybody has their own adaptation. The Lebanese have a version, the Syrians, the Turkish. Even within each nationality there are versions of each version so I always perform a standard one step, one kick, which usually gives me a bare minimum pass (it also works at Greek and Jewish weddings).

I'm clapping to the music and my hands are red and sore but I'm having too much fun to care. I catch Amina's eyes and smile widely at her, mouthing out "*Mabruk*", congratulations. Hosnu is grinning like a man who has been given a new chance at life. My mum and Aunt Cassandra go all teary, even though they've probably spoken five words to Amina in their entire lives and have never met Hosnu. My dad sees my mum's eyes and playfully offers her the tissue in his ear.

When the bride and groom finally make it through the crowd and take their seats on the stage, the music continues for another forty minutes. Mum's going all aggro on Yasmeen and me, wanting us to get up and dance. We stand up and rush to the middle of the dance floor, wedged in among the crowd of bodies so nobody sees us. It's too embarrassing with all the parents watching.

I love Arabic music and as soon as I'm on the dance floor a wave of energy takes over my body. Yasmeen and I start belly dancing, laughing and singing aloud to the familiar pop Arabic song as we shake our hips and torso in different patterns. After half an hour of belly dancing we link hands in the *dabke* line. On my right is an old man who is surprisingly more energetic than me and whose hand is seriously grossing me out with its sweatiness. He grins at me and I wonder where his dentures are. His eyes are aqua-blue and he keeps leaning over to me and shouting out "*Mashallah*" – God be praised – in an admiring voice, confirming to me that he is senile. He praises me on my green eyes, as though they are a product of my handiwork, and shouts over the music to ask me if I'm single. I pretend that I can't hear him. Except, for someone so old, he doesn't look fooled for a second and yells out whether I know his grandson, Ramy Salah, who is "well known" and "very popular" because he owns a mobile phone shop on Bourke Street and drives a Lexus. I squeeze Yasmeen's hand tighter. But she is too busy being interrogated by a tall, broad woman with cherry-red hair, gold bracelets on both arms up to her elbows, and a massive gold cross plunging down her cleavage. Mr Energizer on my right is now asking whether I have a mobile telephone and I tug Yasmeen out of the line. We rush off to the bathroom and explode into a fit of laughter. We gloss our lips, curl our eyelashes, style Yasmeen's hair, fix my hijab and make sure there's no toilet paper stuck to our heels.

"So that old man doing the *dabke*," Yasmeen says when we're back at our table and digging into our entrée. "First set-up attempt?"

"One down," I groan.

"This is my second. The first was in the foyer, when we first arrived. She wanted to know if I was a Muslim, what my TER score was, and did I attend university or technical college. This one now asked me if I was Christian and knew how to cook and speak Arabic. I told her I was a Muslim who could use a microwave and speak a little Urdu, and would that do?"

"No way!"

"She totally freaked out. Luckily you dragged me away in time. She looked like she was getting ready to slam her heels into my toes!"

We spend the rest of the evening perched on a back table, away from the crowd, checking out the selection of guys. We end the night convinced that our short-listed selection are all probably either attached or mummy's boys. Anybody with white socks and black shoes is immediately disqualified.

Nobody is free from prejudice I guess.

35

The story to my parents is this: Leila's mum is OK with Chapel Street but her dad is having a hernia, so under no circumstances should they answer the phone in case he rings for an interrogation seminar. If he needs Leila, there's always the mobile. My dad considers this equivalent to an "accomplice after the fact" (he watched *Law and Order* last night), as he would be betraying the trust of Leila's father. I argue that it is Leila's mum's business what she hides and doesn't hide from her husband, and who are we to interfere in their marital relationship?

Yasmeen and I are pulling a shifty very badly but we've got no choice. It's either that or Turkish matchmaking chat room.

I've been in front of the mirror for three hours. No

kidding. My entire wardrobe is on my bed and floor. I've decided that I hate all my clothes. Everything. I am a girl with nothing to wear. To make matters worse, I put on liquid eyeliner and it smudges. That's when I go berserk. I mean, I'm wearing a hijab, so if my face doesn't look good, what hope have I got? A good manicure? I attack my eyelids with cotton buds but that only makes it worse. My eyes are black and puffy now. Great. I feel well and truly hideous and all I want is to sit on the couch with a packet of Tim Tams and watch back-to-back episodes of *Survivor*.

I feel a teeny weeny bit better after I throw my clothes at the wall, have a bit of a cry and scream at my mum to leave me alone and not to dare enter my room. I eventually scrub my face and start all over again.

It takes me ages to finally look semi-decent. I've highlighted my eyes with eyeliner and mascara, applying some lipgloss and a touch of blush. Yasmeen will be proud. I decide on a baby-pink chiffon hijab with a white cotton headband underneath. I've draped the hijab loosely around my head so that the headband shows, flicking the tail ends over my shoulders and clasping them together with a brooch I bought from a funky jewellery shop on Bridge Road. I go for a long, straight black skirt, a soft-pink fitted cashmere top and pink heels. It's clearly all very centrefold. I still feel ugh, but if "I feel like a supermodel" is ten and "Even my mum would think I'm ugly" is one, then I'm hovering on five. There is no way I'd enter Chapel Street on a Saturday night on a score of one to four.

My mum takes photos of me before the girls arrive. She's gushing that I look like a Barbie doll, with obvious reference to Toy World in Saudi Arabia, not Australia.

Leila's brother, "Sam", drops her off at our house and my mum answers the door. Thank God he's got the manners of a goat because he doesn't bother to say hello, just speeds off in his red 180SX. From the front door I can see the dice hanging down from the rear-view mirror and the "No Fear" sticker covering his back window. His arm is dangling out of the car window, his techno music doof doof doofing, on the assumption that the next few streets are dying to share in his bad taste.

Leila looks stunning. She has massive, doe-shaped brown eyes with a jungle of thick brown eyelashes. She's outlined her eyes with eyeliner and they're so bright and dazzling we should be able to use them as headlights. She's wearing a black silk veil, with a red headband underneath. She's got on a wrap-around red dress, which she's put on over black fitted trousers and red heels. My mum takes one look at her and finishes half a roll of film.

When Yasmeen arrives she starts yelping and squealing, hugging and kissing us, overjoyed that we've opened our make-up bags. Her hair is straightened and kicked out at the back and she's wearing a three-quarter-length black dress.

"You two look gorgeous!" She puts her night bag in the hallway. She's staying over tonight but her bag could probably supply her for a week.

My mum drives us to Chapel Street. We want her to drop

us off at a side street because we don't want to look like utter morons – but she goes all "you're ashamed of your own mum" on me and so I let her take six solid minutes to parallel-park in front of a packed-out fruit juice shop directly outside the Jam Factory complex.

We make quite an entrance in the restaurant. It is beyond embarrassing.

We sit down at a booth and it's one of the best nights the three of us have spent together. Leila is relaxed and uninhibited, cracking jokes and talking about anything and everything but never once mentioning her family. They are irrelevant tonight. As we're eating our chicken and mushroom pastas Yasmeen announces that it's present time and Leila starts to blush.

"You guys didn't have to—"

"*Leila!*" Yasmeen moans. "Don't go all shy and modest and *I don't need presents* on us. It's your birthday! Use and abuse!"

Leila grins. "OK, fine. What did you get me?" she asks.

When Leila has opened the wrapped jewellery box, her eyeballs start to pop in and out like a reversible slinky.

"It's stunning," she whispers, holding up a white-gold chain and oval locket.

"Read the inscription," I tell her. "Sorry about the font size, we had to fit it in."

Leila opens the locket up and reads it aloud: *For your strength & faith, you inspire. Y & A.*

We have a bit of a Kodak moment and hug each other.

283

After an hour the cheesecake arrives and while we're stuffing our mouths, arguing about how many minutes you need on the treadmill for every bite, Leila lets out a startled cry and drops her spoon on the table.

Hakan is standing at the front door, next to a girl wearing a mini denim skirt, black knee-high boots and a top as thin as tissue. It's funny how your brain thinks of the dumbest things at the wrong time. My first reaction isn't where they'll be burying Leila. Instead, I'm actually wondering whether that girl realizes she makes Jessica Simpson look like a brain surgeon, walking around like that when it's fourteen degrees outside. Then the reality of the situation hits me so hard I have to spit my mouthful of cake into a napkin.

"Oh Allah," Yasmeen whispers. Both of us grab one of Leila's hands and don't let go. Hakan storms through the restaurant and up to our table, his girlfriend struggling in her heels to keep up with him.

"What the hell do you think you're doing here?" he asks coldly, his furious gaze fixed on Leila.

"I'm having a birthday dinner, Hakan," she says slowly and calmly. "It's no big deal."

"*Hakan?*" the tissue-top girl pipes up. "Who's *Hakan*? Isn't your name Sam?" He flashes a silencing look at her and she gives him a timid half-smile, stepping backwards and playing with her nails.

"Do Mum and Dad know about this?"

"No, they don't," I say, before Leila gets a chance to respond. "They think she's at my house, because that's what

284

we told Leila. That we were having dinner there. But we lied. It was a surprise and when she arrived at my house, we brought her here. It's not her fault."

"Yeah," Yasmeen adds. "She had no idea."

"*Shut up*," Leila hisses but I squeeze her hand tighter.

"So you two can go around like sluts and drag my sister along with you?"

"Don't you dare call us sluts!" Yasmeen cries.

He ignores Yasmeen, his eyes focused on Leila. "Get your things, you're going home."

"I . . . I. . ." Her face has collapsed into a confused, defeated heap of terror and weariness. She gathers her present and places it in her bag.

"No!" I shout. "We'll take her home. OK? I'll get my mum to pick us up and we'll drop her off."

"She's not going anywhere with you tarts." I want to hit him. I want to yell and shout at him, but for Leila's sake I don't. I ignore him and the veins in my head are popping against my skull from the pressure of keeping my rage at bay.

Suddenly the manager of the restaurant is before us, asking us to pay the bill and leave. Yasmeen and I put money on the table and we all gather our things and walk out, Hakan beside us like a security guard escorting a disgraced patron out of a store. Nearby tables are looking at us and smirking, as though we've proved they were right to think we were troublemaking wogs after all. Our faces burn red as we stand outside, the smell of smoke and aftershave and pizza and alcohol overwhelming us in our dizziness, the icy wind cutting into our faces.

"Please," I plead with him. "Let us take her home. Go out with your girlfriend and we'll explain everything to your parents."

Yasmeen and Leila are standing side by side, their arms linked, teeth chattering, a look of desperate panic on their faces.

Hakan's girlfriend is clutching his arm, shivering in the cold. So she does realize it's freezing, I think, in one of those tangent thoughts.

"Come on, Sam," she coos into his ear, pressing her cleavage up against his chest and caressing his arm with her nails. "Let's leave them. We're meeting the gang at Heat, remember? Kylie and Dave are probably wondering where we are."

His face relaxes for almost a split second and I plunge in.

"I promise my mum will drop Leila off. Look, I'll call her now, in front of you. You go out and have your fun. I'm sorry if we did this behind your family's back, but honestly Leila had no idea. We forced her along. She had no choice."

Retch. Vomit. Oh God, let him say yes, *please*.

"Some Muslim you are," he leers, looking at me up and down.

He wins. I betray Leila and let loose. I can't hold it any more. I feel almost faint from keeping my fury inside and I swear and shout at him for being a hypocritical sexist filthy scumbag. For going ballistic at Leila over an innocent dinner when he's the one going around with a tart, drinking himself blind and smoking dope. For daring to disrespect us and judge us. I can't stop. I see Leila's face crumple into shock and Yasmeen is motioning for me to shut up, but I betray my best friend and lose control.

He takes a step towards me and stares me in the eye. "You bitch," he spits out in a low tone. "You'll never see Leila again."

He seizes Leila's arm and storms away, his girlfriend teetering behind him. Leila looks back over her shoulder and our eyes connect for a moment, but he just walks faster and we stand there, watching them disappear into the crowd.

My mum doesn't say anything on the way home. Yasmeen and I are curled up to one another in the back seat. Yasmeen doesn't stop crying but I'm numb. I can't cry. I can't talk. I can't whisper. It's like I'm under anaesthetic.

When we arrive home my dad is waiting for us in the lounge room. Yasmeen and I collapse on to the couch and my mum sits down next to him at the table.

"What were you thinking?" my dad shouts, running his hands through his hair in frustration. "You know what Leila's parents are like. You lied to us! You lied to them! How could you?"

"It was worth it," I say. "For those first two hours it was worth it."

"Worth it? God knows how much trouble that poor girl is going to be in now. You lied to us, Amal! How could you deceive us like this? And how could you not think about the consequences of your actions? I've always had faith in your good sense and judgement, Amal, but you have really disappointed me tonight!"

My chin is trembling and I'm blinking back tears.

"Amal," my mum says, her voice strangely calm and soothing, "there is never an excuse for lying."

"*Please*," I plead, "you have to call her parents and tell them Yasmeen and I set it all up. They can't think she had anything to do with it. *Please*."

My dad sighs, putting his head in his hands and staring down at the table.

"You're grounded," my mum says, standing up and getting the cordless phone. She walks into the kitchen with it and I hear her speaking to Leila's mum. And then I start sobbing and Yasmeen is holding me and sobbing too.

After half an hour my mum comes out of the kitchen, looking thoroughly exhausted.

"Leila is OK," she says. "I spoke to Gulchin and tried to calm her down. She kept raving on about this nearly ruining everything for her daughter, or something dramatic like that. She didn't make much sense. But I made it clear to her that this was not Leila's idea."

The look in her eye tells me that she knows there's more to the story but she doesn't say anything, and I want to fold into her arms and fall asleep against her chest. But she tells us to go upstairs to bed.

36

I don't dare to telephone Leila's house on Sunday. Yasmeen and I send her a text message but she doesn't reply. We log on to MSN Messenger but she's not online.

"I'll get her to call you when I see her at school on Monday," Yasmeen promises. But on Monday Yasmeen sends me an SMS telling me Leila's absent.

During lunch time I'm sitting with Simone, absorbed with my mobile, sending Yasmeen messages.

"You OK?" Simone asks in a concerned voice.

"Yeah, fine," I answer abruptly. I don't want to tell her what's happened because I'm scared. I know it sounds dumb but I'm worried that she'll think, *Oh typical Muslim nutters. Locking their girls up in the house.* I can't deal with that now.

I can't seem to deal with anything. I just want to know Leila's OK.

Simone doesn't say anything, and I'm grateful to her for that. All I can see in my head are scenes of Leila being yelled at, grounded, taken out of school. I'm so distracted that I don't notice that Eileen has joined us. I look up and she's sitting cross-legged beside me. Both her and Simone are staring at me, expressions of concern on their faces.

"You OK, Amal?" Eileen asks softly.

"Not really. . . I. . . Boy do I so not feel like being at school today."

"When do we ever?" Simone rolls her eyes. We sit in silence for a few moments. Then something comes over me.

"Let's just get out of here!" I cry, pulling them up with me.

"*What?*" Simone asks.

"Let's wag. Go to the beach. Or catch a train to the Dandenongs. Or go go-cart racing. Rollerblading. Let's just get out. I feel like I'm going to suffocate in this place." I can't believe I'm suggesting this. If Ms Walsh finds out, if my parents find out, it will be over. But I don't care. I push my parents out of my brain, throw a fire blanket over Ms Walsh's face, forget what everybody else will say and beg them to leave with me.

And they do.

We sneak out of school, catch a tram to St Kilda beach and then take a ferry to Williamstown. When we arrive, Eileen and I buy massive ice cream cones, Simone buys an apple, and we go for a walk along the pier. It's a gloomy, overcast day. It's like the clouds are ganging up on the sun, refusing to let the rays break through. There's a slight whistly sort of breeze, very fresh, very salty. Like Vegemite in the air, I think, smiling quietly to myself as I think of Mrs Vaselli. We pass a fisherman, who looks at us and laughs.

"Skipping school, eh?" he grins.

We nod and grin back at him.

"Caught anything?" I peer down into his bucket.

"Not yet. But I've got time, and the sea breeze has never bored me yet."

"Good luck," I say.

We sit further up along the pier, dangling our legs over the edge.

"I'd be listening to Mr Piper talk about Stalin now. . ." I say, my voice trailing off.

"Hmm. I'd be in English," Eileen says. "Fantasizing about the moment I finish my exams and jump on the Internet to book an overseas trip."

"Sounds nice," Simone says wistfully. "I'd be daydreaming about walking into class in a size ten and everybody cheering at me and asking me out on a date."

"Everybody?" I tease.

"Yeah, everybody. And Tia would beg me to go along with her to the coolest club so that the bouncer takes a look at *me* and lets us all in."

"I'm going to get you to say, 'I'm beautiful just the way I am' ten times a day, Simone," I growl at her. "No less than ten times a day. Starting from now!"

"No way!" She pushes me away.

"Come on Eileen; tickle her until she says it." We start tickling her and she loses her breath shrieking.

"Come on!" I warn her.

"OK, OK," she gasps. "I'm beautiful just the way I am. Ugh you are *such* a loser. Happy?"

"Say it like you mean it!"

"Amal, shut up will you! How many times do I have to tell you you're not Oprah?" She takes out a cigarette, looking at us self-consciously as she lights it.

"Are you still on that crap?" I ask.

"You can't even do it properly," Eileen says.

"Just a matter of practice," Simone says.

"Wow! Practising how to poison yourself and make your breath reek like the fart of a seagull!" Eileen cries.

"Stop preaching."

"Stop smoking."

"Stop mothering me."

"Stop ignoring me."

"Stop pretending to know what it feels like."

"Stop pretending to hate yourself."

"Will both of you shut up?!" I cry.

"*Anyway*," Eileen says, "it's your life, Simone."

"You've got that right. So anyway, Amal, you haven't even told us what *you'd* be daydreaming about."

I raise my eyebrows at them and lie on my back, my legs still dangling over the edge. They lean back and join me and we stare up at the sky.

"So?" Eileen asks, after several minutes.

"I'd be daydreaming about lots of things," I answer. "About Leila . . . becoming all she's capable of being . . . and walking up to her brother and telling him to shove his face up his rear end!"

"Woah! Reverse a little!" Eileen says. "What happened to Leila?"

I pause, biting my nails as I fix my gaze on one cloud as it moves and collides into the others. I try to follow its movement, its distinct silhouette, as it fuses and melts away. And then I lose track of its shape and I'm left looking at a chaotic mess of fluffy shapes collapsing into each other.

I tell them all about Leila. And they don't tell me it's a Muslim story. They don't tell me it's a Turkish story. They understand it is Leila's story, and I feel ashamed to think that I could ever have doubted them.

37

Nine a.m. Tuesday. Mr Pearse's office. Somebody saw us wagging and dobbed us in. We're punished with a week of lunch time detentions. He excuses Eileen and Simone from his office, and asks me to stay back for a moment.

"Amal, I just want you to know that I don't plan to tell Ms Walsh or your parents about this."

I look at him in surprise, a smile forcing its way on to my face. "Really?"

"Yes. Really." He leans back in his chair, tapping his pen on his knee. "Look, don't think we don't understand what you're going through here. I know you haven't approached the school counsellor. Maybe you should think about it."

I shrug. "What for?"

"To deal with any issues you may be having. I'm not naïve, Amal. I know that people judge you. I'll tell you something personal. My partner is Koorie. When we walk down the street together we can feel people staring, whispering, raising their eyebrows. She's always confronting the assumptions and generalizations. All Koories are alcoholics. All Koories are dole bludgers. You know what I'm talking about. The things the media and politicians churn out for ratings."

"Mmm. . ."

"So I understand what you're going through."

"You're making me sound like I should be on suicide watch, Mr Pearse."

He sighs and shakes his head. "I'm sorry, Amal. I don't mean to cast you as a victim. I just want you to know that if you're having any problems—"

"I'm doing fine."

He doesn't look very convinced. "I thought you should know that I'll be accompanying your team to the interschool debate."

"Er . . . OK."

"If any students are giving you a hard time you will approach me, won't you?"

"Yep."

"You don't lie very well." He gives me a gentle smile and sits upright. Some teachers understand that when it comes to your classmates, even your enemies, there is a strict code of silence. You don't snitch. Mr Pearse doesn't seem to get it.

"Just know that you don't have to put up with bullies."

"Yeah, thanks. Can I go now?"

I make about twenty calls to Leila's house and mobile that night. Finally, at eight forty, her dad answers and puts me on to her.

"Oh my God! Where have you been? Your phone's been off. I've tried your house but nobody's picked up. Are you OK?"

"Hey, Amal. Yeah, I'm OK." Her voice is flat and faded, and my heart twists at the sound of her.

"Did they go psycho? I'm *so* sorry you had to go through it!"

"Nah, forget it. It's not your fault. What on earth have you got to do with them?"

"Why aren't you at school then?"

"I've just been sick. . . Anyway, Amal, I'm sorry but I've got to go."

"Why so soon? I miss talking to you."

"We've got people over."

"Ohh . . . the usual?"

She sighs and her voice is thick with strain. "Yeah, Amal. The usual."

"Oh . . . OK Leila. Well, call me tomorrow then?"

"Yep. OK."

"Well . . . bye, love ya!"

"Love you too. . . Bye."

*

Tonight I'm taking the rubbish out after dinner when Mrs Vaselli waves me over to her front porch.

"You wanting tea?" she asks.

I smile at her. "Um, OK, sure. Just let me tell Mum or she'll think I've been abducted."

Mrs Vaselli doesn't count in the grounding rules so I return in a couple of moments and enter her house. The aroma of freshly baked cake hits me as soon as I walk in. She insists I sit at the table while she makes tea and cuts me a big chunk.

"It smells yummy."

"Of coursing it is. I making za best cake." She grins at me and hands me a plate. "I making one for your mum too. She very busy woman. Always working. I put on plate and you give to her. But you remembering to returning my plate."

I laugh and reassure her I'll bring it back sparkling clean. As I'm sipping on my tea and rambling on about school I notice Mrs Vaselli's white and lavender china tea set stacked on the corner of the bench.

"Have you got visitors?" I ask incredulously, pointing to the china set.

She avoids eye contact and sips on her tea. "Soon... Maybe... We'll see."

"Who?"

"You always asking ze questions."

"Yeah I know. So who is it?"

I can't hold back my astonishment as I've never seen Mrs Vaselli in entertainment mode.

She coughs and shifts in her chair. "Spiro and his wife. You wanting more cake?"

"You called!" I leap from my chair in excitement, nearly knocking my tea out of my hand.

She shrugs her shoulders casually and stares down at her mug. But I know her too well now. I can see the corners of her mouth itching to break out into a grin.

"Is it OK? Is he coming? When did you call? What did he say?"

She looks up and finally smiles, the frown lines in her face loosening away. "We talking now . . . my son . . . we talk now."

"Well it's about time! So what happened? What did you say? Are you going to see them?"

"I no know. Maybe. . . I hoping so. I want fix my house and my kitchen nice for when zey coming . . . maybe . . . zey has work so hard coming now."

"So what happened? I want details. Start to finish."

She laughs and gets up and cuts me another slice of cake. "Stopping with ze questions and eat more cake."

"You want me to finish off an entire cake?" I say, laughing at her. "Leave it for yourself for tomorrow, Mrs Vaselli."

She smiles at me. "No worry about finish ze cake, Amal. I tinking I making plenty more cakes and Greek sweets from now. I making for your family. . . And maybe I be making for my family too."

38

I arrive home from school the next day to find Leila's parents sitting in the lounge room with my parents. Leila's mum is a mess. Her eyes are squashed between puffy eyelids and heavy, sagging bags reaching just above her cheekbones; her face is a swollen pulp, as though she's been crying for days. Her husband is sitting beside her, silent, his head in his hands. My dad is at the dining table holding my mum's hand.

"What's wrong?" I cry, throwing my bag on the floor and standing before them. "What's happened?"

"Amal!" Leila's mum shouts, pointing her finger accusingly at me. "It's all your fault! Where's Leila?!"

"*What*? I don't know what you're talking about!"

"Don't lie to me!" she shrieks.

"Gulchin, you must be calm," my mum says, a look of exasperation on her face. "I know it's hard, but if Amal knows where Leila is she'll tell us."

"What's going on?" I ask, looking desperately from my mum and dad to Leila's parents.

"Leila's gone, Amal," my mum says. "She's run away."

"*When?*"

"This morning. She left a note in her bedroom saying she was leaving home. Has she contacted you?"

I stare back at her dumbfounded.

"Amal?" my dad says. "Has Leila contacted you?"

"Yeah, we spoke last night," I whisper, feeling a sickening wave of fear take over my body.

"Did she give you any clue that she was going?" my mum asks.

"Nothing. We only spoke for a minute or two. She didn't mention anything."

"I thought you good girl, Amal," Leila's mum says. "But you lie to me! I say OK for her to go your house but no go out, and you lie! You make my daughter go out at night like bad girl and she reject good man and now she run away."

I collapse into an armchair and stare in a confused daze at the carpet, not making sense of her words. Leila's mum glares at me as she wrings her hands.

"What do you mean by *she reject good man*, Gulchin?" my mum suddenly asks.

Leila's mum looks up with a tired expression. "I bring good man for engagement to my Leila."

"When?" my mum asks wearily.

"Saturday. He very good man. He from America. Our families from same village in Turkey. When Leila come home that night he was visit with us. He see her walking in with her brother so late and I disgraced, you know? But he still no reject her."

"That's just bull crap!" I say, and she frowns at me but continues to talk.

"Hakan tell us what happen and I so mad! Leila betray me. I go her room and I so upset with her. I tell her I forgiving her if she talk to him, he good man, he interesting to engage her."

My mouth is gaping open. My mum and dad each let out heavy, frustrated sighs.

"Then Leila suddenly screaming and shouting. No respect! When this good man in our house and hearing her! And after I convince him to live here and no take Leila away to America. And he agreed. After weeks talking with him we convincing him to start his business here. I no wanted to be separate from Leila." She takes a gulp of breath and her husband clasps her hand tightly.

Rage suddenly hammers through my head. "Why couldn't you just leave her alone?"

She looks up, startled. "What you meaning?"

"It's not time for her to marry!"

"I know what best for my daughter!"

"This is your daughter's life, Gulchin," my mum interrupts. "There is plenty of time for her to meet somebody and

301

settle down, if she chooses to. She's still so young and her duty, Gulchin, her *Islamic* duty, is to gain an education, to seek knowledge. She has never given you any cause to feel disgraced. You should be proud of her."

She looks at us indignantly. "She marry *now*, when she this age, better for her."

"Why?"

"Because she have nice home and he look after her and she be secure. She visiting me and I teaching her nice recipes and she having babies. She girl, she supposed to be doing this, so why she delaying?"

"What a load of—"

"*Amal*," my dad says sternly.

"— crap!"

"*Amal*," my mum hisses but I cross my arms over my chest and glare at the floor.

"You rude girl," Leila's mum says.

My mum quickly interrupts again, sensing that I'm about to explode. "What happened this morning?"

"All week she moody. This man coming every night for dinner and she sit like statue, no talk or laugh. I begging her to show him how nice she is and how she funny and I asking her to wear make-up. But no, she come out in her boy track pants and she no wear make-up and she no fixing her scarf nicely. I even telling her to show her fringe a little, you know? Fix it up so he see how beautiful her hair is. Allah, he no worry about your fringe in this time, I tell her. And she go crazy at me when I tell her this!"

302

I knock my head back against the back of the armchair in frustration and let out an exaggerated "Ooof".

"Then this morning I knocking on her door and no answer. I go in and she . . . gone. . . We call police and they no help."

I've had enough. "Serves you right!" I suddenly yell, jumping up from my seat. "You don't deserve her!"

"Amal!" my dad shouts.

Leila's mum looks at me in shock. "Why you talk like this to me? I older than you! You show manners!"

"You're just so bloody ignorant!"

"That's *enough*, Amal!" my mum shouts, but I'm beyond control and lash out.

"How could you treat her like that when she could be anything she wants to be? How can you think you're religious? You don't know the first thing about Islam. You picked on Leila when your son is an idiot!"

Leila's mum gasps, holding her hand to her throat as though I've got her in a headlock. "Oh Allah! This girl crazy!"

"Don't you *dare* bring Allah into this!"

She stares back at me, her mouth snapping shut.

"Amal, that is enough." My dad is towering over me now, his eyes ordering me to shut up.

"We go." Leila's mum grabs her husband's hand. She stands up and storms out of the living room to the front door. As she passes me she pauses, looks at me and shakes her head. "I never knowing you like this, Amal," she says. "I always thinking you a good girl. You wear hijab, you praying. You telling me I no know religion. Where your religion when you liar and you talking back to your friend mum?"

Her words suck the wind out of me; I feel as though she's shoved a Hoover down my throat and switched it on maximum power. She yanks her husband's arm and walks out of the house.

39

What do you do when your best friend disappears? Life doesn't stop. There's no intermission when you can lean back in your chair and let the scenes and dialogues you've just watched sink in. It feels like an ABC or SBS movie, where there are no ad breaks. Things roll on and you're expected to keep going. You have no choice but to adjust your screen monitor so that each thought or pain or emotion is on minimizer. So I'm in History and I have to minimize thoughts of where Leila is sleeping while Mr Piper roams the classroom demanding answers to his pop quiz. I'm setting the table for dinner. Don't click on *Is Leila getting three meals a day?* Otherwise I'll break down.

I keep on going to school, hanging out with everybody, doing all the normal, boring stuff in my day. But I feel like an emotional mess. The debate is in a week. I'm dying to back out but I can't bring myself to let Adam and Josh down after all our practice. I'm so nervous I've been waking up at night. When I'm not having nightmares about Leila being somewhere dangerous I'm having nightmares about me bombing out in the debate. I know there's no comparison but that's the way school is. Things just go on and you have to deal with everything on the same level.

I don't feel real. I feel like a clone who's pretending to be me while the real me remains curled up in bed thinking about where my best friend is. The evenings are the hardest. I don't feel like eating. I don't feel like watching TV or working out or talking celebrity goss with the girls on the telephone. I just come home and go straight to my room. My parents tread carefully around me, giving me my space, being really selective with their words like they're scared I'll collapse into a puddle of tears if they say a word which even rhymes with her name.

The only person I get a time-out on life with is Yasmeen. Neither of us has heard from Leila. Leila's mum calls my mum every day to find out if we've had any contact. Her brother calls my mobile telephone, accusing me of knowing where she is and hiding it from him.

I ring all the shelters but nobody will answer my questions. Who's there is strictly confidential and I suppose they have a point, but it makes me furious anyway.

Yasmeen, Simone, Eileen and I patrol the streets, shops, even libraries Leila used to go to, with the false hope we'll bump into her.

It hurts at night, when I'm lying in bed listening to the leaves on the trees rattle in the wind. I stare at the ceiling wondering how easy it is to take freedom and open-minded parents for granted. I wonder if she's better off away from her family. I wonder if she's safe and protected and able to be all she wants to be without loneliness or fear.

Time without Leila makes me feel like I used to on primary school camps. You'd say bye to your parents and then your guts would start to churn and twist and you'd feel so lost and teary that you'd do anything just to see their faces. I feel homesick for her. I miss her face and her smile and the way she makes us laugh and the way she can memorize television commercials and the annoying way she eats an apple and corrects us when we get our grammar wrong and how strong and real and gutsy she is.

On Sunday afternoon Mum takes me to a shopping mall. We split after a while. She wants to spend time looking at patterns in Lincraft, which is as excruciating as counting how many times the letter *a* is used in a newspaper. So I go to the food court to get a drink and as I'm walking I see a takeaway shop advertising for casuals.

I had a casual job last year, working in Hungry Jack's on the weekend. I was pretty cool having the extra pocket money and we used to muck around a lot on our shifts. Mum and

Dad made me quit because of VCE. I gave them ulcers about taking away my "economic independence". Thinking about the stacks of homework the teachers keep dishing out, I guess it probably makes sense. But when I see the advertisement, I have an urge to apply. If I could get just one shift a week, on the weekend, I think I could still manage to study and have a life. So I go to the toilets and fix my hijab and put some gloss on. Then I hover at the counter, waiting for the customers to be served. The shop sells fish and chips.

When the last customer has left, the girl at the front turns to me and asks me what I'd like.

"I'm here about the job . . . how do I apply?"

"Have you got any experience?"

"Yeah, I used to work at Hungry Jack's."

"Cool!" She smiles at me and tells me to hang on a second so that she can call the owner who's out back.

"Hey George! Someone here about the job!"

"Gimme a minute!" he yells back.

"How old are ya?"

"Sixteen."

"Sweet!" She grabs a stash of napkins and starts folding them with plastic forks. "He hasn't had much response to the advertisement, ya know? And he needs someone pronto 'cause the other girl quit and it's bloody impossible just the two of us. The ad's been up there for ages now and we've only got four people come up and ask. Two of them were guys and that was a definite no-no!"

"Why?"

308

"Ah, 'cause he wants girls at the counter. Thinks it looks better, ya know, being served by a girl."

"Oh."

"And the other two girls were too old. Like in their twenties and he wants teenagers 'cause they don't cost as much. Here he is now."

George is a short, fifty-something-year-old man with a perfectly trimmed moustache and beautiful grey eyes. He walks up to the counter, notices me and immediately looks constipated.

"Hi!" I say as cheerfully as possible. "I'm here about the job. I'm sixteen. I've worked at Hungry Jack's so I've got loads of experience." I thought I'd get it all out in one hit.

OK, now there are some people who are tactful. They see somebody they don't like and they bluff their way through the encounter and go full throttle with the avoidance strategies. In a situation like this, there are plenty of exits available to George. "The position has been filled", "We're looking for somebody older", "We don't like people who've worked in the mass consumer fast food industry". But George decides to go straight for the "say what's on your mind" route.

"Sorry, love, we can't accept people like you."

"What do you mean?"

"The thing on your head, love, that's what I mean. It's not hygienic and it just don't look good up at the front of the shop. Sorry, love. Try somewhere else."

I cough, dig my toes into my shoes and try to come up for

air. "What if I wore a beanie? It'd keep all the hair out of the food. *That's* hygienic."

"No good, love. We sell food with an image at the front. I got girls at the front, see? For a reason. Now I'm busy. Thanks for your time but it's impossible." He turns on his heels and goes out to the back room. I'm completely taken aback and stand there, not knowing how to walk away without looking like a rejected loser.

"Sorry about that, hey?" The girl at the counter shrugs her shoulders. "I thought he'd ignore your head thing 'cause of your experience. Don't take it personal, though. If you had a turban he'd freak too. And he made me get rid of my eyebrow earring. I drew the line at my tongue ring. No way I'm giving that one up."

"Yeah . . . sure . . . thanks."

I tell my mum what happened and she wants to make a complaint to centre management. But I'm not interested.

"What's the point?"

"At least they'll be aware, ya Amal. We have to raise awareness that these things happen!"

"Mum, I don't want to, OK? It's not worth it."

"What do you mean, it's not worth it?! Of course it is! Then the next time some girl tries to find a job they'll know this kind of discrimination is unacceptable!"

"No! I'm not going to make a big deal about it, OK? I just want to go home."

"Ya Amal, you have to stick up for yourself. You can't cave in like this."

"Who's caving, Mum? I'm just . . . look I just want to go home. I JUST WANT TO GO HOME!"

"Why are you yelling? Don't yell at me like that, Amal!"

I look at her and burst into tears. We're in the middle of the shopping centre and people are staring at us. A veiled mum and her daughter bawling in the shops. There are times you just need to disappear. It has to happen, your body tells you, or you will become hysterical and combust. I run through the crowd and out of the centre, to where our car is parked. My mum runs after me, calling out my name, but I ignore her. I get to our car and lean against it sobbing so badly that my head feels drenched with the sweat of it. My mum rushes up to me and engulfs me in a massive hug. "Oh how silly you are my darling Amal," she says. She squashes my face against her chest and I blubber and fumble my thoughts against her jumper.

"Mum, maybe I shouldn't have worn it. . . Maybe I was stupid. . . Where am I going to go now? It's just going to hold me back. . . The debate's this week and I'm so scared. People are going to laugh, I know it."

She cups my chin in her hand and looks into my eyes. "You're so silly, ya Amal. You can do anything you want, don't you know that? You're going to make us proud up there. It will only be a problem if you make it one."

"Mum?"

"Yes?"

"I miss Leila. . . I could do this if she was in the audience cheering me on. She had all the guts and spunk and she ends

311

up running away. I want things back to normal with her safe next to us. Nothing makes sense."

She doesn't say anything, just hugs me tightly and gently helps me into the car.

40

I've got that sweaty-palm thing happening. The plait under my hijab feels itchy against my skin and I feel I'd rather be hole-punched in the forehead than go through with the debate.

We arrive at Chelsea Grammar School by school bus at six thirty on Thursday evening. The entire trip consists of Mr Pearse giving us you-can-do-anything-if-you-put-your-mind-to-it pep talks, and Tia scanning me over as I practise my cards on Eileen and Simone. Adam is sitting with Josh and they're both going through their cards. Adam looks my way and winks at me. I flash him a smile and give him the thumbs-up sign.

Things between Adam and me aren't like they used to be.

I don't suppose I should expect them to be. The late-night telephone calls and long chat sessions on MSN are gone. We still hang out as a group some lunch times but I can tell that the spark between us isn't there any more. The other day we were all studying in the library. I asked him whether he'd spoken to his mum recently and if things had changed at all. He shook his head and immediately changed the subject. I'm pretty certain that he won't be opening up to me about his mum or anything truly personal any more.

Maybe he feels betrayed by me. I just thought we were becoming closer friends. But if he did sense that I had the hots for him and that I was sending out signals that I wanted to be with him then I feel like a hypocrite. I would have been playing with his mind. I would have been betraying my own faith too, because belief means nothing without action.

It's all very confusing and if it was the movies we'd probably kiss and make up and things would go back to normal. Except in our case it's the kissing part that's holding up the making up.

Mr Pearse insists on taking photos of the teams and so we pose before him with sheepish smiles or I'm-too-cool-to-smile scowls. I survey the hall for my parents but don't see them.

Our adjudicator unlocks the hall and we file in. His face is a work of art: bright hazel eyes in a tanned canvas chiselled to perfection. He has dreadlocks down to his waist, an earring in his eyebrow and a stud earring in the cleft of his chin. Not really my look but he's making Tia drool.

314

Adam, Josh and I take a seat at the front of the room. The other side walks in. Three girls. Two of them look like they want to get intimate with a toilet bowl. The other looks so damn self-confident that I start to panic. Her lips are curled up in a smug half-smile, her head is up like she's got a Granny Smith wedged between her chin and neck, and her chest is sticking out like overcooked puff pastry.

The adjudicator raps his pen on the table and Mr Pearse and the teacher for the other side start their shooshing frenzy. At that moment my parents walk in and start waving to me like I'm on a boat departing to Tahiti instead of three metres away. I do a grimace mixed up with a grin and they get the message, stop waving and get the video camera out instead. I try not to self-combust from embarrassment until I notice two other parents with their cameras out too.

The adjudicator starts to introduce himself. "Hi. My name is Timothy. I'll skip a long intro. I study law. I'm in my second last year. Tonight's topic is 'Should Australia become a republic?' On the affirmative is McCleans Grammar School and arguing in the negative is Barnia Girls. Good luck. First speaker start." He flashes an utterly captivating grin at us.

The first speaker, Emily, is pretty good. Adam and I write furiously, passing on rebuttal points to Josh, who's flicking through our notes trying to decode our illegible handwriting. Rebuttal is definitely the most challenging part about debating. The adjudicator is testing your ability to respond to the points raised by the speaker before you. You have to think on the spot and come up with an intelligent comeback line that conveys an argument beyond "I disagree with that point because it's crap".

Emily gets a round of applause and I lock gazes with Simone and Eileen, who give me the thumbs-up. Josh is next, and after a few seconds of fumbling nerves during rebuttal, gets into the argument which he's practised before, with a solid, aggressive voice and overly excited use of hand gestures, especially when he's pointing to the other side like they're vermin. He's getting stuck in to it and Adam and I are getting conceited, thinking we've won. I glance sidelong at the other team and the puff pastry girl is hunched over her desk writing out her rebuttal. She looks up for a moment and our eyes connect. She gives me a scowl. I pull an arrogant face. She smirks and I narrow my eyes as I prepare to go for the rebuttal kill.

I listen to the other side's second speaker, Natalie, who rips through Josh's speech but then delivers a performance two minutes under time. We're about to break out in a hymn. She plonks herself down in her chair and scrunches her cards in her hands. Emily smiles reassuringly at her but the third speaker gives her a frustrated look. For a moment I feel sorry for her. But Mother Teresa departs from me within a second when I remember what I'm here for. To win over the adjudicator hunk and return victorious to Tia, I mean Ms Walsh, I mean my parents, I mean Mr Pearse, I mean my school. OK, to win, period.

It's Adam's turn now and Josh slaps him encouragingly on the back. He gives me a nervous look and I cross my eyes at him and grin. His face relaxes. He stands up, takes a deep breath, and then proceeds to detonate the other side. He knows his palm cards by heart and doesn't even have to so much as glance at them. He's demanding backup to their claims, contradicting their arguments, trying to show them up as clueless wannabes more suited to a career in face painting than debating. We keep looking at the other side, taunting them with our smug nodding until I realize my turn is up soon and the butterflies start playing basketball in my stomach.

The third speaker is Carmen, the smirking one. She is brilliant. Pulverizes Adam into dust. Makes Josh look like one of the Wiggles delivering a speech in Pig Latin. The audience stares back, open-mouthed. Mr Pearse looks on edge. His encouraging winks don't fool us for a moment. My hand is cramping up as I go into a whirl writing out rebuttal points. I glance at the audience again and my eyes connect with Tia and for one second, one minuscule nanosecond, I detect we're on the same wavelength: she's also worried we'll lose. It's the only time we're connected together against another object – not each other.

Carmen doesn't walk back to her chair. She glides as if on a red carpet. She's just about to start doing a royal wave. Our eyes lock and then and there I decide that I want to do a combined Science and Law degree because one day I want to be wearing a wig in court, pulverizing my opponent too.

I do the fastest internal recitation of some Koranic prayers, smooth my trousers and shirt out, stand up, position myself in front of the room, look out at everybody and debate.

I've been injected with the formula for confidence and butt kicking. Not in spite of my hijab but because of it. Because I want to prove to everybody that it's just a piece of material and that I'm here, representing my school, supporting my team, kicking some serious rear ends. Carmen had better scuttle herself off to the maid's quarters because there isn't going to be any royalty around here except our team. With every card I start believing that my team line symbolizes the holiest of truths. I go Chosen People on the other team. Mr Pearse is beaming with pride. My mum is trying to save her mascara. My dad is zooming in the lens, grinning wildly at me. Simone and Eileen are dangling off the edge of their seats, stuck in a permanent thumbs-up. Tia is covering her mouth with her hand, trying to stifle a smile. The dreadlocked hunk is writing out notes furiously and I finish my speech wishing that Leila had been here so that she could have seen that I tried to make her proud.

We win the debate by one point and Carmen and I are tied best speakers. Unorthodox decision, but Timothy talked for fifteen minutes analysing our strengths and couldn't make up his mind in the end.

It's quite possibly the best moment of my year. I am floating and Adam and Josh are grinning wildly. My parents are flashing their cameras and holding back woo hoos. Simone and Eileen are clapping after everybody else has stopped. I'm pretty sure Mr Pearse is having a this-is-why-I-

318

became-a-teacher moment, because he's gazing at us like we've sewn up the hole in the ozone layer. We all spend twenty minutes outside the classroom reliving moments, sharing our euphoria. It's fantastic.

My parents take me out for gelato in Lygon Street and make me feel even better, if that's possible. *So articulate, ya Amal. So persuasive. So confident.* So needing a bigger scarf now that my head has expanded and is blocking the car's rear window.

I tell them I've finally worked out what I want to do at uni and that I'm thinking about whether I want to be a scientist with a law degree or a lawyer with a science degree. They hear law and go absolutely ga-ga on me. *Just like your uncle! Another lawyer in the family! Oh how you will make us proud!* What is it with parents and law degrees? It seems like a group of barristers and doctors patrol the maternity wards telling expectant parents that eternal bliss, the answers to all life's mysteries, and honour and prestige will be granted to their children if they study law or medicine. Like society would really function if everybody were qualified to either cure the sick or sue the doctor.

I call Leila's mobile, but it's still switched off. I ring her house but nobody answers. So I send her a text message anyway: HEY SWEET, MISS U 2 MUCH. GUESS WHAT? AM PUTTING LAW DOWN ON MY UNI PREFERENCES. MAYBE WE'LL BE IN CLASS 2GETHER AGAIN! WOULD BE GR8. I MISS U. SALAMS.

I go to bed on a bit of a high. In the scheme of my life, it's only a debate, right? But I feel like I've turned a corner tonight. Call it what you want. Proving myself. Competing as an equal. Living up to my potential. Whatever way you want to analyse it, I go to bed feeling like nothing can stop me.

41

I walk in our front door and the trampoline starts going in my chest again. Leila's mum is sitting on the couch next to my mum. I stare at her. She stares back. My mum is throwing furious looks at me but I ignore her.

"My daughter talking to you?"

"No." My mum tenses up and then hurls an ultimatum at me in Arabic to stop being so cruel and rude. I plonk myself down on a chair.

"She hasn't called," I force out in as civil a voice as possible. She nods and I'm taken aback. I was expecting a long list of accusations. I notice her face. It's so thin and drawn. It's not just that she's lost weight. There's something else. It's like the anger and tension have fallen away. There's something so quiet about her face now.

"I . . . no cope," she says softly, looking at my mum.

"I scared . . . I . . ." She coughs and my mum squeezes her hand.

"Just tell me this, Aunty. You grew up without any freedom. So why do you want Leila to go through the same?"

"*Amal*," my mum whispers.

Leila's mum looks at me wearily and heaves a huge sigh. I'm dumbfounded. She should have at least cursed me to purgatory by now.

"You think I no have freedom? I feel free. I have my own house and my own life and I happy. Why you always say bad thing about this? Why you judge me?"

"Because you didn't have choices, and now you want to take Leila's choices away too. And that's not what Islam is about."

"You think my culture I just throw away? It is my culture. It is me. All I know is how I grow up and what my mum taught me. It is my village culture and my family culture and my home culture. If you losing your culture you becoming nothing. Are you wanting have no culture?"

"I'm picking and choosing what I like and what I don't like. But Islam is where my rights come from, so if some crappy cultural rule says I have to chuck out my education or sit at home for life, then stuff it." I'm expecting her to well and truly lose it now. But she simply sighs again and stands up.

"I tired now," she says to my mum. "I go home and sleep. My husband he try cook dinner tonight. He upset for me you know? So he say you rest, I cook." She chuckles softly. "He no even know how boil the egg."

My mum smiles and hugs her and they walk across the room to the front hall. I look at her as I stand awkwardly in front of my chair. She turns back to look at me.

"If Leila calling . . . just tell her I want her home. I . . . let her go school and we no talk marry now . . . just. . ." She stops and shrugs her shoulders, biting on her lip to distract attention away from her quivering chin.

I don't know what to say or do. She nods at me and turns back to my mum, kissing and hugging her goodbye.

I sit down on the couch confused. I've never understood Leila's mum and I've never wanted to. I always thought she resented Leila. All she did was yell and scream and criticize her. But tonight she didn't even challenge me when I insulted her. And what's even more staggering is that she's actually compromising. Never in a million years could I have imagined her backing down.

There's something so different in her eyes now. Something maternal, and it's a shock because I've never associated the word maternal with Leila's mum. I've always understood her in terms of conflict and stress. Arguing with Leila, complaining about Hakan, fighting with Leila's father, pressuring Yasmeen. All I saw was a bitter, backward woman who only cared about clean dishes, ironed tea towels and marrying her daughter off.

323

But I think I was wrong. Somehow her love for Leila seems no less than my own mum's love for me.

I feel guilty. I never tried to bring Leila and her mum together. I never gave myself the chance to see things from Leila's mum's perspective and to understand her fears. It was easier to dismiss her as an ignorant villager. All those times I laughed behind her back with Yasmeen, ridiculed her paranoia about us being harassed on public transport or her obvious denial about Hakan.

It's not that I was arrogant. It's the fact that I felt that somehow, because I'm being educated and brought up in an open-minded environment, I had the *right* to be arrogant and superior.

All this time I've been walking around thinking I've become pious because I've made the difficult decision to wear the hijab. I've been assuming that now that I'm wearing it full-time, I've earned all my brownie points.

But what's the good of being true to your religion on the outside, if you don't change what's on the inside, where it really counts?

I've been kidding myself. Putting on the hijab isn't the end of the journey. It's just the beginning of it.

42

Ramadan begins. We wake up at 3.45 a.m. to eat our *suhoor*, our pre-dawn meal. I can't really stomach more than a slice of toast and a hot drink. My dad insists that I drink tea as it quenches the thirst. I'm up for any piece of advice, given I won't be touching any food or drink, including water, from dawn until dusk.

I remember my first Ramadan fast. I'd begged my mum to let me fast from dawn until dusk "like the grown-ups". I was in Grade Four. She let me fast until recess. Ramadans passed and recess became lunch time, lunch time became an afternoon snack. Pretty soon I was fasting for the full haul.

It took me some time to realize that Ramadan is not just about hunger and thirst. I guess that when we're a McValue meal away from relieving a hunger pain in a world where millions of people are dying of starvation, empathy does more to your conscience than a news report.

But there are pig-outs.

Boy are there pig-outs. After-dusk gorges. I know it defeats the purpose, but after sixteen hours I've got meat and salad and bread and Tim Tams and cheese and tomato melted on Turkish toast and *maklobe* and tortellini and carrot cake and pizzas with the lot minus the lot and souvlaki and sitting under an ice cream tap with my mouth wide open. . . Pretty terrible, actually.

I remember understanding what Ramadan was all about when I was in Grade Six, at a birthday party. It was the usual primary school scene: cake, fairy bread, chocolate, lollies, chips and not a single Muslim friend connected to my family who could lag on me if I cheated. It took half an hour and I caved. Big time. I wiped out the Mars bars, squashed CCs on top of my party pies and ravaged through the jelly beans. And then, when we were playing musical chairs and I was burping and hiccuping proof that I'd been a fat guts, I was overwhelmed with guilt. I broke down in tears, got disqualified from the game (I sat down to cry, which was considered hogging a chair) and went home early.

But it kind of dawned on me then that at the end of the day nobody knows what I do behind closed doors. Except God. One of my all-time favourite verses in the Koran is when God says, "We have created man and know what his

326

soul is whispering within him. We are closer to him than his jugular vein".

Boy does that verse give me the shivers. I think about my jugular vein, how it collects the blood from my head, runs it down my neck to unite with my other major veins, and I suddenly grasp how certain I am that God is watching over me. Sometimes I get this temptation to sneak into the kitchen and eat a biscuit, or to take a sip of water when I'm gargling my mouth. My parents won't know. My friends wouldn't have a clue. But I guess that's just not the way it works.

Despite Mrs Vaselli disapproving of my fasting (she thinks it's a waste of time given that I don't have salvation) she's insisted I visit her whenever I can after dinner to eat dessert with her. She always seems to be baking cakes now. When we're polishing off a batch of scones I try to dig for news about how she's going with her son.

"Tings be good. It take time. But zey be good."

Naturally, I think this is an invitation for me to ask her a zillion questions. "What did he say when you called? Did you talk to his wife? When will he be visiting you?"

She smiles quietly and tells me to help myself to more tea. "We starting new, Amal. It take time... Now you drinking more tea or you fainting at school tomorrow. Next year you trying Lent wiz me. Better for you."

"No problem, Mrs Vaselli," I say and she grins at me.

"I think I'm going mental," Simone says when she picks me up from my house for a walk in our local park after school. "Want to know why?"

"Spill it."

"I think. . . I'm not sure. . . I mean, I could be wrong. . . I know I'm wrong . . . it's just a guess—"

"*Simone*."

"OK . . . do you think Josh might like . . . me?"

"Well DOH!"

Her eyes widen in surprise. "Really?"

"*Simone*, stop being a Neanderthal, will you? It's bloody obvious he's interested in you!"

"Well, OK, little things keep happening and I don't know if

they mean anything because I just can't imagine that he'd like me."

"Stop! Have you got a pen and paper?"

"*No.* Why?"

"Just check your bag and I'll check mine. Come on, let's sit down over there at that bench."

She looks at me incredulously but follows me over. We both rummage through our bags and manage to produce a sharpened lip liner and a piece of paper.

"What are you doing?"

"We're going to write it down. Make a list of all the little things you say he does which might show he likes you and the reasons why you think he doesn't."

"You have issues."

"I know but just accept it and start listing."

This is what she comes up with:

Reasons why Josh might like me

- *Just a coincidence??? E.g.: next to my locker when I'm there & starts up a conversation so when I'm finished packing my things away we walk off together & talk (?)*

- *When something funny happens in class he looks my way to lock eyes with me(?), to see if I'm laughing*

- *Called me a couple of times. Says it's about school work but that conversation lasts 2.5 seconds & then he's changing the topic talking about all kinds of stuff (?)*

- *St Kilda day. Did he deliberately want to sit next to me on roller-coaster?*

Reasons why Josh might not like me
- *Cannot write down or Amal will probably try to have a Dr Phil moment with me*

When she's finished, she passes the list over to me.

"What's with all the question marks?"

"What's wrong with them?!"

"Forget it! Well then, what's with this Dr Phil comment? You know you can say what you want to me."

She explodes into a fit of laughter. "Really now?"

"Fine. Anyway, based on this list you have nothing to worry about. He's obviously got the hots for you."

"Guess what Mum said last night? She comes into my room when I'm finished on a call with Josh and she sits me down for a D & M session."

"Don't you just hate those?"

"Big time. She goes that she's so overjoyed that a guy has *finally* shown an interest in me. And then she goes that I should start a crash diet – apparently Liz Hurley does a watercress soup diet and she's heard it's simply *fab* – so that I can quickly lose some kilos before – check this out – he loses interest."

"Why don't you just tell her that if she refuses to see the real you she should just go and legally adopt a celery stick and raise it as a carrot so that she can stay out of your life?"

"I'll go look up the adoption agency when I get home."

"Anyway, want to come over to my place now? Try to work out what you're going to say when he asks you out?"

"I thought you'd never ask."

My parents take me to the movies on the weekend to pass the time before we break our fast. Dusk is at eight forty-three tonight. Ramadan has fallen at the beginning of summer so daylight saving is mercilessly stretching it out for us.

We've timed it and we can start to eat about twenty minutes into the movie. Well, twenty-three minutes to be precise. When you're fasting, even a minute counts. Personally, I don't feel we've gone overboard with the food stock. Neither does my dad. My mum thinks we're both mad. She's brought in a small popcorn and two sushi rolls. She's a little disgusted by our itinerary: a jumbo butter popcorn, a packet of salt and vinegar chips, one box of Pringles, four sushi rolls, a king-size packet of Maltesers, liquorice sticks and jelly beans.

OK, it could be viewed as sickening but today was a long haul. Usually I'll sleep in until some obscene Saturday afternoonish time and then whittle my day away watching old Elvis movies and trying out different colour nail polish in my trackies and Disney slippers. Instead, I was up at eight this morning, reading through all my saved hotmail chat sessions with Leila, going over all the stuff we'd written to each other over the year. Then I spent three hours on the phone with Yasmeen. That took me until twelve, which basically left me with eight and a half hours to go.

But weekends are a breeze compared to fasting at school. By recess time I'm just about ready to fall into a coma. Luckily I don't snore because I've managed to catch a few minutes of snooze time in some of my classes. Simone and Eileen have been so supportive. At lunch time they find a quiet shady corner in the school and lie down with me for a lazy nap. Adam and Josh have also joined us a couple of times. It's cute because they're reluctant to eat or drink in front of me, even though I tell them that I have absolutely no problem with it. The other day Adam took out some chewing gum and was passing it around. He was about to offer me when he realized I was fasting. He was so sweet and apologetic I wanted to kiss him. Not literally, of course.

Anyway, eight forty-three finally arrives. I can't really tell you what happens in the movie after that. I kind of get distracted. By five past ten the movie has ended, my stomach is cramped up with about three days' supply of food and my mum is getting a big head with her "I told you so" spiel.

It's at ten forty, when we're back home and I'm sprawled out on my bedroom floor contemplating voluntary admission to the emergency ward to have my stomach pumped, that my mobile phone rings and I hear Leila's voice for the first time in almost two months.

"Amal, it's me."

Her voice is so hushed and tiny that it's hard to hear her. But I instantly recognize it.

"Oh my God! Leila? Where are you?" And then I burst into tears and she bursts into tears and she actually asks me if my parents would mind if she visits.

One hour later and I'm opening the front door to a skinny wreck. Leila's face is practically hollow; her cheekbones are protruding, her eyes are widened and seem to be transfixed in a permanently horrified gaze. She wraps her arms around me and I hug her so tightly I'm scared her fragile body will snap like a toothpick. Then my mum rushes to her and we're hugging and sobbing until my dad comes in, closes the door, guides us gently to the family room and goes to make us a cup of tea.

"How's Mum?" she says after we've dried our faces and are curled up on the couch with tea and sandwiches. Leila is in the middle, my arm is rested on hers, my mum is beside her, holding her hand.

"She's . . . in a very bad state," my mum says.

Leila closes her eyes and nods.

"I couldn't handle it any more," she says, her face crumpling. I hold her tightly and let her cry on my shoulder. She finally finds her breath and dries her eyes.

"This time it was an American-Turkish guy. Perfect match. Our grandmothers were apparently from the same village. I . . . maybe I overreacted by running away. I . . . just got so tired."

"Where did you stay?" I ask.

"At a women's shelter in the city." She shudders. "It was horrible. . . There were women who'd been beaten to a pulp by their boyfriends. Or raped or molested. Women with their children, hiding from abusive partners. Teenage girls kicked out of home because they're pregnant. Some of them didn't even know who the father of their baby was. Druggies clutching on to their babies and desperate to shoot up. Just . . . awful stuff. . ."

She's silent for a while and then continues: "I feel so . . . I don't know. I miss home. I want to feel safe again. Like, ninety-five per cent of the time Mum was on my back about marriage while my brother was getting away with murder, but I just believed so hard that if I got through high school then I'd have a ticket to uni and a new life and independence. I just wanted to get through VCE. Isn't that funny? You'd think I was shooting up heroin the way she carried on. . ."

"What happened on that Saturday night?"

"Hakan took me home. Of course he was swearing and shouting at me the whole way. He was so angry. I just sat there, not saying a word. I didn't even want to dignify him with a response and it infuriated him. All I could think about was how terrified I was and how crazy that it was all over a birthday dinner! And then, from being terrified I went to being angry.

"When we arrived, there was another guy in the house, sitting on the couch, drinking tea, sucking up to my parents. My mum was practically bribing me, telling me she'd forgive my betrayal if I considered this man, who owns his own business and whose capital is in American dollars!" She lets out a humourless laugh.

"I'm so sorry, Leila," I say, "for getting you into trouble. We never should have done that to you."

She looks at me intently. "I never do something I'm not comfortable with. This has nothing to do with you or Yasmeen. That night was still perfect for me."

I nod my head, fighting back tears.

"Leila, I know it may mean little to you now," my mum says after some time, "but Gulchin came here in an absolute mess the other week, begging us to tell you she's sorry and will never do it again."

"She did?" She looks up in surprise. "She's sorry?"

"Yes," my mum says. "When she first came here she was so convinced that she was right. That she was trying to save you and look out for your best interests. But this time she was like another woman."

Leila leans back in the chair staring in thought at the carpet. "If I knew that she wouldn't do it again, I'd go back. For a roof over my head. For the five per cent happy times. For the feeling that I'm not somebody out on the streets. I'd go back and study and get what I want and then I wouldn't be vulnerable ever again. I'd have choices, do you know what I mean?"

We nod our heads at her.

"So how can I be sure?"

My mum puts her arm around her. "I think you can be

sure... Of course, I'll drum it into her that she risks losing you if she doesn't change but ... you mean more to her than even your brother does. She's given up on him. She's so easy with him because she's lost hope. You're her only daughter. You have to be as strong as you were before and keep reassuring her that you aren't losing your identity or morals by studying."

"Mr Aziz could get involved," I add, "like at the end of Year Ten when she wanted to pull you out of school."

"Yeah..." she whispers, smiling. "I always could rely on him. Every school excursion he'd call home and tell her he'd ripped up the note refusing me permission to attend. Remember Year Nine camp?"

"Smudging mousse all over Dilba's face while she slept? How could I forget?"

"That might never have happened if he hadn't told her he'd personally undertake that I wouldn't meet any men or boys, disgrace myself or be seen in public alone."

My mum shakes her head in disbelief and Leila shrugs her shoulders. "You're right, he has been there for me. Do you think this time...?"

I jump up, grab the phone and thrust it into my mum's hands.

"Leila, would you like me to call?" she asks.

Leila pauses in thought. "No. I think I should."

My mum finds her the number and Leila holds the phone, breathing heavily and biting her nails as she stares at the wall, her face creased in thought. She sits there for twenty minutes, not saying a word. I want to say something but Mum holds me back and we just sit in her silence, respecting her time. And then she peers down at the phone and dials the number, and I know I'm looking at one of the bravest people I've ever met.

Mrs Vaselli was, of course, right. Life isn't like the movies. People don't change overnight. People don't go from arrogant and self-righteous to ashamed and remorseful. They don't suddenly give in when they've spent years taking out. No doesn't magically become a yes. You don't go from wanting your daughter to throw her high-school certificate out in exchange for a marriage certificate to being Melbourne's leading Education and Independence for my Daughter advocate. I guess Leila must have known that. That's why she paused before she dialled Mr Aziz's number. She knew that no matter how aggro and menacing he could get (and this man is pretty good at making you wish you invested in bladder-control remedies when he gets all fired up), it was still a leap of faith to think her family would change.

But that's what Leila's always been about. Faith. Faith that she'll do something in her life. Faith in people. Faith in God. Faith that she knows who she is and what she wants and what her rights are. Things you take for granted and don't think about.

Within half an hour of Leila calling Mr Aziz, he's at our house. I've never seen him in jeans before. That's another

337

left-field thought. He's Leila's knight, minus the shining armour, plus the balding head, grey beard and hairy ears.

He talks with my mum and dad and Leila and then drives her home. It's past midnight now. We hear from her at four in the morning, sixteen and a half minutes before the break of dawn (remember: every minute counts in Ramadan). Mr Aziz has just left their house and Leila is eating toast with jam, drinking cocoa her mum made her, and reassuring me that there is hope.

44

My end-of-year exams fall within the second last week of Ramadan. So my usual routine of overloading on chocolate and chips to survive maths modules and history essays isn't an option. But when the sun sets, and I've stuffed myself at dinner and the chicken and rice and *maklobe* and *fatoosh* are straining against the lining of my stomach tempting it to bust, I'm full of energy to attack my textbooks. I feel like a vampire who comes alive after dark. That's not a very nice way to think of a religious experience but it's what hunger does to the mind.

I'm trying to memorize some calculus formulas when Simone calls me. She manages to speak for an entire minute without me understanding more than three per cent of what she's said.

"Simone! Slow down! I can't make out what you're saying! Something about Josh, the colour red and you wanting to jump off the Rialto towers? What the hell has happened?"

She laughs. "Oh my God, Amal! Josh and me have been sending text messages to each other for the past hour! We started during *Everybody Loves Raymond* and it went through to *Big Brother*. That's ages! And I've replied, so all up we've officially had a fourteen-text-message exchange! Isn't that unbelievable? I mean, come on, that's kind of cool isn't it?"

"Wow! That's awesome! What did he say?"

"He started with this message out of the blue: HAVE U EVER WONDERED WHY WE SAY APARTMENTS WHEN THEY R ALL STUCK TOGETHER? So I sent one back saying: HAVE U EVER WONDERED WHY PHONETIC ISN'T SPELLED THE WAY IT SOUNDS? Then we kept sending, like, jokes like that, you know, corny stuff you get in email forwards and try to pass off as your own invention, and then he said, and I quote, WHY R YOUR LIPS ALWAYS SO RED? DO U WEAR LIPSTICK ALL THE TIME?"

I burst out laughing. "Are you kidding? Just like that he asked you?"

"Yes! He actually noticed something about me, Amal! *Me.* It's just too unbelievable!"

"Yes, Simone, he is mentally unstable for being attracted to you. Call the men in white suits."

"Anyway, I didn't know how to reply. I was having a panic

attack trying to think of something witty or cute to say back. The more I thought about it the longer the time was passing between the reply and I was freaking out because before it was like instant replies and suddenly there's this huge, long pause. Then I finally came up with something pretty ordinary, NO I DON'T WEAR LIPSTICK, because my creative muse had passed its expiry date by that stage."

"And?"

"He replied by asking me if I wear blue contacts!"

"Oh my God, he's in love with your eyes!"

"And for a second I went blank again. Then something came over me, Amal, and I thought, to hell with it, I'm going to bloody flirt!"

"Finally!"

"Don't get excited. That lasted about three seconds."

"NO!"

She laughs. "Only joking. I was shameless. I replied: NO, THEY R MINE AND IN CASE UR WONDERING MY DAD ISN'T A THIEF."

I pause. "Huh?"

"Don't you get it?"

"*NOO!*"

"Come on! You know that pick-up line: *Is your dad a thief because he must have plucked the stars from the sky and put them in your eyes.* You must know it."

"Oh my God! Of course I know it! But it doesn't fit! Did Josh get it? What did he reply? That could have been text message suicide!"

She bursts out laughing. "No, he didn't get it. He didn't reply either."

"What? He could have pretended to get it. How could he ignore you like that? How could he be so rude?"

"Relax, Amal. He didn't reply because he called."

"Josh called?"

"Yes. He called to tell me that I'd officially written the worst text message response in teenage history and would I go to the movies with him tomorrow night."

"I need oxygen. Somebody get me oxygen. You totally expose yourself and the boy of your dreams asks you out in response. Oh my God, Simone!"

"Amal, I feel like I'm floating around my bedroom. It doesn't feel real. But it is! Josh Goldberg asked me – not Tia – to the movies! It's going to be my first date and it's going to be with Josh!"

Eileen and I spend the following afternoon with Simone, working out what she's going to wear and fixing her hair and make-up. I'm in charge of wardrobe and Eileen is in charge of make-up. Simone's hair is silky straight so she doesn't need to go through the whole blow-drying, teasing or hairspraying drama.

"Don't make me look like a drag queen, Eileen! I just want a little bit of mascara and some gloss."

"Eyeshadow?"

"Nope."

"Blush? You know, for cheekbone contouring?"

"Hmm . . . OK."

"Jeans or pants?" I ask.

"Whichever makes me look slimmer."

"Probably black pants. It's pretty mild tonight so you can wear this really nice top to accentuate your waist."

"No way! I want a jean jacket to cover it all up."

"It's not tarty, Simone. Do you think I'd let you walk out tarty? *Hello*? Are we forgetting that you're being dressed by a girl who basically only needs to put sunblock on her hands and face?"

Simone groans in defeat.

"OK, OK. I'm just not used to wearing fitted tops."

"You'll look fabulous, stop stressing."

"Simone! Stop fidgeting! The mascara's smudging."

"High heels, but not too high. Accentuates the calves."

"I thought I was wearing pants?"

"So you'll feel good knowing that your calves are accentuated. Dress for how it makes you *feel* as well as how it makes you *look*."

"Amal, if you don't shut up with the cheesy lines and stop making Simone fidget and twist in her chair I'm going to stick this mascara wand up your nose."

That night Simone sends me a text message: WE KISSED.

343

45

I receive my exam results just as Ramadan ends and our three-day festival, *Eid al-Fitr* (Festival of Breaking the Fast), begins.

I get an A grade average for my exam results and send my parents into a *dabke* around the dinner table. My dad wants to photocopy my marks and put them in a photo frame. Excuse me? Maybe in another lifetime. I'm excited but there are some things that are beyond daggy.

The first day of *Eid al-Fitr* falls on a Tuesday in the last week of school. I've been granted permission to take the day off. I wake up early with Mum and Dad and pray the *fajr*. We don't go back to sleep. We read the Koran together in our pyjamas for an hour and then we watch the sunrise from our veranda over cups of sweet mint tea. We have a couple of hours until we go to the mosque for the *Eid* prayers. We don't have a mosque in our area but ever since I can remember we've attended the one in Preston. It's the first mosque in Victoria and I've grown up listening to the sermons of the *Imam* there, who was one of the original founding members. He's my all-time favourite. He has the most peaceful, gentle personality and a wicked sense of humour. Whenever I listen to him I feel uplifted and inspired.

My mum cooks up a massive breakfast for us while my dad rushes out to buy freshly baked bread. We then sit and devour *falafals*, scrambled eggs and minced meat with *homous*. After a month of tasting food only after sunset, it feels strange to be eating breakfast again. I always feel a little sad and nostalgic at *Eid* breakfast. Ramadan sure is hard but I really do love the whole atmosphere of it.

We're running late to prayers because it takes me a while to get ready. I ironed my hijab but then it got static-infected and the shape wasn't working and I was getting a migraine until Mum found the non-static spray and fixed the emergency before I committed hari-kari with the safety pin.

So now my dad is driving like a maniac as he tries to find parking in the street in which the mosque is located. My mum is lecturing him about speeding and how wrong it is to disobey traffic laws and endanger other people's lives and does he really think that he can face God after ignoring the zebra stripes after the roundabout?

My dad eventually manages an appalling parallel park and we then power-walk to the mosque, getting stopped every five metres by friends wrapping us in huge hugs and greetings of peace and *Kola Sana Winta Bikhair*, "May every year bring you happiness", or else the condensed version of "Happy *Eid*" (for Aussie-born Muslims like me who can't pronounce Arabic to save their lives).

My dad gives us both a kiss and joins the men, and my mum and I join the women. We take a seat on the carpet, and ladies with donation buckets walk through the lines. After enduring a month's reminder of what it means to be hungry and thirsty, everybody is quick to open their purses.

I notice Leila and her mum in the middle row and Mum and I move to sit beside them. It's the first time we've seen Leila's mum since she came to our house.

I know people don't change overnight. I know that separating your upbringng from who you are is like trying to separate flour from butter in a cake. But there's something different in Leila's mum today; when she sees me she embraces me warmly, kissing me on the cheek and saying, "*Eid Mubarak*", (another version of Happy *Eid*).

Then the call to prayer starts to sound through the loudspeakers, preparing us for the communal prayer where we thank God for the food we have after a month of fasting and pray for those without. It's a haunting, beautiful reminder that the time has come to stand humble before God and I get goosepimples listening to it.

I glance over at Leila and her mum and I just know that they feel the same way.

All the stuff I said at the start of semester, about not caring about pimples, my body image, etc. It was all crap with a capital C. I wake up this morning, the last day of school, with a pus-filled zit the size of a golf ball in the worst geographical position possible: at the bottom tip of my right nostril. Consequently, I look like I have a piece of snot hanging from my nose. Just as I'm busting the pimple my mum walks in and proceeds to lecture me about facial scarring and leaving the pimple to dry out in its own time. I scream at her that she's (a) ruining my life; (b) completely out of tune with the kingdom of teenagers; and (c) clearly intent on making me a social outcast for the rest of my school life. She gives me a what-can-I-do-with-my-rude-ignorant-daughter shrug and storms out of the bathroom, leaving me in peace to carry out my zit-removal operation.

I mean, who is she kidding? Theoretically I guess I do have a greater sense of my own individuality now. Even so, I'm not willing to commit social suicide by exiting the house, *on the last day of Year Eleven*, with a zit resembling a snot attached to my face for the entire school population to write up in our year book.

Fat lot of good all my efforts do. In home room I get the following comments: *You need a tissue; When you chuck a sneeze, it's nice to wipe up please; Woah! we need an aerial shot of that thing; Does it have a name?*

347

The last two comments come from Adam. So I just pucker up and blow him a kiss. He can't help but grin. The moment truly deserves a theme song.

At lunch time Adam, Eileen and I proceed to grill Simone and Josh about their date. But they both just blush and giggle and go into let's-gaze-into-each-other's-eyes mode. One thing Simone does tell us in between classes is that she's quit smoking. Josh hates the smell on her. He also realized why she was doing it when he took her for pizza after the movie and she wanted to light up to avoid the garlic bread. Apparently he went ballistic and spent the rest of the night telling her how gorgeous she was the way she is. Eileen and I just about do cartwheels around the lockers.

So Josh and Simone are now a couple and as much as Eileen and I are thrilled for them, they're in their own world and there are no visiting visas for us at this fresh stage. As for us single babes (self-esteem begins from within), we spend the rest of lunch time yelling at Adam to stop taking photos of us with his mobile phone. So far he's taken three of my zit, a couple of Eileen's eyelashes and one of his teeth (he had a bit of lettuce stuck and didn't believe us so we told him to take a photo and see for himself). A pretty good tool if you don't have a mirror handy.

During the day Ms Walsh approaches me and offers me belated congratulations for my best speaker award. OK, so I'm a nerd deep down, craving the approval of the big-shot principal, because for some reason my stomach goes all gooey and fuzzy. "You've made this educational institution proud," she says.

"Well you never can quite predict what being institutionalized can do to a person," I say, sticking my foot well and truly down my larynx.

For a second she looks at me suspiciously. But then she does something I've never seen her do before: she gives me a sincere and warm smile. "Rebuttal always was your good point," she says. "Enjoy your holidays, Amal."

I'm left standing in a dumbfounded trance.

After school, we all go to Timezone in the city and spend a month's supply of pocket money trying to beat each other at Daytona. It feels like the happiest of times. Even though Simone is still reading diet magazines. Even though I can get paranoid and oversensitive about how people react to my hijab. Even though Leila's brother is a creep and she's had a rough time. There are just moments captured in your life when you don't seem to care about the "even thoughs".

Things have changed for the better for Leila. She's allowed to go out with us now and her mum is slowly relaxing. She's even started taking an interest in what Leila's learning at school. Leila brought home the BBC production of *Pride and Prejudice* for an English assignment and her mother watched it with her. Apparently she was very impressed with Mrs Bennet's matchmaking skills.

I'm looking forward to the holidays. I'm looking forward to summer days and nights with Simone and Eileen. I'm looking forward to conversations with Adam. I'm looking forward to visiting Mrs Vaselli and watching her eyes rumba and salsa as she tells me the latest news about her son. I'm looking forward to watching Josh go completely ga-ga over Simone whenever she walks into the room. I'm looking forward to feasts with Aunt Cassandra and Uncle Tariq, daggy DVD nights with my parents, dreaming and laughing and going out and gossiping with Leila and Yasmeen.

Some people might find this ironic, but when I think about it, it's mainly been the migrants in my life who have inspired me to understand what it means to be an Aussie. To be a hyphenated Australian.

It's been the "wogs", the "nappy heads", the "foreigners" the "persons of Middle Eastern appearance", the Asians, the "oppressed" women, the Greek Orthodox pensioner chain-smoker, the "salami eaters", the "ethnics", the narrow-minded and the educated, the fair-dinkum wannabes, the principal with hairy ears who showed me that I am a colourful adjective. It's their stories and confrontations and pains and joys which have empowered me to know myself, challenged me to embrace my identity as a young Australian-Palestinian-Muslim girl.

Anyway, I've decided I'm through with identity. The next chapter in my life isn't going to so much as mention the word. Instead, I've decided I'll write a new list. I've done To Wear or Not To Wear. I've had To Go To Court or Work In A Lab. I'm going traditional now. Straight to the source, right from the horse's mouth.

To Be or Not To Be.

But you know what? This time I don't need a list. I don't even need to think about it. Because something tells me that I already know which side is going to win this one.